MW00986214

All is not yet lost

A Novel By

K.L. Kovar

All Is Not Yet Lost
Copyright © 2023 K.L. Kovar
First Edition April 2023

ISBN: 9798393676186

This work may not be reproduced or distributed without written permission of the author.

This is a work of fiction. Names, characters, places, and incidents are either the product of the author's imagination or are used fictitiously. Any resemblance to actual persons, living or dead, events or locations is entirely coincidental.

Cover art by Dione Moon

For more work by K.L. Kovar, please check her Amazon page or contact her at angiebernie22@gmail.com

Dedication

To Sheldon Isenberg and to all the helpers in the world who make a difference.

Chapter 1

Friday Morning, April 6, 2018

It was the last day of what I would forever think of as normal life. After this day there would always be a before and an after.

The yellow heads of the jonquils lining the driveway nodded in the light breeze that promised another warm spring day. I turned into the parking lot of the Franklin County Free Clinic, humming a song — "You Are My Sunshine." I smiled as I realized the earworm was the result of hearing a pharmaceutical ad on the television just before I left home.

Only two vehicles were in the parking lot — the battered green truck driven by the clinic director, Dr. Kahn, and the iridescent blue Honda that belonged to Kammie, the supply clerk. The clinic wouldn't open until eight o'clock. Dr. Kahn had set this meeting for six-thirty, before the Friday morning rush of patients descended on us.

I sighed as I opened the Blazer door. I hated early morning meetings. My two kids didn't leave for school until eight-thirty, and Kyle would oversleep and miss his ride. Don would drive him, but he'd yell at Kyle. Not a good way to start a school day for a senior who was barely passing his classes. And LaRissa wouldn't eat breakfast, taking advantage of my absence to abstain. At fifteen, she'd become withdrawn and obsessed with her weight. She'd lost so much that I was thinking of making an appointment with the pediatrician to be sure there wasn't a health problem. I opened the back door of the car and retrieved

1

my purse and the stack of papers from the seat. *Another day, another grant to write. Focus, Jana!*

The clinic door was locked, but it opened abruptly as I fished in my purse for the key.

"Good morning, Jana," Kammie said. She held open the door and took the stack of papers. "Dr. Kahn's waiting for us in his office." She leaned forward and whispered. "And he's on a tear today. He wants to fire John."

"Why does he want to fire John? It took us a year to find a pharmacist who would work for the salary we can pay." I shook my head in disbelief. "We can't get along without a pharmacist. Our patients can't afford to buy drugs, and we need free drugs from pharmaceutical companies. We have to have a registered pharmacist to dispense, or we don't get donations."

"Apparently, John screwed up two prescriptions. Gave birth control pills to an eighty-year-old patient instead of a blood thinner and vice versa. The pills look alike, small, white, and in a monthly strip. The blood thinner lady noticed that she had the wrong prescription and brought it back. No harm. But Dr. Kahn is fuming."

She stopped talking as we saw the doctor standing in the doorway of his office. His dark face was set in his perpetual scowl, and he gave a preemptory wave toward the door.

"Tell you more later," Kammie said as we entered the office.

"Sit down, both of you," Kahn said. He took a seat at his desk and looked at me. "Jana, I just got word that we weren't awarded the grant for a new X-ray machine. I thought you told me it was a sure thing." He stared fixedly at me with his black eyes.

"It should have been," I said, frowning. "They were planning to award fifty of those, and we fit all the criteria. I'll find out what happened." I shuffled through the papers on my lap. "I have two other grant applications I think we should go after." I laid two thin stacks of paper held together with binder clips on his desk. "This one's for lab equipment. I know you've been wanting a new autoclave. The other one would support the salary of a diabetes educator for two years." I glanced at Kahn to get a read on his interest.

"Those sound fine," he responded, mollified. "Go get to work. You submit these things, and it takes six months for the funding agency to review and award them. We need everything now." Kahn said. "Now, we need to discuss finding a new pharmacist." He went into a tirade about John, ending with "We need to get rid of him as soon as we can hire someone else. Jana, you're in charge of recruitment. Get to it!" He turned to Kammie. "You stay. I think there's a problem with missing supplies. We need to set up a secured system, and you will be responsible for monitoring who's taking what supplies and how many." His voice rose and his accent became more prominent as he spoke—sure signs that he was about to embark on a lengthy list of complaints.

I glanced sympathetically at Kammie as I gathered my papers to leave. They'd been through this before. Dr. Kahn had a suspicious streak that caused him to micromanage each pen, mask, bedsheet, and gauze roll. The staff would be unhappy, and Kammie would get the brunt of their complaints.

My office was a cubbyhole behind the laboratory with no windows and a single 100-watt light bulb dangling from the ceiling. My gray metal desk was in the center of the room to maximize the lighting. A laptop computer, a comfortable chair, and a small printer sitting on a wobbly table were the only other furnishings. Stacks of files, reference materials, and books occupied two corners of the room. I sat down at the desk, picked up a highlighting pen, and opened the grant announcement for the funding of the autoclave. I was halfway through the detailed instructions when my cell phone chimed.

Caller ID said Franklin County Regional High School was calling. "What has Kyle done now?" I muttered as I swiped to accept the call. "Hello, this is Jana Spencer."

"Mrs. Spencer? This is the attendance secretary at Franklin High. Your daughter, LaRissa, isn't in school today. Is she sick? Or does she have another approved absence?" The woman on the other end of the line had a cheerful, light voice. I could hear the public announcement system echoing in the background.

"I'm not sure," I said. "I had to leave before she got up this morning. My husband was there. Maybe LaRissa didn't feel well, and he let her stay home."

"Well, if she's sick today, be sure to send an excused note with her when she returns to school," the cheery voice replied. "And let your husband know that, in the future, he should call in to the office if your daughter is sick. Now, you have a nice day."

I put the phone down, then picked it up again and punched in Don's number. He hated being called at work, but I needed to be sure LaRissa was all right. The phone rang five times before it was picked up.

"What?" Don's voice was irritated. "I'm under a truck, and this is not a good time."

"I just got a call from the school saying LaRissa is absent today. Is she sick?"

"She was already gone when I knocked on her bedroom door. Her bed was made, and her phone and purse were gone, so I figured she'd had some early thing at school and one of her friends picked her up."

"Well, she's not at school," I said, my voice sharp. Don was too cavalier about LaRissa, letting her do whatever she wanted. Unlike his approach to Kyle, who he constantly criticized.

"Maybe she's just taking a day off to go hang out somewhere," Don chuckled. "Something you and I did a couple times, right?" There was shouting in the background.

"Gotta go. That's my boss yelling about this truck. See you tonight."

I stared at the phone after Don ended the call. LaRissa never missed school. That was her social life—band, theater, school paper. She didn't have a boyfriend, and she hung out after school with a small circle of girlfriends. LaRissa had always been the perfect child. Lately, though, she was beginning to show signs of typical teenage sullenness. *Well, she's going to be grounded for a month for this little escapade.* I punched LaRissa's number on my cell. The call went to voicemail. *Two months!* I frowned and rubbed my temple. Then I picked up the highlighter and went back to the grant application instructions.

Chapter 2

Friday Evening, April 6, 2018

I was fuming by the time I got home that night. Dr. Kahn had yelled at me again for not winning more funding for the clinic, and his tantrum made me miss the deadline for sending a form that would have made us eligible for another grant. The red Check Engine light had come on when I was halfway home. And LaRissa still hadn't answered my calls. In fact, the last time I called I got a message saying her mailbox was full.

Don was in the kitchen when I walked in the house, staring into the open refrigerator. "There's nothing in here to fix for dinner," he said.

"Call Pizza Hut. And make a salad and some scrambled eggs for Kyle." I slammed my purse and papers down on the counter. "Is LaRissa home? I've been calling her all day. She's not answering or calling me back."

Don frowned. "She's not. I asked Kyle if he knew where she is. He acted a little strange, stuttered a little, and then said he had no idea. Maybe we should call her friends."

I could feel a migraine coming on. Pinpricks of pain and my vision was getting wobbly. "Where's Kyle?"

"In his room playing a video game."

"I'm going to talk to him. Call Pizza Hut. Supreme pizza on one side and whatever you want on the other." I kicked my shoes off and went upstairs.

Kyle had his music turned up full blast. I knocked three times then opened the door. He was lying on the bed, his lanky six-foot-three-inch body sprawled face down. "Kyle!" I shouted. He rolled over and stared at me as I went to his iPod and clicked it off. Kyle's eyes were red, and his shoulder-length brown hair was straggling in his face. "Have you been smoking pot in here?" I sniffed the air in the room. No acrid aroma, and the window wasn't open. I sat down on the bed.

"You're always accusing me of something," Kyle whined, his voice cracking. He swung his feet over the side of the bed and sat up. "No, I haven't been smoking pot. My eyes are probably red because I didn't sleep much last night. What do you want?"

My only son. My heart hurt for him. He was struggling in school and spent all his time in his room listening to music and playing video games. He had Type 1 diabetes and had had to drop out of soccer last year after collapsing on the field. The constant monitoring of his blood sugar levels and need to go to the school nurse's office for insulin embarrassed him. The few friends he'd had in elementary school had gradually deserted him when he began acting out in high school. I patted his leg. "I'm getting a little worried about LaRissa. She skipped school today, and she's not answering her phone. Did you see her last night?"

"She was at the social at the church, with her besties," Kyle said, his voice flat. "I didn't stay. That's the last I saw of her."

"You didn't drive her home?"

"She told me she'd get a ride with a friend. I went to the arcade and played pinball for a couple hours and came home." He glanced at me. "I know you said I should stay at the social and drive her home, but she told me to get lost. Her friends all laughed."

"What time did she get home?" I asked.

"How would I know?" His face was sullen. "I was in here listening to my music. It's not like she'd stop by and want to tell me all about her great evening."

I rubbed my forehead. "It's okay, Kyle. I'm sure she got home safely. But I want to call a couple of her friends to see if they know where she's been all day. Who was she with at the social?"

Kyle reeled off three names. I knew all three and their parents. "I'll call them now. Dad is getting dinner for us. Come down in fifteen minutes."

6

He nodded and reached to turn the iPod back on, full blast. I got up and left. My headache was getting worse.

LaRissa's friends had no idea where she'd been all day. All of them denied having given her a ride home from the social. "She was in a bad mood, Mrs. Spencer," LaRissa's best friend, Bailey, had said. "Hardly hung out with us at all. I saw her with a couple of older boys. But I don't know who they were."

Over pizza, after Kyle had devoured his eggs and gone back upstairs, I told Don what I'd learned. "Nothing. No one knows where she went today." Tears sprung to my eyes. "It's eight o'clock at night, and it's been more than twenty-four hours since we've laid eyes on her. I think we should call the police."

Don swallowed the last bite of pizza. "She'll be really pissed if she walks in and there are cops here. Or worse, if they find her someplace with her friends and drag her home. All kids do stupid things like this. Maybe we should wait till morning? If she's not back by then, we'll call the police."

The Imitrex I'd taken for migraine wasn't helping much. "I need to lay down in a dark room," I said. "I think you should drive around and see if you spot her. She might be at the mall or the Green Grill."

"Or one of those places in the park where we used to hang out," Don said, smiling. Fairview was a small town: three traffic lights, half a dozen restaurants, a strip mall, Walmart, and one high school. Don and I had gone to that high school and knew all the places where teens went to get away from parents. Of course, that was twenty years ago. "I'll clean up here then go drive around." He stood up and brushed pizza crumbs off the table.

"Thanks, sweetie." I grimaced as another wave of pain shot through my head. "Maybe you'll find her. Wake me if I'm asleep when you get back."

Don didn't wake me. And LaRissa was still missing when I staggered downstairs the next morning.

Chapter 3

Saturday morning, April 7

Don's face was drawn as he greeted me in the kitchen. Dark bags shadowed his eyes, and he hadn't shaved. "I was out until two this morning searching for her. I didn't find her, and she hasn't come back," he said. "It's time to call the police. Either something's happened to her, or she's run away."

I started shaking and dropped into a kitchen chair. Don put a hand on my shoulder. "Coffee?" I nodded, and he went to the counter and poured a cup. I took it, holding the cup with both hands. The strong aroma assaulted my senses, and my stomach lurched. I scrambled to my feet, dropping the cup, and ran to the sink. The acid taste of bile burned my throat as I vomited. I rinsed my mouth and splashed water on my face before returning to the table. Sinking into the chair, my voice hoarse, I said, "Call them."

Don looked at me, his blue eyes worried, then handed me a towel to wipe up the coffee before picking up his phone. He went into the living room and made the call. I could hear his muffled voice but not what he was saying. When he returned, he sat down across from me.

"They're sending a couple of deputies. Are you okay now?" I gave him a blank look.

"I'm going to go wake up Kyle. They'll want to talk to him," Don said. He picked up the towel and dropped it on the counter. "Can I get you anything?"

"Some crackers, maybe." My stomach felt like a hot coal was burning a hole in it. Don took a box of Saltines from the cupboard and set it on the table.

"Okay?" I nodded, and he went to the stairs to wake Kyle. Don had always been my rock. We'd found each other in high school. I'd been overwhelmed when the tall, black-haired, blue-eyed football star every girl wanted had asked me out. He turned out to be smart and funny and wanted only me. He was an extrovert, charming everyone he met. I was an introvert, quiet and organized, and devoted to him. We went steady for two years and knew we'd be together forever. I never looked at another man. Despite some hints from jealous girlfriends, I was sure that he wanted only me. We went to the same college, lived together off-campus, and married two weeks after graduation. Our lives had been perfect, despite a few ups and downs.

Don and Kyle came down the stairs and joined me in the kitchen. Kyle rubbed his eyes and ran his fingers through his dark hair. He looked like he hadn't slept much either.

"What's up?" His head drooped, and he didn't meet my eyes. "Dad said LaRissa's still missing. I don't know anything," he mumbled. "I need to get to the Final Quest." He looked at the clock on the kitchen wall. "I promised I'd be there to help unload boxes." For the past four months, Kyle had been working on Saturdays for a friend of Don's who owned a comic book and video game store. It was one of the few things he looked forward to every week.

"We know you don't know anything, Kyle," Don said. "But the police will want to talk to you—to all of us. I'll call Bob and let him know you won't be coming in. You need to be here."

The doorbell rang, and I jumped up. "They're here." My hands started shaking again, and I felt like I couldn't breathe.

"I'll get it," Don said. "Come on, let's all go in the living room." He took my hand and led me into the living room, then settled me in the big armchair before opening the door. "Thank you for getting here so quickly. Please come in."

I watched, trying to breathe, as the two deputies clanked into the room. The older one introduced himself, "I'm Deputy Tolman. You called about a missing daughter." Don nodded and escorted them into the living room.

The young female deputy— "Barrett" on her name tag— was tall and had broad shoulders, with blonde hair pulled into a tight bun. She took a seat on the sofa, a clipboard and pen in her hands. I found myself wondering how she came to be on the police force, my mind wandering away from the purpose of her visit. I liked to watch cop shows on TV and began creating a backstory for her. I was abruptly pulled from my avoidance distraction by her partner's gravelly voice.

"Your report says your daughter's missing?" The older deputy – "Tolman –took off his hat and laid it on the side table by the sofa but didn't sit down. I stared at him, my mind registering his obvious advanced years. White hair, buzz cut, slight potbelly, though the width of his shoulders suggested he had at one time been a weightlifter.

"Yes," Don answered. "She didn't make it to school yesterday and didn't come home the last two nights. We haven't seen her since she left for the church social on Thursday evening." He sat down, heavily, on the arm of my chair. "We've called her friends, Deputy. None of them have seen or talked to her since Thursday night. Last night, I drove around to all the places where she might be—where high school kids hang out. Nothing."

Kyle was slouching in the doorway to the kitchen. Tolman fixed his eyes on Kyle and scowled. "And who are you?"

Kyle flushed red. "I-I-I'm her brother. I don't know anything." His shoulders slumped, and he added, "But I'm worried about LaRissa too. She's never been in trouble before. Not like me." His voice trailed off.

"And what kind of trouble have you been in?" Barrett asked.

Don waved his hand, dismissively. "Nothing, really. Just bad grades and bad attitude. Normal teen boy stuff. Let's get back to LaRissa, shall we?"

"Tell us about your daughter, then," Barrett said, looking at me. "Has she run away before? How does she do in school?"

I sobbed and covered my face with my hands. My throat was thick with tears, and I couldn't answer.

Don jumped in. "I've put together a list of her friends and her school schedule. Her cell phone number, maybe you can track that? Also, a description of her—height, weight, hair and eye color. No tattoos or other distinguishing features." He handed a sheet of paper to Barrett. "She's a straight-A student, involved in lots of activities, and . . . really, never been in any trouble at all. Do you need a picture?" Don went to the fireplace mantel and picked up one of the framed photos. "This is LaRissa." I glanced at it as he carried it over to Barrett. LaRissa was laughing, holding a beach ball, dressed in shorts and a T-shirt with her long blonde hair blowing in the wind. That trip to Florida last year was one of the best family trips we'd ever taken.

Barrett took the picture. "Is it okay if we take it out of the frame? We'll want to make copies to distribute." At Don's nod, she began disassembling the frame.

Deputy Tolman cleared his throat. "Look, folks, most teens who disappear have run away. They often come back in a day or two. She may walk in the door in an hour. We'll take your report and circulate her picture and description, but the odds are that she'll come back on her own. It's only been . . . what . . . thirty-six hours since she was last seen. If she does come back, you let us know right away. If not, a detective from our office will be contacting you tomorrow. He'll want to interview each of you, in detail, and begin contacting her friends and others who might know something."

"You mean you're not going to start searching for her now?" Don leaped off the arm of the chair, his face contorted. "You need to take this seriously and start now!" His hands balled into fists.

"We'll send a description and her picture out, and our patrols will be on the lookout for her," Barrett said, her voice calm. "If she's wandering around the area, afraid to come home, someone may spot her. There's no evidence of foul play. You said when you called this in that she had her purse and cell phone with her. It looks, right now, like she took off on her own. If she doesn't come back by tomorrow night, I'm sure there will be a full investigation. In the meantime, as my partner said, be sure to contact us if she comes back or if you hear from her."

Don was fuming as he slammed the door after the deputies. "They're not going to do anything," he snapped. "Protect and serve, my ass!" He bent over me. "I'm going to organize a search party. And call the newspaper—get them to write a story about LaRissa being missing." He strode around the room, anger in each step. "Kyle! You get on the phone with your sister's friends. Tell them we're organizing a search party and they should ask everyone they know to help. Tell them to meet here at one o'clock. I'll call the neighbors and my friends from work."

Kyle muttered something I couldn't hear.

"What did you say?" Don shouted at my son. I covered my ears and huddled in the chair.

"I think she's just hiding out with one of her friends because she missed curfew last night and she's afraid to come home," Kyle said. He sidled away from his father who was walking toward him, fire in his eyes. "But I'll go call them and anyone else I can think of." He headed up the stairs to his room.

Don came over to me and knelt next to the chair. "Are you okay? Can you call people?"

I shook my head. "I can't, Don," I whispered. "My migraine is back." I looked at him, desperate. "And I'd just cry, talking to anyone."

"All right. You go to bed, take a pill. Kyle and I will get things going. I'll call your friend Sarah. She'll help round up a posse of searchers." He helped me up from the chair and guided me up the stairs to our bedroom.

I closed the curtains and lay down on the bed. Images of LaRissa flashed through my brain. I sobbed and pulled a pillow over my face.

Chapter 4

Saturday evening, April 7

It was full dark when I woke. I ached all over, like I'd gone through a harrowing workout at the gym. The migraine was gone, though, and my stomach rumbled in complaint. I hadn't eaten anything since last night's pizza. Downstairs, there was noise of people coming and going. I sat up abruptly. Was LaRissa home? Please let her be home, my mind was screaming. I knew she wasn't, though. Don would have come and told me if she was.

I got up and went into the bathroom. The image in the mirror shook me. My normally sleek brown hair with one white streak was tangled and lank. There were dark circles around my bloodshot hazel eyes, and deep wrinkles lined my forehead and bracketed my mouth. I turned on the shower full blast, and cold. When I stepped out, I was shivering, but my mind was clearer than it had been. I dressed and brushed the tangles out of my hair. I squared my shoulders and sucked in my stomach. I didn't want to face whatever was going on downstairs, to talk to people, to thank them for helping. But I knew it was necessary.

My next-door neighbor and best friend, Sarah, greeted me as I walked into the kitchen. She was wearing an apron over her ample waist and hips. A smear of what looked like mustard decorated the tip of one of her thick red braids. Her eyes were compassionate as she put a hand on my arm. "They're all out looking for her, Jana. I'm sure they'll find her soon. The girls and I are making sandwiches and keeping the coffeepot full for when groups of searchers stop by to report the areas they've swept." Her three daughters, all older than LaRissa, looked at me, uncertain how to react. "You come sit down and eat something. There's ham and cheese sandwiches and peanut butter and jelly. Or I can heat up some soup for you."

My stomach growled again, loud enough for Sarah and her daughters to hear. "You do need to eat something," Sarah said. "Keep your strength up!"

"A peanut butter and jelly sandwich sounds good," I told her. "And a cup of coffee."

She opened a cupboard door and took out a small plate. I sat down at the table, where she placed the sandwich in front of me. Sarah told her daughters to go into the living room, then she poured out coffee for herself and me.

"No news yet," she said. "About thirty people are searching. They've covered most of the west side of town so far. Don organized search areas and assigned each of the seven teams to specific areas. My girls have been on their phones calling everyone they know at school, telling them LaRissa is missing and asking them if they know anything about where she went — or with whom — after the social Thursday night. I've been on the phone with the teachers and school staff too." Sarah taught home economics and English at the high school. "So far, no leads. But lots of people are looking for her." She looked at me. "I'm sorry, Jana. I know this is a nightmare for you." Her voice dropped to a whisper. "I never told anyone this, but Siobhan ran away a couple years ago. We had a fight about that boy she was seeing. The one with the tattoos and the motorcycle? I forbade her to see him, and she took off. Didn't come home till the next night. Bill and I were so worried we didn't know what to do. She finally came back on her own and said she'd spent the night at a friend's house." Sarah reached out and rubbed my shoulder. "I'm sure she's okay. The teen years are hard — for girls, especially." She smiled. "To say nothing of how hard they are for parents."

I tried to smile back. From the expression on Sarah's face, it was likely my smile was more like a grimace. "Thank you for all you're doing, Sarah. I'm just terrified that . . ."

"I know," she said. "But keep your chin up. Don told me the police officers who were here said most missing teens come home on their own."

The front door slammed open. I jumped, startled at the noise. Don rushed into the kitchen, followed by several men and women. He stopped when he saw me. "You're up. Migraine over with?"

I nodded. "Have you found her?" My tone was hopeful, but the expression on Don's face frightened me.

A man behind Don dropped a purse on the table. I recognized his face but couldn't think of his name. He stepped back as Don picked up the purse and took out a cell phone. "Larry's team found LaRissa's purse under the bleachers on the football field. Her phone's in it too. She wouldn't have left them on her own. Someone has her. We need to call the police so they can get a unit out to the school to look for evidence." His voice was rough and thick, and his hands were trembling. He dropped the phone on the table and went into the next room, holding the card the deputy had given him.

I picked up LaRissa's phone and scrolled through her phone calls. Eight from me, a couple from friends. None that I didn't recognize. I switched over to check her text messages. A dozen from friends since Friday evening. She hadn't responded to any of them. I laid the phone down and buried my head in my hands. Sarah put her hand on my shoulder but didn't say anything.

"I talked to the deputy," Don said when he returned to the kitchen. "They're on their way here." He pulled up a chair next to me. "Are you okay?" Don had been solicitous since my bout with breast cancer three years before. I'm in remission, but the anxiety every time I went in for post-treatment tests was overwhelming for both of us. "You should go upstairs and rest. I can meet with the police."

A surge of anger swept through me. "No! My daughter's missing, and I don't need to rest. I need to find her." I pushed him away. "Stop hovering over me." I stood up. "Where's Kyle? He should be helping too." My eyes swept the room. "We all should be doing something to find her! Not sitting here drinking coffee and eating sandwiches." Sarah's green eyes were round as I shoved the sandwich away. Her mouth opened and then closed as she turned to put the plate on the kitchen counter.

Don watched me as I marched out of the kitchen, intent on dragging Kyle out of his bedroom. I could hear him saying something to the crowd in the kitchen as I ran up the stairs. Probably telling them I wasn't well, and they shouldn't take it personally, I thought. I reached Kyle's closed door, knocked once, and threw the door open.

"What's wrong with you? Why aren't you out helping to find your sister?"

Kyle removed the earbuds. "What?" His face was pale, and he looked as though he hadn't showered in days. There were crumbs on his bed and crumpled Cheetos bags on the floor. My anger surged again.

"I said what's wrong with you. You should be out searching for LaRissa, like all of our neighbors and her friends." I picked up his gaming console and threw it across the room hard enough that it dented the drywall.

"I don't know where she is. You know she doesn't even like me talking to her at school. How could I help?" He huddled back on the pillows. "I'm a screwup, like Dad's always telling me. I'd just get in the way of those people trying to find her."

"You're her big brother—family! You should be worried about her. Everyone else is," I said, my voice softer. "Now go take a shower and get dressed. The police are on their way here. Some of the searchers found her purse and phone at the school. That means she must have been there after she left the social." I put my hands on his shoulders. "If you have any idea who she left the social with, you need to tell us. Now."

He pulled away from me and stood up. "I don't know anything. I've told you and told you that." He stomped to the bathroom.

"Take your glucose level," I yelled as he slammed the door. I took a deep breath.

The two deputies from yesterday were in the living room when I got back downstairs. Don was standing beside Deputy Tolman, holding LaRissa's purse.

Tolman shook his head. "You should have left it where it was, so the crime scene investigators could view it *in situ*. There may be other evidence there." He raised his voice. "How many of you were at the site when the purse was found?" Five people raised their hands. "How many touched the purse or any of the contents?" Two of the five raised their hands. "Okay, we'll need to get shoe impressions and fingerprints from all of you, so they can be compared to any others we find. Deputy Barrett and I need someone to come with us and show us exactly where this evidence was found. We'll tape it off as a crime scene and get the crime scene unit and a detective on the scene."

Don pointed at Larry, a neighbor from the end of the block. "Larry's team found it. He should go." Larry nodded and picked up his jacket. Deputy Barrett opened a large plastic bag she'd been holding and told Don to drop the purse inside.

"Do you need her phone too?" Don went into the kitchen to retrieve the phone from the kitchen table where I'd dropped it. "Her mother took it out and checked the messages and phone calls." He saw me standing in the doorway. "I don't think she found anything helpful."

Tolman grimaced. "Of course, she checked it out," he grumbled. "We'll need your fingerprints, too, ma'am." He handed the phone to Barrett, who put it in a small plastic bag and wrote something in black ink on the bag. "With your permission, we will check your daughter's room to see if she left any note or anything that may give us an idea who she might be with. My partner will stay and do that, while Larry can take me to where you found the purse."

I followed Tolman and Larry to the front door. "I want to go with you."

"No can do, Mrs. Spencer. We need as few people contaminating the site as possible. I'll report back to you when the scene's controlled and the crime scene guys arrive." He said this quietly. "I know it's hard, sitting and waiting. But the best chance we have of finding your daughter is if we handle the investigation according to protocol. Now that it looks like your daughter may have . . . well, we still don't know what happened, but a detective has been assigned and will meet us at the scene. He'll follow up with you."

I started to argue with him. I needed to see, with my own eyes, where LaRissa had been when she dropped her purse. My breath caught in my throat as I realized—where she'd been when she was abducted. Tolman firmly closed the door in my face, and seconds later I saw the flashing red and blue lights as his cruiser pulled away. Don took my hand and led me back into the living room before leading Deputy Barrett upstairs to LaRissa's room.

Chapter 5

Saturday night, April 7

The Fairmont sub-office of the Franklin County Sheriff's Office was in the basement of the city hall. The sandstone building was nearly a hundred years old, and a local citizens' group had applied to have the building designated a national historic site. It lacked adequate heating and cooling, and the electric system was in serious need of upgrading. The space shared by the eight-person department was limited, with most of the deputies sitting in cubicles in the large open space.

Detective Alphonse Simmons, by reason of seniority, was the lead detective and had his own office. He'd been off duty when he'd received the call from the sheriff; he was just sitting down to a dinner of fried perch and french fries. A missing Fairmont girl—forty-eight hours—and evidence that there might have been an abduction. The sheriff ordered him to get to the office to meet the deputies who'd taken the initial call, pronto. Simmons had put the fish in the refrigerator, changed from his off-duty clothes to the baggy pants that cradled his generous belly, a wrinkled blue shirt, and the one tweed jacket he wore anytime he had to interview citizens.

Fifteen minutes after answering the phone, he groaned as he sank into the ergonomic chair in his office. He rubbed his right knee. The three hours he'd spent playing catch with his twelve-year-old grandson the previous night had wrought hell with his joints. He vowed to insist on pitching the next time—easier on the knees of a sixty-two-year-old man only eighteen months from retirement.

He rifled through the pink slips on his desk. One was a follow-up from the lab, and another was a call-back from a store owner whose shop had been burgled the previous week. He picked up the phone to call the lab, then hung up when he saw Tolman and his partner heading toward his office.

Tolman strode in and hung a haunch of the edge of the desk. "Still refusing to put a couple chairs in here, Al?"

"Yup," Simmons said. "Cuts down on the amount of palavering that I have to listen to. What's up with the missing girl? Another runaway who'll show up after we spend a lot of time looking for her?"

Barrett stepped into the room and put a file folder on Simmons's desk. "That's what we thought till this evening. The father organized search parties and one of them found the girl's purse and phone under the bleachers on the football field. Lou had one of the searchers show him the spot where they found the purse and phone and called in the forensics guys. I did a quick search of the girl's bedroom. No notes or indication of who she might have been with Thursday night. She does have a laptop that we might want to look at to see if there's anything relevant on it."

Tolman added: "Of course, the searchers walked all over the area and rummaged through the purse before they called us. So, it'll be unlikely there's much for the forensics guys to find that could help."

Simmons opened the file folder and skimmed through the report. "Missing since Thursday evening, huh? Not long." He held up the picture of LaRissa. "Good-looking girl. Any previous problems? Boyfriends?"

"It's all in the report," Barrett said. "Read it and then we'll head back over to the scene. Sheriff Smith said to make this a priority." She shuffled her feet impatiently while Simmons returned to the file folder, reading each page, and placing it upside down on his desk.

Simmons finally put the papers back in the folder and lumbered to his feet. "Okay, it looks suspicious all right." He pulled his tie to bring the knot closer to his neck. "Let's go."

There was no traffic on a Saturday evening, and the drive to the high school took five minutes. Simmons followed the cruiser in his ancient Ford 150 pickup truck and parked next to Tolman on the edge of the football field, near the east bleachers. "You guys stay here while I see what's going on. If I'm not back in a few minutes, take off," Simmons told the deputies. "No point in you wasting your time here. I'll head over to the parents' house after I talk to forensics."

Four cars and the forensics van were present, and lights shone through the bleachers. Yellow crime scene tape surrounded the area, and Simmons ducked under it. He approached the two people setting up the lighting to illuminate the area. "You guys got shoe covers?" He pulled out latex gloves from his back pocket and slipped them on. After putting covers on his shoes, Simmons moved up to stand beside the lights. "Where's Pearson?" He looked at the woman who was holding the lighting. She pointed to the right corner of the taped-off area.

"Over there, crawling under the seats. He's been taking pictures and measurements of footprints and picking up trash. But it's probably a lost cause. There was a pep rally here on Friday afternoon, and a half dozen searchers who found the purse trampled all over the area."

Simmons grunted and walked away. He bent down to peer under the bleachers. "Pearson, finding anything interesting?"

The investigator raised his head, which collided with the underside of the bleachers. He turned toward Simmons and began moving on hands and knees until he was out from under. "Finding a lot, none of it likely relevant," he said, standing up. He was shoulder-high to Simmons and wiry, with thinning light brown hair standing up around his ears. A dozen plastic bags tied to his belt held detritus he'd bagged and labeled. More bags, awaiting filling, spilled from the pockets of his pants. "Lots of footprints around the area where the purse was found, but I suspect most are from the searchers. No signs of a scuffle. And most of what I've been finding look like items left over from the pep rally." He grimaced in disgust. "Some condoms—used— back under there. Don't know what the younger generation is thinking. We never did the dance under the bleachers. Too dirty and too visible."

"Know what you mean," Simmons grunted. "But something must have happened here. Teen girls don't leave their phones behind voluntarily. When will you finish up?"

"A few more hours. Then it'll take a couple days to process what we found," Pearson said, smoothing his hair down. He sighed and rubbed his back. "I'll give you a call when we have anything to report." He dropped to his knees and crawled back under the bleachers, flashlight shining on an area to the right of where he'd been working.

"Okay, I'm going to the girl's house to talk to the parents." Simmons strode away without saying anything to the three other investigators. He got in his truck and plugged in the address.

Chapter 6

Saturday night, April 7

My anxiety level rose as I watched the vehicles pull away. I was shaking, inwardly and physically. Deputy Barrett came downstairs after a few minutes.

"I didn't find anything in her room that would help us," she said. "We may want to look at her laptop to see if there's anything on it that might indicate who she might be with. Maybe tomorrow. For now, I'm heading to the school to check in with the forensics team and my partner, and I'll brief Detective Simmons. He'll be over to talk to you sometime this evening."

I thanked her and watched her leave. Sarah came and stood beside me.

"What can I do to help, Jana?"

"The deputy didn't spend much time up there. I'm going to search her room myself," I mumbled, my voice cracking. "Maybe there's something—a note or phone number—that can tell me who she was talking to that we don't know about. Or what might be behind this."

"Okay, come on. I'll help you." Sarah put a hand on my arm and drew me toward the stairs. As I followed her, I saw Kyle and Don talking in the kitchen. Don's face was grim, and Kyle's was distraught. I felt like I should be doing something to smooth the situation between them. But it was too much. I didn't have the energy, or the will, at this point to be the peacemaker.

The door to LaRissa's room was slightly open. I looked around in dismay. Everything was jumbled, out of place. LaRissa was a neat freak; everything in her room had to be exactly in its place. Her bookshelf was organized by category, author, and title. She organized the clothes in the dresser and closet by type, season, and color. Pictures and posters were hung carefully, using a level and tape measure. "I have to fix her room before she comes back," I said. "She'll be upset if it's like this." I could hear, as if from afar, a note of hysteria in my voice. I rushed over to her dresser drawers and began straightening and refolding the items in the top drawer.

Sarah put her arm around my shoulders and pulled me away. "Jana, let's do this systematically, while we search." Her voice was gentle. "We'll search and then put everything exactly where LaRissa would want it. Okay?" She smiled. "Let's start with her bed. Then we'll do her desk, the dresser, and the closet."

My eyes darted around the room, frantically. She led me to the bed and placed me on one side while she circled to the other side. "Duvet first. Lift and shake." I robotically followed her directions, and we raised the duvet in the air, shook it, and then folded it. "Okay, nothing there. Now the sheets." Sarah bent to lift the top sheet up. By the time we were down to the mattress, I was taking deep breaths and was calmer.

Sarah and I slid the mattress off the bed. A black composition book slid to the floor as the mattress landed with a thud. I bent and picked it up.

"What is it?" Sarah took a step toward me as I opened the cover.

Inside, on the first page, there was a sketch of a little girl. She was huddled in a corner, head buried in her arms. The picture was framed by black slashes that looked as though they had been drawn harshly, some of the slashes scratching through the paper. I sucked in a deep breath. The drawing was frightening. The child radiated terror and despair, with long hair covering her face and her shoulders bent inward and self-protective. LaRissa had always been artistic, but I'd never seen a picture she'd drawn that was so . . . frightening.

"Nothing," I said, firmly closing the cover. "Looks like math homework." I laid the composition book on the dresser. "Let's keep searching. Move the box spring." I lifted one side of the heavy box spring and pushed it off the frame.

"Okay, nothing here except a few dust balls. Her room sure is neater than any of my girls'," Sarah said, smiling. "Let's put the bed back together then start on the dresser drawers."

I nodded, and we quickly reassembled the bed and bedding. I was careful to line up the sheets, blanket, and duvet precisely, as LaRissa had made it.

We had just started working our way through the dresser when the doorbell rang. I could hear Don talking to someone before yelling for me to come downstairs. I looked at Sarah, who shrugged. She started to leave the room. I went to the dresser, picked up the composition book, and slipped it under my sweater.

"Tell Don I'll be down in a minute," I said to Sarah. She headed down the stairs, and I went into the spare bedroom. The composition book was burning a hole in my skin. Were there clues to what LaRissa has been up to? Mentions of people she didn't want me to know about? No time to look through it right now, but I had a feeling it held information that might help find her. My mind was whirling in confusion. I just knew this was too personal . . . too revealing . . . to share with anyone. Not the police, and not even Don. I wasn't even certain I wanted to know what was in it. I went to the bedroom closet where our winter clothes were stored and slid the book into a deep pocket of my gray Burberry coat.

When I got downstairs, Sarah was on the phone in the living room and Don was waiting impatiently, his expression irritated. "The detective is here. He wants to talk to both of us in the kitchen." He put his hand on my arm and led me into the kitchen. "This is Detective Simmons. He has some questions for us."

The detective was sitting at the kitchen table, his hands around a cup of coffee that, I assumed, Sarah had poured for him. He stood up. Simmons was tall and old, and I thought I heard his knees creak as he rose from the chair. His appearance didn't give me much confidence. He was rumpled, with what was probably a mustard stain on his tie and thinning gray hair that looked like it hadn't seen a comb for days.

"Please sit down, Mrs. Spencer." His voice was hoarse, like he'd swallowed something rough that had hurt going down. "I have a few questions for you and your husband, and then I'd like to talk to your son." I slid into a chair across from him. Don sat down and took my hand.

Simmons coughed a harsh bark. "Sorry, I'm just getting over a cold. Now, would you begin at the beginning? When did you last talk to and see your daughter? And were there any arguments or problems that you think might have affected her mood before she left on Friday night?"

I tensed up. Was he trying to blame us for her disappearance? Suggest that we'd somehow driven her away? "She was fine! Normal all day on Thursday. I dropped her off at school. She was here for dinner, then she and Kyle, our son, left to go to the church social. Nothing seemed different. Just our usual routine. At least till the high school called Friday and said she wasn't in school." My voice, in my head, sounded far-off, echoing. I looked at Don for affirmation. He nodded and then began providing details that I'd left out. LaRissa had been short and irritable with him on Thursday evening. He'd told her the dress she was wearing—with a thigh-length skirt and low bodice that revealed her cleavage—wasn't appropriate for a church social. He'd demanded she change before she left the house. LaRissa had argued with him. When he'd threatened to not let her go to the social, she'd had tears in her eyes when she went upstairs and changed into more modest pants and a sweater. She'd left the house minutes later, saying her friend was picking her up.

"Do you know what friend picked her up?" Simmons looked at Don, his rheumy eyes sharply focused.

"No, I don't know!" Don retorted. "She's always had a lot of friends, and we've always trusted her. There was no reason to interrogate her."

"I think she was meeting her friend, Brenda, who lives down the block," I added. "Brenda usually drives when they're going somewhere. LaRissa's only fifteen, so she doesn't have a license yet."

Simmons ruffled through a notebook he'd set in front of him. "That's Brenda Caswell?"

I nodded.

"Okay, I'll be talking to her to see what she may know. Now, tell me about your relationship with your daughter. Was this argument Thursday night unusual?"

Don and I looked at each other. "Yes," I said.

"Lately, she's been a bit difficult," Don said, interrupting me before I could go on. "LaRissa's always been an easy child, but in the past few months she's been showing signs of what I call 'teen angst.'" He smiled, as he looked at Simmons. "You know, what most teens go through. Resenting being asked to do chores. Arguing with us about little things, like the dress. We all went through it, right? Pulling away from our parents. Trying to be independent."

Simmons made a neutral noise and looked at me. "Is that what you've seen, Mrs. Spencer? Sometimes a child is different with each parent."

I gave him a hard look. "No, I haven't seen that. LaRissa has always been polite and certainly not rebellious." I thought for a moment, then added, "She's been a bit moody lately, not talking a lot about school and friends. But I wouldn't say she's been resentful or argumentative. Not with me, anyway."

Simmons just nodded and jotted something in his notebook. "So, you didn't actually see who picked her up?" Don and I both shook our heads. "Okay, I'll want to talk to your neighbors. Maybe see if anyone has a security cam that might show something."

I was getting exasperated. "Detective! We know she went to the social! Her friends saw her there. Talked to her. But she didn't leave with them. Isn't that what you should be focused on? Who she left with? That should be your starting point, shouldn't it?" My voice was getting shrill, and I took a deep breath. "Not how she was getting along with her father and me."

Simmons put his pen down. "Yes," he said, calmly. "Yes, we will focus on who she left the social with. But your relationship with her . . . what she was thinking . . . may be important. It may help us figure out what caused her to leave the social with someone other than her usual friends. There's still a possibility that she's run away and will show up soon."

"Without her purse and phone?" Don's anger was rising. I could see the flush around his ears that usually indicated rage just beneath the surface. I put a hand on his arm to calm him. He shook it off.

"We don't know what happened that resulted in her purse and phone being dropped. Yes, it's suspicious, but not definitive," Detective Simmons said. "It's possible, yes, that she was abducted. Maybe by someone she knows, maybe by a stranger. We don't know. There also could have been an accident. I have someone checking hospitals within a hundred-mile radius, just in case. I also have my people interviewing her friends and others who were at the social Thursday night. We've distributed her picture and a BOLO to law enforcement in the state. Don't think we're not taking this seriously, Mr. Spencer. We are." He rubbed his forehead, his eyes steady on Don. "Now I'd like to talk to your son. He was with her at the social and may have information that is useful."

"Kyle told us he saw her there, but she told him to get lost," I responded quickly. "She refused to ride home with him, so he left. He would have told us if he'd seen anything or anyone that he thought was important. He told me he left after a half hour and went to the arcade for a while and then came home." My anxiety level was rising, feeling protective of Kyle who wouldn't handle an interrogation well. "The two of them are so different. They're not close at all. I wish they were. . ." My voice trailed off.

"I just need to talk to him," Simmons said. "Maybe he'll remember something that's helpful. Or maybe not. But I do need to talk to him."

Don stood up and went to the stairs. "Kyle," he yelled. "Come down here!" I heard Kyle's music shut off and his bedroom door open.

"I think his father and I should be with him if you're going to interrogate him," I pleaded. "He has health issues."

"He'll be fine, Jana. He doesn't need mama bear to protect him," Don said. "We'll go in the living room, Detective. Would you like another cup of coffee?"

Simmons shook his head and stood as Kyle came into the kitchen. "No, thank you. I'll talk to you again after your son and I finish up."

Don led me into the living room. Sarah was still on the phone and nodded at me. I looked back to see Kyle staring at the detective, his face pale. "He needs us with him, Don. He's only a boy."

"A boy who's three inches taller than I am. And eighteen years old. That's an adult, legally. Would you rather they take him down to the police station and talk to him in an interrogation room? Besides, I really don't think he knows anything more than what he told us. It's not like LaRissa considers him a close confidante." Don put his arm around my waist and pulled me to the sofa.

"Would you like that sandwich now?" Sarah asked, putting her phone in a pocket. "I have a couple dozen wrapped in plastic in the refrigerator."

"And some coffee would be good," Don said. "I don't expect we'll get much sleep tonight."

I nodded distractedly. I could hear the murmur of voices in the kitchen, but not the words. Sarah ducked into the kitchen and quickly returned with a plate of sandwiches, a coffee carafe, and a stack of paper cups. She poured three cups of coffee and set them on the coffee table. "It'll be all right, Jana," she comforted. "They'll find her soon, or she'll call, or come strolling in the door." She patted my shoulder. "Eat. You need to keep your strength up."

I picked up a sandwich and peeled the plastic off. Peanut butter and jelly. Three bites in my stomach started roiling. I sat back, straining to hear the conversation in the other room, but the voices were quiet. Don ate heartily, two sandwiches and half of a third. Sarah sat silently, watching me with concern.

After twenty minutes, I heard Kyle's footsteps pounding up the stairs. Then his door slammed and his music blared full blast.

"See, he's fine," Don said. Uh-huh, I thought. The door slam and full-blast music didn't convince me he was fine. More like hiding out, as usual. We both stood and went into the kitchen.

"Well, did Kyle give you anything useful?" Don asked.

"Some," Simmons responded, not looking up from the notebook he was writing in. "He did see her talking to a group of young men that he claimed he didn't know. Said LaRissa was flirting with one of them and gave me a description." He tucked his notebook in his pocket. "I'll see if there was video at the church social. We may be able to identify the men. And I'll ask her friends if any of them took pictures on their cell phones. It's not much, but it could shake out a lead to who she left with."

He stood up. "To be honest, Kyle knows more than he told you. Or me. There was something about his story that raised my interest. Do you know what arcade he went to when he left the social? I'll check out his alibi with them."

"Alibi! Are you considering him a suspect?" My voice rose, and my hands rolled into fists.

"Sorry, Mrs. Spencer. I don't mean alibi as in he's a suspect. Just I need to verify his story. Know for sure where he was Thursday night. If he was at the arcade, that'll be all I need to know. If not, I'll need to talk to him again."

"Calm down, Jana," Don said. "The detective is just doing his job. It doesn't mean he thinks Kyle did something to LaRissa." He looked at Simmons. "Thank you, Detective. What's next?"

"One more question. Did you see your son when he returned home Thursday night? What time was it?" He picked up his pen and poised it over his notebook.

I looked at Don and shook my head. "I went to bed early. Don, were you here when he came back?"

"I went next door and watched the game with Bill, my neighbor. Didn't get back till after eleven," Don said. "He was home then. I could hear a video game playing in his room. But I didn't stick my head in, so I don't know exactly when he got back."

Simmons made a note. "Okay, then. You two stay close to home while we do what we can to find your daughter. If you hear from her, or from anyone who might know where she is, call me right away." Simmons handed us each a card. "This is the number where you can reach me, day or night. I'll be working the case, and if we learn anything new, I'll be in touch with you." He nodded at both of us and went to the front door. I could see he was limping and wished they had assigned a younger, more active detective. His age and physical condition didn't reassure me that he'd be "on the job night and day" as he'd promised.

I went back in the kitchen, thanked Sarah for her help, and told her to go home and get some rest. She hugged me and slipped out the side door.

"The searchers are still working," Don said, looking at the clock. "They said they'd keep going till midnight. I'm going out to join them. You hold down the fort here."

"Take Kyle with you," I said as he put on his jacket. "He needs to feel like he's involved, helping. It's not good for you to leave him out."

Don rolled his eyes at me, then ran up the stairs. I heard him talking to Kyle. After a few minutes, he came downstairs with Kyle trailing after him. "We'll be back after midnight. Try to get some sleep," Don told me.

When they were gone, the house was deadly quiet. I turned on the TV to local news. A picture of LaRissa flashed on the screen and I gasped. The young woman reporter was talking about LaRissa being missing and asked anyone who knew her whereabouts to call the number on the screen. I frantically clicked off the television and collapsed in a chair, unable to think anymore.

Chapter 7

Sunday morning early, April 8

I woke just after midnight from a restless sleep plagued by dreams I couldn't remember but left me on edge. Downstairs, Don was shouting. I quickly put on my robe and opened the bedroom door. Rushing down the stairs, I found Don standing over Kyle, who was lying face down on the floor.

"What are you doing?" I was yelling and panicky. Kyle pushed himself up and scuttled away from Don and me. Don's face was red and furious. "What's happening?" Kyle was moving on all fours toward the stairs. I grabbed Don by the shoulders. "I need to know what's going on!"

"What's going on? I'll tell you what's going on," Don shouted, his voice hoarse. "We're all out searching the east side of town. I assigned Kyle to cover two square blocks. When he didn't show up at the meeting place, I went looking for him. He wasn't searching. He was sitting on a park swing, listening to music." Don fished in his jacket pocket and pulled out earbuds. "I confiscated these, and then he knocked me down trying to get them back." Don threw the earbuds on the floor and then smashed them with the heel of his boot.

Kyle made a dash toward the stairs as Don advanced toward him, fists raised. I heard his footsteps scrambling up the stairs. His bedroom door slammed, and I heard the lock snap shut.

"Yeah, run, you little jackass!" Don took a step toward the stairs. I jumped in front of him.

"Don, stop it! Calm down and tell me what happened, exactly," I said. I reached out and took his hand. "This isn't helpful. Come over here and talk to me." Don visibly shook himself, which he did when he was trying to regain control. He put his arms around me and led me over to the sofa.

"I don't know what's wrong with him," Don said. "He seems unwilling to help search for LaRissa. He avoids talking to the other searchers. I'm beginning to wonder if the detective is right—maybe he does know more about where she is or who she's with, and he isn't telling us."

"You don't believe that, Don. I know that Kyle cares about LaRissa. He's just overwhelmed with all that's going on." My heart was breaking for Kyle, and I didn't know how I could convince Don that his attitude was hurting, not helping. "You know he's always found it difficult to handle chaos, confusion. I think he's terribly worried about her. But his reaction to his fear is to withdraw, shut down."

Don took a deep, rasping breath. He took my hand. "You're right. It's just that I'm so angry about all this. When I saw him sitting on the swing, nodding his head to music, I exploded. Grabbed him by the hair and dragged him back to where the other searchers were waiting for their next assignments. And screamed at him." He looked at me, shame-faced. "Not good. What can I do to fix this?"

"Don, I'm not handling this well either. But we've got to all pull together to get through this as a family. Kyle needs us as much as LaRissa does." I leaned over and gently kissed his cheek. "I'll go talk to Kyle right now. You go back to the search. Or go back and close the search down for the night." He nodded and walked to the door, his shoulders slumped.

The door closed, and I heard the car engine start. I took a deep breath and went upstairs. I tapped lightly on Kyle's door and turned the doorknob. Locked, as I figured.

"Kyle, it's Mom. Let me in." There was a muffled sound from inside.

"Kyle! Open the door now." No response. "You do know I can unlock this door with a kitchen knife, right? Don't make me go downstairs and get one."

The bedsprings squeaked, and I heard Kyle shuffling toward the door. He opened it a crack. His face was tearstained and pale. "I don't want to talk right now," he muttered, his eyes staring at a wall across the room. "Just leave me alone."

"I'm not going to leave you alone," I said, pushing gently against the door. "We need to talk." He stepped back, and the door swung open. Kyle turned his back on me and headed for the bed, where he lay down and pulled the covers up over his head.

I sat down on the bed and stroked his back. "Look, Kyle. Your dad is sorry for what happened tonight." My voice was soft and calm. Kyle had often been overwhelmed and scared as a child, and I had always been the one who could soothe him, bring him back from the dark place he withdrew into. "Do you understand how frightened he is that something has happened to LaRissa?" Kyle didn't move or respond. "The most terrible thing for a parent is to think their child is lost and in danger. I'm frightened, too, you know. If it was you missing, both your dad and I would be just as scared." A muffled disbelieving sob emerged from the bedclothes.

"It's true," I went on. "And sometimes when people are afraid—terribly afraid—they take it out on other people. That's all that happened tonight. Your dad was holding in a lot of fear, and it exploded on you. He's sorry, really he is. And he'll tell you that himself when he gets back and gets some sleep. And I know you're scared too. For LaRissa." I let that sink in for a moment. "I have to believe that LaRissa will be okay. She'll come home on her own, or the police will find her. But until that happens, we need to all get through this as a family. Your father loves you, even when he's hard on you. And I love you. And we need to be kind and support each other." I kneaded his back through the comforter.

The bed covers stirred and Kyle peered out at me. "I don't know, Mom. I don't know anything. But Dad shouted at me in front of everyone and pulled my hair and accused me of . . . I'm not sure what, but I think he's thinking I'm hiding something and don't want to help find LaRissa." His voice cracked on his sister's name. His face, what I could see of it, was pale. "I don't know anything," he whispered.

I stroked his cheek. "I know you don't, Kyle. I know. But please think about what he's going through and forgive him. He doesn't think you're deliberately lying about what LaRissa did on Thursday night, he's just desperate to find her. It'll be all right." I smiled at him. "The detective who talked to you said he would check with the arcade to verify that you were there. Once he's done that, your dad will know you're telling the truth. And if you can join in the search tomorrow, that will help. Not that you'll necessarily find her, but it will show you're doing your part." Kyle whimpered and pulled the covers up again. "Okay?"

A muffled sound came from under the covers, and I took it as an affirmative. "Try to get some sleep. We all need to keep our strength up and tomorrow—actually, today now—will be the day LaRissa is back. We'll get through this, Kyle. Really, we will."

The motion of the covers suggested a nod. I patted him again, turned out the lamp, and went out of his room. I hoped I'd helped repair the damage to my fragile teen boy's psyche. I hoped.

Chapter 8

Sunday morning, April 8

Sarah woke me at ten Sunday morning. She knocked and came in holding a cup of coffee. I extricated myself from under the covers, ran my fingers through my hair, and sat up.

"Any news?" I took a sip of coffee.

Sarah sat down on the edge of the bed, her face somber. "Nothing new," she responded. "Don and Kyle left about eight to meet the search teams. Don said to tell you they'd be back this evening and not to wait up for them."

I looked at her, questioning.

"Bill told me about their argument last night." Bill, Sarah's husband, was the football coach and PE teacher at the high school. "It looked pretty bad, but they seemed okay this morning."

A wave of relief washed through me. "It was awful," I said. "I thought Don was going to hit Kyle—or worse—when I came downstairs after hearing Don shouting. I talked Don down, and it sounds like they must have talked after I went back to sleep." I shook my head. "We're all so stressed." I sipped my coffee, head down, not wanting Sarah to see the tears that suddenly flooded my eyes.

"I know you are," Sarah said. "Anyone going through this nightmare would be." She put a hand over mine.

I looked at her and didn't say anything.

"Anyway, I've been making more sandwiches for the searchers. There are reporters out front, and some cameras from

TV stations. I called the police and asked them to send a patrol car to keep them off your property. One of them was on the lawn, trying to take pictures through the windows. Not that they would get any except shadows of my ample form holding bread slices and a knife." She smiled. "I doubt they'll want to put that on TV. But I've closed all the blinds and curtains downstairs. If you're ready to get up and come downstairs, it's safe."

I threw the comforter back and swung my feet over the side of the bed. "I guess I'll take a shower and get dressed. I'll be down in a few minutes." I leaned over and hugged Sarah. "Thank you. You're a rock. I don't know how I'd get through this without you."

She hugged me back. "I'm here, whatever you need. And my girls are on errand duty, so you can put together a list of what you need from the grocery store, and they'll pick it up." She stood up. "You want breakfast? Soft-boiled egg on toast and orange juice, maybe?"

"Sure. Fifteen minutes and I'll be down." I looked around for my phone. Frowning, I patted the bed covers. "Did I leave my phone downstairs?"

"You did. It's in the kitchen and has been going off a lot. I let the calls go to voicemail. Probably more reporters and friends who've heard that LaRissa is still missing. You can check them when you come down." She went to the door. "Breakfast in fifteen minutes!"

I sat on the side of the bed, thinking and monitoring my state of mind: worry, but not despair—despite the nightmares during my restless night. I'd even had the recurring one that started when I was a child: me, panicky, running through a dark forest, knowing something or someone was chasing me. And knowing something terrible would happen if I was caught. I shook my head and stood up, thinking maybe I was due for a refresher therapy session. But Dr. Hannigan had retired, and I really wasn't up to starting over with someone new. Besides, somehow, I was sure LaRissa would be home soon. She had to be.

Downstairs, I ate breakfast and scrolled through my phone calls. There were a few old friends—just calling to say they were thinking of me—and several calls from news reporters. I deleted the latter without listening to messages. The last call recorded was from the Franklin County Sheriff's Office. News? I doubted it. If there was anything new to report, the detective on the case would have shown up at our door.

"Anything important?" Sarah poured me another glass of orange juice and sat down at the kitchen table, nibbling on a chocolate chip cookie. She'd brought a large platter of cookies with her.

"Not really, but I need to listen to messages." I punched in the number for my voicemail. *You have nine new messages.* The first one was from my mother. She lives in a retirement community in Florida and ordinarily we talk only once or twice a month. We'd never been close. Our political and cultural values were diametrically opposed, and it was difficult to stick to the few topics that didn't lead us to a point where I could visualize her pursing her lips and frowning on the other end of the line. Apparently, she hadn't heard the news about LaRissa. Thank heavens for being an only child and having no relatives left living in the area. Her message was just something about having big news to tell me. I hit the number for "save" and went on to the next message.

The next four were from friends who expressed their concern and offered the usual "anything we can do to help, just call." The sixth call was from Kammie, my colleague at the clinic. *Jana, I heard about LaRissa being missing. Oh god, I'm so sorry! Listen, don't worry about anything at the clinic. I'll let Dr. Kahn know first thing in the morning and tell him you won't be in. Please, please, let me know when they find her. And . . . well, just don't worry about the clinic.* There was a long pause, followed by *I'm so sorry this is happening. Bye.* I half smiled. I could see Kammie, flustered, not really knowing what to say, but managing to call anyway. I hadn't given a thought to the clinic or the two grants I was writing since Saturday morning, and I didn't intend to. Priorities, Jana. I deleted a couple of scam call messages.

The final message was from Detective Simmons, left at three o'clock this morning. *Mrs. Simmons, I'm calling to tell you we're actively working on your daughter's case. As part of that, I'd like to talk again to Kyle. I'm going home to get a few hours of sleep now. But I'd appreciate it if you could have him at the Fairmont sheriff's office Monday at 2 p.m. He can ask for me. If you have any questions before then, feel free to call me after 9 a.m. today.* Simmons' voice was tired and hoarse and, again, I wondered again if he was up to this investigation.

When the message was over, I sat staring at my phone.

"Are you okay, Jana?" Sarah was looking at me, concern on her face.

"Yeah. That last message was the detective assigned to LaRissa's case. He wants to talk to Kyle tomorrow." I glanced at her. "I don't know why he needs to talk to him. Kyle's already told him everything he knows. And he said he hadn't seen LaRissa after he left the social that night."

"Well, you did tell me the detective said he thought Kyle knew more than he said when he was interviewed before. Maybe they just want to see if he's remembered anything else."

"Maybe. But I think I'd better call Don and tell him about this," I said, picking up my phone. The call to Don went to voicemail. I left a message for him, asking him to call me as soon as he got the message.

"I think I'm going to do laundry," I told Sarah as I got up from the table. "I usually do it on Saturday, but yesterday was a lost day. This waiting is the worst thing. I'd rather be out with the searchers so I could feel like I was doing something to find her. But the police said I needed to stay in the house in case LaRissa came back. I really don't want to talk to anyone, except for you, and I can't focus enough to read or watch TV." I stood up. "So, I'm going to do laundry." I tucked my phone into my jeans pocket.

"You do that," Sarah said. "I'll clean up the kitchen and run the vacuum. All these people traipsing in and out are leaving dirt and mud on the floors."

Don called back when I was in the basement, loading the second load of laundry into the dryer. "What's up? We've got a few more hours of the search ahead, so Kyle and I will be home around six or seven."

I told him about the call from Detective Simmons.

"He wants to talk to him at the sheriff's office? That sounds more like interrogation than just talking to him," Don said. "I don't like this. I'm going to call Simmons and see what he's thinking. Also, I want to find out if we can be in the room with Kyle when Simmons is talking to him."

"Well, Simmons said we could call him today after nine. He was going home to sleep when he left the message."

"It's eleven now. I'll let you know what he says." Don hung up abruptly.

He called back twenty minutes later. "That SOB wouldn't tell me anything except he had some additional questions for Kyle. I asked him if we could be with Kyle while he was questioned and he said an emphatic 'no.' That Kyle was eighteen and he didn't have the right to have his parents in the room. I told him I was going to call a lawyer to be there, and Simmons said that was my prerogative." He muttered some epithets about Simmons' parentage before going on. "Find a lawyer. Preferably one who knows something about criminal law. Not Larry, he just does wills and real estate. But call him and ask him for a suggestion." I could hear voices in the background. "Gotta go. Call Larry!"

Sarah was hovering in the doorway. "Everything all right?"

"No, not all right. The detective wants to talk to Kyle again tomorrow and says we can't be in the room when he questions Kyle. Because Kyle is technically 'an adult.'" I air-quoted the last two words. "Now Don wants me to track down a criminal lawyer and get him on board to be with Kyle tomorrow afternoon."

Sarah came in the room and sat on the arm of the chair across from me. "Look," she said. "I'm sure they don't think Kyle had anything to do with LaRissa going missing. That's absurd! But they may think he does know more than he told them. Like, he actually knows who the guys were that LaRissa was talking to at the social and, for some reason, is afraid to name them."

I shook my head. "That doesn't make any sense. Why would he be afraid to name them?"

"Well, think about it. What if they—or at least one of them—had sold Kyle drugs, back when he was using? He wouldn't want to rat the guy out, right?" Sarah had written a couple mystery novels and had a vivid imagination. Not vivid enough to have gotten the books published, though, despite her efforts to find a publisher.

"I doubt that's a thing, Sarah," I said, dismissive of her fantasies. "Anyway, I need to call Larry Stevenson and ask him who we should call that has criminal law experience. I'm going upstairs."

By the time I'd talked to Larry, called the lawyer he'd suggested, left a message, and finished the laundry, Don and Kyle were home. Don had explained the situation to Kyle, who didn't take it well and went directly up to his room.

"I'm just waiting for the call back from the lawyer," I said.

"If you don't hear from him soon, call Larry again and get another name," Don said. "No way I'm letting Simmons bully Kyle into some sort of admission or confession. I'm going to take a shower."

"Sarah left a stew in the oven. I'll make a salad. You need to eat," I said as Don pounded up the stairs.

My phone rang as I was setting the table. It was the lawyer, James Barrow. I answered and briefly explained what was going on. Barrow agreed to be at the sheriff's office at one-thirty on Monday; he wanted to meet and talk to Kyle before the interview. I agreed and hung up.

More waiting. More to worry about. There was still no sign of LaRissa. And now I had to worry about Kyle too. I dropped into a kitchen chair and buried my head in my hands.

Chapter 9

Monday afternoon, April 9

"Al, they're here. You want me to take them to the interrogation room?" Deputy Barrett stood in the doorway of the coffee room.

Detective Simmons looked up from the table where he was eating a corned beef and Swiss sandwich. "Yeah, take them to Room Three." He grimaced. "Only one with a comfortable chair—for me, anyway. Who all is here?"

"Kid's lawyer is with him. And the father. Father told me the mother stayed home in case the girl shows up."

Simmons nodded and went back to his sandwich. He crammed the last piece into his mouth and hauled his bulk up to stand. The coffeepot was nearly finished re-filling, and he waited till the last few drops fell before limping over to pour his cup full. As he finished, Sheriff Smith strolled in.

"Doing your usual and keeping the witnesses waiting?" The sheriff poured a cup of coffee, turning his back to Simmons.

Simmons grunted. "Longer they wait, the more they get anxious, Jack. And anxious can be good."

"Well, don't keep them waiting too long. The lawyer they brought along is Barrow. He charges $250 an hour. Don't want to run up a big bill for them, unless you figure the kid is responsible for his sister's disappearance. Election's coming up, and I don't want to have to deal with a harassment complaint."

"Barrow, huh? Brought out the big guns." Simmons lifted his cup to his lips. "Now that's interesting. Barrow's the only lawyer in the county who's had experience in murder trials. Makes me wonder."

"Most likely, they just called the first lawyer whose name they recognized. Anyway, take it easy on the kid. He's in my son's class and, from what I hear, he's got some serious health problems." Smith fixed Simmons with a glance. "You don't actually suspect him, do you?"

"I suspect everyone. Always. But I'll take it easy until I have some reason to treat the kid as a perp."

"Let me know if anything comes from your interview. The girl's been missing since last Thursday night—almost four days. Doesn't look good."

After the sheriff left, Simmons lowered himself into a chair at the sole table in the small room. He absentmindedly rubbed his right knee and glanced at the clock on the wall. *Ten more minutes should give them time to work up a sweat.* He sipped his coffee and leafed through the sports section of the newspaper someone had left on the table. When he finished reading a story on why his team was one-and-nine for the year, he refilled his coffee cup and headed toward the interrogation room.

Inside, Kyle Spencer was sitting at the conference table, his shoulders slumped and his long hair hiding his face. On one side of him, James Barrow was reading some papers that he quickly stuffed into his open briefcase before closing it. He stood up.

"Detective Simmons, good to see you. Although the situation is surely unfortunate." Barrow rested one hand on Kyle's shoulder. "My client is here voluntarily, and he wants to help in any way he can." Barrow was tall, slim, and blond-haired. His tailored suit was dark blue, matched with a light blue shirt and navy and white striped tie. His wrist was encircled by a gold Rolex watch. Barrow stretched his arm over the table, hand extended.

"Yeah," Simmons grunted. "Haven't seen you since the Holzman trial." He gave a brief grasp of Barrow's hand and lowered himself into the chair opposite Kyle. "We can probably keep this brief. I just have a few questions." He looked around the room. "No father?"

"I told him he should wait outside," Barrow said. "I'll fill him in after we finish."

"Okay, then. Kyle . . ."

The kid startled at hearing his name. He straightened in the chair but kept his eyes on the table.

"Kyle, how about you start with going over again what happened Thursday night, the last time you saw your sister." Simmons leaned forward, propping his head on his hands.

"Well, uhh. Just like I told you. LaRissa rode to the social with her friend, Brenda. I went a little later. When I got there, she was hanging with her friends. I went over to her and told her that Mom said we had to be home by ten and I'd drive her." Kyle looked up. "Brenda always stays till the end, and we had to leave earlier. Anyway, LaRissa just laughed at me and said I should get lost, that there was no way she was going with me. Her friends all laughed at me too. So, I took off. I didn't want to go in the first place, but my mom said I had to make sure LaRissa got home by curfew." He paused and swallowed. "That's the last time I saw her."

Simmons nodded. "Yes, that's what you told me when we talked before. Where did you go after you left the party?"

"I told you that too." Kyle's voice cracked on the last word, and he turned red. "I went to the arcade over on Main Street, played some pinball, and left to go home a little before ten."

Simmons sat back in his chair, then slammed his hands on the table. "Okay, that's what I have a problem with, Kyle. I went to the arcade and talked to the manager who was working that night. He doesn't remember seeing you Thursday evening. And he has a video surveillance system. I looked at it, and I didn't see you there. Started at six-thirty and ran through the tape all the way to midnight, when they close. No Kyle." He paused and waited.

A few drops of sweat appeared on Kyle's forehead. Barrow held up a hand.

"I need to talk to my client for a minute, Detective. Could you please step out of the room?"

Simmons slowly stood up. "Five minutes." He picked up his coffee cup, walked out, and closed the door behind him. The coffeepot was empty, so he washed it out and set up another pot to brew. Once it was done, he poured a cup and went back to the interrogation room.

"Ready to start again, Kyle?" Simmons sat down.

Barrow looked at Kyle. "Go ahead, Kyle."

"I-I-I didn't want to sound like a l-l-loser," Kyle stuttered. "It sounds like I'm a loser with no friends or anything if I say that I left the social and just walked around for hours." His eyes brimmed with tears, and he angrily brushed them away. "LaRissa's friends all laughed at me, and I was embarrassed. So I just walked around. I thought it sounded better to say I went to the arcade."

Simmons stood up. "There's a map of the town on the wall. Why don't you come over here and trace for me where you walked that night?" He studied the map for a moment, then picked up a pushpin and put a red-tipped pin in. "This is the church. Where did you go from there?"

Kyle lifted his hand and pointed to the left. "I-I-I think I went to the park."

"Which park?"

His face flushing, Kyle stammered, "Th-th-the one with little p-p-ond."

Simmons picked up another pushpin and pressed it into the map. "What did you do there?"

"S-s-sat on the bench by the pond."

"For how long?"

"I-I-I don't know," Kyle said, after a pause. His eyes were downcast. "An hour? Then I went home."

"Okay, you went home. What time did you get there?"

"I d-d-don't know. Nine?" Kyle's voice cracked on the last word. He slumped back in the chair and covered his face with one hand.

A sharp knock on the interrogation room door interrupted Detective Simmons' next question. A uniformed deputy opened the door. "Detective, you're wanted at the front desk."

Barrow stood up. "I think it's time for a break, anyway. Kyle, can I get you something to drink?" Kyle shook his head and slid down farther in his chair.

"I'll be back in a few minutes," Simmons said. "Don't go anywhere. We're not done here."

Barrow sat back down as Simmons left the room. "Kyle, talk to me. I need to know if there's anything you're not telling the police. Did you go anywhere else that night? See anything that might be related to your sister's disappearance? Anything you tell me is confidential. Completely." He looked at Kyle, who had his eyes closed and didn't respond.

"Kyle! They seem to believe you're not telling everything you know. Are you?" Kyle shook his head.

The interrogation room door was flung open, and Simmons rushed in. "We're finished for now," he announced, his voice angry. "You can go home. But I'll want to continue this later. I'll let you know when."

Kyle straightened in his chair. "I can go home?"

"Yes, go home! Get your father and go home," Simmons said. "I'll be in touch this evening. Now get out of here."

Barrow stood up. "What's going on, Detective? Have you found LaRissa?"

"Just take your client and leave. I'll be in touch later—like I said." Simmons held the door open and motioned to them to go through it.

"We're leaving," Barrow said. "Kyle, come on. Let's find your father and get out of here."

Kyle struggled to his feet and followed Barrow out into the hallway. They walked toward the building entrance, where Kyle's father was waiting. Don put his hand on Kyle's shoulder and looked askance at the lawyer. "What's going on? Two deputies came running in, talked to the person at the front desk, and then one of them pulled Simmons out of the room you were in."

"Simmons didn't say anything," Barrow answered. "He just terminated the interview and said we'd pick it up again later. It may have nothing to do with your daughter." He patted Kyle on the back. "You did okay in there, but we should talk before you meet again with the detective. Now, I'm going back to my office. You should both go home. Call me if you hear from the police, and don't say anything to them without me there."

In the car, Don turned the ignition on but didn't pull out. "What did the detective ask you about, Kyle? Any idea?"

"He wanted to go over what I did after I left the social, I guess. I know it was dumb of me when I told him I was at the arcade. He checked their video cam and found out I wasn't there." Kyle glanced at his father. "I'm sorry I lied about that. It just slipped out 'cause I didn't want to say I was wandering around town alone. Are you mad?"

"No, Kyle. I'm not mad. It was dumb, like you said. You shouldn't ever lie to the police, and now you know that," Don said. "But no harm done. Let's get home. Your mother will be worried."

Chapter 10

Monday evening, April 9

Don and Kyle got home a little after five. Sarah was in the kitchen making a chicken casserole for dinner. I'd already finished making a chef salad and had rolls baking in the oven.

"How did it go with the interview?" I asked after hugging Kyle. He didn't meet my eyes.

"Apparently, the detective checked his alibi and found that he wasn't at the arcade," Don said. "Like he said, dumb move. That's why Simmons was interested in talking to him again." He patted Kyle on the shoulder. "But now he knows that lying to the police isn't ever a good idea."

"Were you able to be with him while the police were talking to him?"

"No, but Jim Barrow was there." Don frowned. "Detective Simmons ended the meeting suddenly, after another deputy came in and told him something. But Simmons told Kyle he'd want to talk to him again. Jim said to call him right away if they wanted Kyle to come down for another interview."

"Okay," I said, frowning. "Simmons didn't say why he was stopping the interview?"

Don shook his head. "I asked, but he said he'd be in touch with us if there was anything new to report."

My mind was conjuring up scenarios, some of which made my stomach roil. I sat down on the sofa.

"The casserole will be done in forty-five minutes," Sarah announced. I hadn't noticed she had come into the room while we were talking. "Anything new from the police?" When Don told her there wasn't, she went to the closet and took her jacket out. "Well, call me if you need anything. I'm heading home to fix dinner for the horde."

"Thanks, Sarah," I said, standing up. "I don't know what we'd do without you." I hugged her and walked with her to the back door. "See you tomorrow?"

"I'll be here right after school lets out," she said. "Try to get some rest." Sarah gave me a small smile. "It's going to be okay, Jana. I just know they're going to find her soon." She squeezed my hand and went out the door.

I heard Kyle's footsteps on the stairs and, seconds later, music playing. I went back into the living room. "Is he okay? He didn't say anything, and he looks anxious."

"He lied to the police, Jana. Now he says he was just walking around town by himself after he left the church social. Went to Green Park and sat on the bench for a while. Unless there were cameras he passed by, he doesn't have an alibi." Don looked worried, and that made me worried. "I think he knows something he's not telling us or the police."

"Like what?"

"I don't know. Maybe he knows who she left the social with? Maybe he's afraid if he tells the police, whoever it was will come after him? I just don't know!" The frustration in Don's voice was obvious. "I need to talk to him and find out what's really going on." He took a step toward the stairs, and I grabbed his arm.

"Leave him alone for now, Don. You're worked up, and that'll put him on the defensive. I'll talk to him after dinner, okay?"

Don shrugged away from me. "Okay. I'm going out to my workshop to try to finish the bookshelf I'm making. Call me when dinner's ready."

Dinner was strained. Kyle asked if he could take a plate up to his room. "I have a trig test tomorrow. I'm studying."

"You're not going to school tomorrow," Don said, his voice raised. "What's wrong with you? Your sister is still missing. Besides, that detective said he wanted to continue talking to you. You need to be available when he calls."

48

Kyle slumped in his chair. He picked up a fork and stirred it around in the casserole. "I'm not hungry anyway."

"You need to eat, Kyle. Did you take your blood sugar before dinner? What was it?" I worried about another diabetic seizure, something he'd had a couple times in the past when he wasn't eating on a regular schedule.

"It was fine. 135. I'm okay. And not due for insulin till eight o'clock," Kyle muttered. "Can I just go upstairs? I need to study even if I'm not going to school. I don't want to get behind and fail a class and not graduate next month."

"Just go!" Don shouted suddenly, slamming his hand on the table. "I don't understand you. Don't you care about LaRissa being missing?"

Kyle fumbled with his plate, stuck a fork in his pocket, and scurried out of the kitchen. I heard his steps on the stairs and then the music starting.

"You're being too hard on him. I know he's worried about LaRissa. And think what he's been through today—being interrogated by the police? He's stressed, and that's dangerous for him."

Don scowled at me. "You're babying him. He's eighteen, an adult, and he needs to begin acting like a man. Not hiding from difficult situations." He stood up. "I'm done. I'll be out in the garage." He grabbed a dinner roll and strode out of the room.

I stared after him, then got up and started cleaning up from dinner. Casserole and salad in the refrigerator, rolls in a plastic bag to the breadbox, dishes rinsed and put in the dishwasher, and the counter and table wiped clean. I sank into a kitchen chair when I was done. My family was falling apart, and I didn't know how to fix it. Don was always angry with Kyle and me. Kyle seemed hopeless and lost. What would he even do when he graduated? He wasn't interested in college or trade school. He told us he wanted to work full-time at the Final Quest, and it seemed like comic books and video games were all he was interested in. Don said he should join the military— "Make a man of you." But with his diabetes, I was sure the military wouldn't take him. It really felt hopeless to me too. I took a deep breath. I needed to talk to Kyle, smooth things over about his father, and see if he'd talk to me about the night LaRissa went missing.

The doorbell rang as I put my hand on the banister. My breath caught in my throat, and my heart raced. The police? Have they found her? I rushed to the door and opened it. Brenda and her mother were standing on the doorstep. "Can we come in?" Florence, Brenda's mother, put out her hand to touch my arm. "Brenda's told me something that I think you should know. It might help the police to find her."

"Of course, come in." I escorted them into the living room and waved them to the sofa. "Please sit down. Anything that can help will be more than we have right now."

Brenda was nervous. I could see she didn't want to be here. She took a seat at the end of the sofa farthest from where her mother was sitting. Flo was an imposing presence, nearly six feet tall and 200 pounds. She had one of those personalities that rammed their views through any opposition, as I'd discovered when she and I were on opposite sides in a school board meeting about social science education standards.

"I asked Brenda tonight about LaRissa's behavior at the social," Flo said. "She didn't want to tell me, but I knew something wasn't right. I can always tell when my kids are being evasive, and that's what she was doing. You need to hear this, but it's not pleasant." She fixed her gaze on Brenda. "Tell Mrs. Spencer what you told me."

Brenda cleared her throat, her eyes downcast. "I'm sorry, Mrs. Spencer. LaRissa will hate me for this."

"For what?" My voice was gentle.

"LaRissa's been in a bad place for the last few weeks. I don't know what happened to her, but something had her angry and sad, all at the same time. She wouldn't talk about it, really. But I knew she was wrestling with something." Brenda glanced at me. "Something bad. Then, on the way to the social, she told me she wanted to get . . . fucked." She blushed and looked at her mother. "I'm sorry, but that's the word she used. I said what's wrong with you? But she just said I wouldn't understand and that she was going to go with the first boy she found at the social who was willing to do it with her." Her eyes brimmed with tears. "There were some older boys there. She went up to one of them and said something to him. He laughed and nodded at her. I saw her dancing with him and went to get some punch, and when I got back, she was gone."

50

"Do you know who the boy was? Or any of the other boys he was with?" Finally, possibly a real lead.

"No. I never saw them before. One of the church people might know who they are. I'm sure they don't go to our school," Brenda said. "I thought she'd come back, but she didn't. I waited at the church for a half hour after the social ended and then left. It was already past ten-thirty, when my mom expected me home."

I thought for a moment. "I appreciate your coming and telling me this. I think the police will want to talk to you so you can give them a description of the boy LaRissa was with. And tell them the time frame for when you noticed she was gone." I stood up. "I'll call and let them know you have information. All right?"

Brenda looked scared but nodded.

Flo stood up. "I thought you needed to know. I hope it will be helpful but, really, I'm concerned that LaRissa may not be the type of person I want Brenda to be friends with. It sounds like she may need counseling when she comes home." She pursed her lips disapprovingly.

A wave of anger rolled through me. I bit back the response I wanted to make. "Thank you for bringing Brenda to talk to me, Flo. I'll take it from here, but the police will want to talk to her themselves."

"I'll be sure she's available when they do call. Now we'll take our leave." She nodded at Brenda, who stood and followed her mother to the front door. "Good luck," Flo said.

After they left, I was at a loss. Should I call Detective Simmons right now? I needed to tell Don first, or he'd be angry. I could hear the buzzing of the saw in the garage and resolved to go out and tell him before calling the police.

The doorbell rang as I reached a decision. When I opened the door, Detective Simmons and Deputy Barrett were waiting. Both had grim looks on their faces.

"May we come in, Mrs. Spencer?" Simmons didn't wait for my answer and walked into the living room. Barrett followed him and closed the door. "Is your husband here?" Simmons asked.

My heart was pounding, and I couldn't catch my breath. I nodded and sank down in a chair before pointing toward the garage. Deputy Barrett went through the side door that opened to the garage. The sound of the saw stopped, and I could hear Don's voice. Seconds later he and Barrett were in the living room.

"Why are you here? Tell us," Don demanded. He stood beside my chair, his hands clenched into fists.

"Please sit down, Mr. Spencer," Simmons said.

"I don't want to sit down! Just tell us!"

Simmons nodded. "All right. I'm sorry to tell you that a body was found this afternoon. It appears to be your daughter."

Don advanced toward Simmons, fists raised. "No. You're wrong! It's not LaRissa." I watched his face crumple as he stopped and put a hand on the back of the sofa to steady himself. "No, you're wrong," he repeated in a whisper. "It can't be LaRissa." Deputy Barrett went to him and gently led him to the sofa. He resisted for a moment, then sat. Anger washed over his face. "Where was the body found?"

I felt like I was in a glass cage, far away from what was happening, but able to see and hear. Their voices were tinny and remote. I could see Deputy Barrett watching me as she answered Don.

"The body was found at the school, Mr. Spencer. This afternoon."

Simmons added, "It's why I terminated my interview with your son. We suspected we'd found your daughter, but I didn't want to alarm you until we knew for sure it was her."

My mind cleared. Kyle. I had to tell Kyle. He couldn't find out from the police or from the internet. I scrambled to my feet and raced for the stairs. I could hear Don calling my name as I got to the top landing. I ignored him and knocked on Kyle's door, then threw it open without waiting for a response. "Kyle," I gasped out and then began sobbing.

"Mom? What is it?" Kyle got to his feet and stood in front of me. He reached for my arm and pulled me into his room, closing the door.

I couldn't say anything. My mouth was moving, but no sound was coming out. I couldn't breathe, and a deep cold swept through my body. Kyle caught me as my knees gave out. I could faintly hear Don slam Kyle's door open before I blacked out. When I came to, Kyle was sitting on the bed beside me, tears streaming down his face. Don was holding out his hand with three Xanax tablets in it.

"Take these," he commanded. "You need to rest. I'll go with the police and identify LaRissa." He paused. "The body. Maybe it's not LaRissa." His eyes were red, and his hand trembled as he held out the pills.

I sat up and swatted his hand away. The pills scattered, flying through the air. "I *don't* need to rest. What I need is for you not to tell me to deny how I'm feeling by drugging myself." I stood up. "LaRissa needs me. She needs her mother to be there for her, hold her hand, kiss her goodbye." The cold seeped through me, along with adrenalin. "I'm going with the police. See her, tell her . . ." My voice trailed off as the enormity of the moment caught me. I stood up, ignoring Don, and turned to Kyle. "Kyle, call Sarah. Ask her to come over and stay here till I get back." I went downstairs.

"Detective, I'm going with you to identify the body." My voice was firm, and my eyes were dry.

"I don't think that's a good idea, Mrs. Spencer. Your husband can do the identification."

"I'm going," I repeated. I went to the closet and took out a coat.

Simmons looked helplessly at Deputy Barrett. She walked over to me and put one hand on my shoulder. "Mrs. Spencer, you really don't want to do this. It's better if you remember your daughter smiling and happy. The good times."

I jerked away from her. "My daughter needs me, and I'm going."

By this time, Don had come downstairs. "Jana, they're right. You stay here and I'll go. It's better if it's me. We don't both need to do this."

"Why? Because you're the strong one? The one who protects and makes everything right?" My voice was flat and cold. "Sorry, Don, but you couldn't protect LaRissa, and you can't make everything right this time. I'm going. You can stay here with Kyle or come too. I don't care." I opened the front door. "Are you ready?" I glanced at the two law enforcement agents and stepped outside.

Chapter 11

Monday evening, April 9

Don drove us to the morgue. It was in the basement of the Fairview City Hospital, where the medical chief served as the county coroner. Despite Don's attempts to dissuade me from going in, I was determined to see LaRissa—to be certain, myself, that it was her. I think some part of my brain was hoping the girl they found at the school was someone else's daughter. When the car slowed in front of the hospital, I opened the door and got out before Don could park. "I'll meet you there," I flung over my shoulder as I hurried away.

The bright fluorescent lights of the lobby made everything stand out in relief. It was like a movie was playing out, and I observed myself walk to the front desk and ask for directions to the morgue. The receptionist gestured toward the elevators and told me to turn left when I reached the basement. Don was just entering the lobby when I pushed the "B" in the elevator and the doors closed. I wondered why I was so angry with him. The elevator chimed, and the doors opened. A left turn, two doors, and the sign that read Morgue told me I was where I needed to be. Detective Simmons and Deputy Barrett were waiting outside the door.

"Mrs. Spencer, Dr. Acker, the coroner, isn't here yet," Simmons said. "He's on the way. Where's your husband?"

The elevator chimed, and Don came around the corner. "There you are. I thought I saw you in the elevator when I came in upstairs," he said. "Detective, Deputy, let's get this over with." His voice echoed loudly in the empty hallway.

Simmons repeated what he'd just told me. "The coroner texted me to say he had an emergency case come in and would be here soon."

Don glowered at the detective, his face twisting in anger. "You dragged us down here without checking with him first? Thanks, thanks a lot." His voice rose. "It's not like we have nothing to do except stand around thinking that may be our daughter lying on a slab in there!" He slammed his fist against the door to the morgue. I was thinking I should try to calm him down, but I decided it wasn't my job. Simmons could handle him.

I leaned back against the concrete block wall of the hallway and closed my eyes. Within seconds, Deputy Barrett was next to me. "Are you all right, Mrs. Spencer?" I opened my eyes and stepped away from the deputy. Across the hall, Simmons pulled Don away from the morgue door and was leaning close, talking to him.

"I'm fine. Just tired."

"You really don't have to do this," Barrett said, her voice soft. "Your husband can make the identification. I can drive you home."

I stared at her. "It's my job, Deputy. I'm her mother. She needs—deserves—to have her mother with her now." I gulped down a sob, then stood up straight and leveled my shoulders. "It's my job." My voice was steady.

We waited almost twenty minutes until the doctor/coroner showed up. He was tall and very thin, with a shock of black hair standing up in tufts. His white coat was stained and rumpled. I thought how tired he looked as he shuffled down the hall. Odd what one remembers.

"I'm sorry to have kept you waiting" were his first words. His red-rimmed eyes met mine. "I'm very sorry."

"We understand," I said, holding my hand out to shake his. "Thank you for coming." Don glared at me. "Please, let's go inside and do what we came here to do." I moved past him to be first through the door.

Dr. Acker swiped his ID badge against the scanner next to the door and held it open for me. The reception area was small, hardly bigger than a closet. The two chairs and a small side table crowded the space. Medical posters exhorting people to wash their hands and get vaccinated lined two walls. It was claustrophobic with five people crowding in.

"Please take a seat. It'll be a few minutes before we're ready to bring you into the room where we hold the bodies," the doctor said. He motioned to Simmons to follow him into the adjoining area.

I sat. Don paced the small room, three strides by three strides, unable to stand still. Barrett sat down next to me. "Are you sure you don't want me to take you home?" Her concern was evident. I shook my head.

The door to the inner sanctum opened. Dr. Acker nodded and held it open. "We've arranged for you to view the body through a window. It's not necessary for you to come all the way into the morgue."

I shot to my feet. "No! I need to see her up close. Hold her hand. Touch her. I have to do that to be sure it's her."

The doctor nodded. "I understand. We thought it would be easier for you though. There's some . . . some things you might not want to see." The sadness in his eyes hurt my heart.

"It's something I have to do," I whispered. He nodded again.

Don pushed past me. "Where is she?"

Simmons was standing halfway down the short hallway. He motioned to Don and waited till Don reached the large window in the wall. Don staggered as he turned and looked. He let out a croak of anguish, and tears streamed down his face. "It's her." He glanced frantically at me, his eyes swiveling to Simmons. "It's her. LaRissa." He turned away. "I've identified her. Now we can get out of here." He rushed back toward me and grabbed my arm. "Come on."

I wrested my arm away from him and walked forward. "Dr. Acker, I need to go in that room and see my daughter." My voice sounded calm and distant in my ears. It was like I was watching myself walk forward. "Take me in there."

Don pushed past Deputy Barrett and yanked the door to the reception area open. I heard the door close as Dr. Acker gently took my arm and escorted me to the door at the end of the hall. "Through here, Mrs. Spencer," he said, opening the door.

A wave of frigid air hit me. It was so cold in the room. LaRissa hated the cold. *She shouldn't be here*, I thought. We turned a corner into a large room. Bright, harsh lights illuminated the metal table in the center of the room. I approached slowly, counting my steps, counting the seconds when I could still believe it wasn't LaRissa. The sheet-draped body on the table faced away from me. I reached out and touched the sheet covering her feet and moved on to the head of the table. The sheet had been folded back to the shoulders. LaRissa's skin was pale, making the bruises on her neck stand out. Her long blonde hair was tangled, with what looked like mud and gravel clumped in it. "Oh, LaRissa, you would hate this," I whispered. I turned around to Dr. Acker. "Can I brush her hair?"

"No, ma'am. I'm sorry but the medical examiner will want to collect any evidence that may be on the body."

"Were her eyes closed when she was found?" I was glad they were closed. I knew I would break if they weren't. Lifeless eyes of my daughter would be too much to bear. "Can I touch her?"

He nodded and I rested my hand on the shoulder exposed by the sheet. Cold and dry and not living. I leaned down and kissed LaRissa's cheek. A soft kiss. "Goodbye, my sweet girl," I whispered. "I love you."

I thanked the doctor and walked out of the room, my head high. He followed me, turning off the lights. Simmons and Barrett were waiting in the hall.

"Your husband left," Simmons said. "I told him Deputy Barrett would take you home when you were ready."

"When will the body be released? I'll need to make arrangements." The cold that had seeped into me in the morgue seemed to help keep me calm.

"It'll be a few days, Mrs. Spencer. We need to have the medical examiner come from the state office. I'm not sure how long it will take for her to get here," Simmons said. "We're too small a county to have one on staff. Dr. Acker's office will call you when the medical examiner releases the body."

"Thank you for your help, detective." I nodded at Barrett. "I'm ready to go home now."

Chapter 12

Monday evening, April 9

Sarah opened the door as I stepped onto the porch. She hugged me and guided me into the house. I broke then, clutching her and sobbing. She held me and rubbed my back for several minutes. I finally stopped and collapsed on the sofa. Sarah sank down beside me and took my hand.

"I'm so sorry, Jana," she said. Tears streamed down her face. "So sorry." She wrapped her arms around me again, and I pressed against her. I needed her warmth after the cold of the morgue. I needed human contact and reassurance and to feel, somehow, that I could survive this. I knew I had to survive this, to be strong for Kyle. Now my only child. He would need me.

"Kyle?" I whispered his name.

"He's in his room. I tried to get him to stay with me down here, but he wouldn't. He said he needed time. I've knocked on his door several times. He answered, but said he wanted to be alone, so I didn't go in his room." She got up. "Let me get you something. A cup of tea?"

"No, thank you. I need to talk to Kyle," I told her. I realized I didn't see Don. "Where's Don? Did he come back from the hospital?"

"He did. I could tell from his face that the news wasn't what we hoped. But he didn't stop to talk to me, just rushed upstairs and went in the bedroom and slammed the door."

"He didn't even stop and tell Kyle?" I frowned. "Really? He didn't think our son needed him?"

Sarah put her hand on my shoulder. "Don't be too hard on Don. This is overwhelming, horrible for all of you. His reactions right now aren't normal. Let him grieve in his own way for tonight. Things will look different in the morning."

I barked a harsh laugh. "How are they going to be different in the morning, Sarah? LaRissa will still be dead."

She looked at me, her eyes filled with tears. "What can I do to help?"

I struggled up, out of the sofa, and took her hand. "Nothing tonight. I'll talk to you in the morning. I'll have to make funeral arrangements, call my mother and Don's parents. They'll let the rest of the family know." I shook my head. "I know you have school tomorrow, so I'll manage till you get off work."

"The principal has closed school tomorrow, Jana," Sarah said. "The news about LaRissa is hitting everyone there hard. He's going to arrange grief counselors for the kids when school reopens." She went to the closet and got her jacket. "I'll go now. You call me if you need anything—anything at all tonight." She slipped on her jacket. "I'll be over in the morning. If you're asleep, I won't wake you. But I'll be here waiting to help with whatever you need." She hugged me tight. "I'll be here."

I waited till I heard the back door close before going upstairs. Kyle. My troubled boy-child. I knew he needed me, but I wasn't sure I'd be able to be what he needed. I steeled myself and went upstairs. Kyle's room was silent—no music, no pings and booms from video games. I knocked quietly on the door. "Kyle?"

He didn't answer, so I opened the door a crack. He was lying on his bed, fully clothed, with his arm across his eyes. "Kyle? Are you awake?"

Kyle stirred and sat up. "I want to be alone," he croaked. His body was slumped over, head down. He dropped back to a prone position and threw his arm across his face again.

I went in the room and sat down on the bed beside him. "Oh, Kyle. I know you're hurting. We're all hurting. But we all need to . . ." I stopped, not sure what we all needed to do. He muttered something and rolled to his side, away from me. I gently put my hand on his shoulder and pulled him back to face me.

"LaRissa is gone, and that's a terrible thing. You're not alone though. You need to know that." He made an anguished sound before pulling away from me. "I need you to help me plan her funeral, Kyle. It needs to be what she would want, her friends, her music, flowers she loved, anything special you can think of that would reflect LaRissa's world."

Kyle squeezed his eyes shut, then opened them wide. His face contorted in an angry scowl. I shrank away from him as he sat up and swung his feet over the side of the bed.

"You think I know what she'd like? She hated me! Her friends all laughed at me," Kyle shouted. "She was the perfect one, right? And I'm the screwup. Sorry, Mom. You only have the screwup left."

I didn't know how to respond. I shook my head and reached out for him, but he scrambled away from me and got to his feet. "She wasn't so perfect!" Kyle's laugh was bitter. "You and Dad thought she was, but you were wrong!" He went to his closet, slipped on his shoes, and grabbed a jacket. "I'm going out for a walk. Don't ask me again to help you with the funeral. I don't know if I'll even go."

My mouth dropped open as he slammed out of the room. I heard his feet hit the stairs two at a time, then the front door slammed. What did I do wrong? I should have left him alone, I thought. Let him grieve in whatever way he needed.

I left his room and walked down the hall to LaRissa's room. I opened the door and stood for a moment. The scent of her favorite perfume—Vera Wang's Princess—wafted out. I'd bought it for her for her fifteenth birthday, and she wore it every day. I slowly closed the door and leaned against the wall in the hallway. The scent still surrounded me, evoking all the times she had laughed as she ran out of the house, excited to go to a dance or hang out with her friends. Too much.

The master bedroom door was closed, and no light seeped under it. I didn't know whether Don was asleep or awake. Either way, I didn't want to go in there. If he was sleeping, fine. Let him sleep. If he was awake, I didn't want to talk to him right now. I was angry. Maybe one of the stages of grief? Being angry? My understanding of the theory was that one would be angry at oneself, but it had been a long time since I read Kübler-Ross in graduate school. Maybe the anger was directed at anyone around you? I was too tired to think straight. The guest room was at the end of the hall, and I slept there that night. Every time I closed my eyes, pictures of LaRissa lying in the morgue appeared—the bruises, tangled dirty hair, and her delicate shoulder and collarbones. She was so lovely in life, and so still and cold on that table. In my troubled dreams, a single tear rolled down her cheek. I woke as the sun peeped through the window at dawn. My face was wet with tears, and I physically ached all over.

Chapter 13

Monday, April 16

It was five days before the medical examiner released LaRissa's body. The day after I identified her body, I woke remembering that I hadn't told Detective Simmons about Brenda's visit to me—LaRissa's state of mind at the social and the young man she was dancing with. I called him after I was dressed. Sarah had been over, made coffee, and left a note that she was going to the grocery store and would be back soon. After calling Simmons, I went looking for Don. His car was gone. Kyle was gone too. The remainder of the morning had rushed by as I called people— my mother, Don's folks, a few close friends—to tell them about LaRissa. Somehow, I got through it and was ready when Sarah told me she'd made an appointment with the funeral home for the afternoon.

Henry August, the funeral home director, was waiting when we arrived. He was a quiet and kind man. He walked us through the details that needed to be decided on: obituary notice, cemetery, casket, the clothes we wanted LaRissa dressed in, flowers, wake, funeral service, and more. I was numb, unable to think, but Sarah helped. She offered suggestions, and I nodded or shook my head. At the end, we'd decided on a simple casket, no embalming, a simple graveside service with family, a few close friends, and Pastor Edgemen to say a prayer. "I don't know when they will release the body," I told Henry. "It may be a few days or a week." He told me he understood and would wait to hear from me. His shirt had a mustard stain that looked like a basset hound—it's funny what you remember in times like this. On the ride home, I'd mentioned it to Sarah. She said she hadn't noticed it.

I woke the morning of the funeral in a panic. I'd dreamed of horrors, LaRissa screaming for me and covered with blood. My face was wet with tears, and my heart was pounding. It took fifteen minutes for me to recover and calm down. I could hear Don moving around in the hallway, opening and closing doors, talking to Kyle. I was still sleeping in the guest room. Don hadn't remarked on my absence from what had been "our" room. We hadn't exchanged words other than the necessary for a week. One small part of my mind recognized that this was strange, but I couldn't deal with any other emotional situation. After a shower and dressing in a black dress and stockings, I carefully put on makeup—something I seldom did, but I needed a mask to protect me from people.

When I went downstairs, Don was dressed in a dark suit and tie. Kyle was similarly dressed, slumped in a chair in the living room, ear buds in. "Do you want something to eat?" Don's voice was careful. Polite, as he would address a stranger.

"I'm going to make some toast and have a glass of orange juice," I told him.

"Your mother called. She said she'd meet us at the cemetery."

I nodded and went in the kitchen. My mother had arrived three days before, ready to take over funeral arrangements and handle everything. She was irritated when I told her the arrangements were already made. She argued that what we'd planned was inappropriate. She wanted a two-day wake, church service, flowers in abundance. We'd had a screaming fight. She'd stormed out and checked into the Best Western. I was glad she didn't want to ride with us to the funeral.

When Kyle, Don, and I arrived at the cemetery, a small crowd was already at the gravesite. We parked and trudged along the gravel path. My mind was disassociated from what was happening, noticing grave markers of people I had known, thinking about the last time I'd seen them. Pastor Edgemen saw us and slowly walked in our direction.

"Don, Jana, Kyle, I'm so sorry. LaRissa was a lovely young woman, with so many good things in her life." He clasped my hand in both of his. "I know this is hard, but God will help you through it."

Don thanked him and walked ahead to the gravesite. Kyle followed him, head down, stumbled over the edge of a marker, and righted himself. He looked around to see if anyone had seen his clumsiness, then stood apart from the dozen people who were waiting for us. Pastor Edgemen was still holding my hand and murmuring some words probably meant to be consoling. I gently removed my hand from his and went forward.

The excavation was covered with a green cloth. The casket—a simple style, wooden, with classic lines—was resting on a gurney draped in a cream-colored velvet cloth. Dozens of yellow roses, LaRissa's favorite, covered the top of the casket. My heart broke as I envisioned LaRissa lying inside, in the simple white flannel ankle-length nightgown with a single rose-colored ribbon at the throat. Soon to be lowered down into the grave and covered with dirt. I suppressed the scream of agony I felt inside. Sarah stepped up to me and took my hand. "You're okay," she whispered. "I'm with you." I looked at her blankly.

She led me to the row of white chairs that were set up a few feet from the casket. I dropped into the chair on the end. Sarah stood beside me, holding my hand in a firm grip. Don, Kyle, his parents, and my mother took the remaining seats. Other friends and family members stood behind and beside the row of chairs. Pastor Edgemen began talking, but I couldn't comprehend what he was saying and looked up at the clouds floating above. It seemed to me the day should be dark with rain. Not sunny and warm. In the distance, I could hear music. My eyes drifted to the football field where the band was practicing. I recognized the piece they were playing. The middle school graduation last year, when LaRissa had walked so proudly, had included that piece of music.

Sarah squeezed my hand, bringing me back to the present. Everyone was standing and reciting the Lord's Prayer. I mumbled along, numb and cold. Pastor Edgemen concluded with a prayer from Ecclesiastes, and people began converging on me.

"Jana, I'm so sorry."

"I'm sorry for your loss."

"Please, if there's anything we can do, call me."

I clutched Sarah's hand, my heart pounding, as a wave of panic swept through me. I couldn't breathe. "Sarah, help me," I gasped.

Sarah understood. She put her arm around me and pulled me off to one side, away from the people who were trying to be kind, compassionate, to show me their support. "Do you want to go home?"

I shook my head. "But I can't be here anymore."

She turned to Don. "I'm going to take Jana home, Don. She's not feeling well. Tell Bill I'll see him at home, will you?" I saw Don nod and turn to the next person who wanted to express condolences.

We walked to Sarah's car and got in. "How about McDonald's drive-thru? A cup of coffee or tea." I nodded as Sarah started the car and pulled onto the road.

"Should I have stayed, Sarah?" I asked as we pulled into the drive-thru lane. "They hadn't lowered the casket into the ground. Was I supposed to stay for that?'

"No, sweetie. They do that after everyone leaves. It's too hard to be there for that." Sarah patted my hand as she pulled up to the drive-thru order microphone. "Coffee or tea?"

"Coffee, please. I didn't go to the restaurant with Don and everyone." I was beginning to feel guilty for not doing what was expected.

"Everyone will understand."

We sat in the parking lot drinking coffee for nearly an hour. "I'm ready to go home now," I finally said.

Don and Kyle were still gone when we got home. I went to the guest room and lay down. I must have fallen asleep, because I woke when I heard loud noises coming from LaRissa's room. I staggered out of bed and went next door to see what was making the banging and thumps. Don was in there, throwing her books into large trash bags. Four bags full of her clothes and shoes and stuffed animals were lying on the bed. "What are you doing?!" I gasped.

"She's gone, and I don't want to see all these things that remind me of her," Don said. "I'm clearing out her room and taking everything to Salvation Army." I grabbed his arm as he reached for another book from her bookcase.

"Stop it! Stop!" I was furious with him. I snatched up a stuffed rabbit, LaRissa's favorite that she kept on her bed, and hugged it to me. "You can't do this!"

He glared at me. "You want to preserve this room as a memorial to her? A holy site? She's gone, Jana. We need to move on. Turn this into something else that doesn't remind me every day. The funeral's over. She's gone, and we need to know that. Move on."

"I hate you," I whispered. I went around the room, picking up items and clutching them to my chest. The remains of LaRissa. Don didn't stop throwing books into bags. He ignored me as I salvaged what I could. It was clear I wasn't going to stop him.

My arms full, I went back to the guest room and laid the few things I'd saved on the bed. I lay down, surrounded by them. *Where's Kyle?* was my last thought as I fell asleep again.

Chapter 14

Wednesday, April 18

How long are you supposed to stay at home after someone dies? Near as was known, LaRissa had died thirteen days before now, but the funeral was only two days ago. The etiquette of death was difficult to discern. But I couldn't stay home anymore. Not with Don determinedly eradicating every trace, every sign that LaRissa had ever lived in our home. Last night he came home with cans of off-white paint, drop cloths, brushes, and rollers that he lugged up the stairs to LaRissa's room. I observed him from the kitchen but didn't say anything. I had nothing to say. He'd hauled all her possessions to Salvation Army, removed her pictures from the mantel in the living room, and scrubbed the floor and windows and sills in her bedroom. All traces gone.

We still weren't talking. I had moved all my clothes and toiletries out of the master bedroom into the guest room. Sarah tried to talk to me. She said that divorce was common when couples—who had been happily married—lost a child. She gave me the name and telephone number of a counselor who specialized in situations like mine, and I smiled and tucked it in a drawer in the kitchen. I had no desire to talk to Don, with or without an intermediary. Why? I didn't know. I figured I would sort out my thoughts over time. Till then, I had enough to cope with.

Kyle, for one. He'd withdrawn completely. He didn't come out of his room except for bathroom trips. I delivered food to him at regular intervals; his diabetes meant that I couldn't let him become erratic about his meals. Breakfast at eight, lunch at twelve-thirty, a mid-afternoon snack, dinner, and a low-carb snack or drink before bedtime. He didn't object to my food deliveries, and he did eat. But he hadn't said a word to me since the funeral. Just nodded when I talked at him. Or ignored me. I wondered if the therapist Sarah had recommended dealt with teen boys. Maybe when I was stronger, I'd call him. I wasn't ready, yet, to talk to a stranger and put my anguish into words.

This morning I rose at seven, got dressed, brushed my teeth and hair, and—after a glance in the mirror—decided a touch of blush and mascara might make me appear less worn. I went downstairs and made Kyle's breakfast and put two protein bars, half of a turkey sandwich, an apple, and two bottles of water in a bag to tide him over till dinner. I knocked on his bedroom door and opened it. He was at his desk with a geometry book open and a pad of paper in front of him.

"Doing homework?"

He nodded but didn't look up.

I set the food on his bed. "Good. Your teachers told me they'll let you finish your assignments at home for as long as you need. I'll drop your homework off tomorrow morning." He nodded again.

"I'm going in to work today, so I left food for lunch and a snack for you." He didn't respond to that. "Be sure to monitor your blood sugar and call me if any problems show up. Okay?" He nodded, eyes fixed on his math book. "I'll see you around five then." I put my hand on the doorknob and looked back at him. He was watching me, his face drawn, dark circles under his eyes.

"Mom?" His voice cracked.

I turned to face him.

"Mom, are the cops going to talk to me again?"

I frowned and walked over to him. "I'm sure they will, Kyle. Detective Simmons told your father that he'd give us a few days to get past the funeral, then set up another appointment to talk to you. Are you worried about it?" He nodded. "Well, Mr. Barrow will go with you to the interview. He said he thought the police think you know more than you've told them so far— especially about the boy LaRissa was with." I held myself back from asking him if that was true. I didn't want him to think I distrusted him too.

"I don't," Kyle said, his voice low. "I don't know anything."

I rested my hand on his shoulder. "I know, sweetheart. And the police will know that, too, after you talk to them again. Don't worry. They have to be thorough, and interviewing you is part of their procedure. Now eat your breakfast, and I'll see you tonight."

His eyes swiveled back to the geometry book before he nodded.

"Eat! Now!" I said in a firm voice. That caused him to smile. A slight smile, but more than I'd gotten from him in days. I left for work feeling encouraged.

The day at the clinic was exhausting. Not because I did a lot of work. I didn't. But because people who worked with me didn't know what to do or say. I could feel it when I passed them in the halls. Some would stop me and say a few words about how sorry they were, others avoided me, ducking into a room if they saw me in the hall. I didn't blame them. I never quite knew what to say to casual friends and acquaintances who suffered tragedies. "I'm sorry for your . . . loss, divorce, accident, arrest." What else could be said? Other than the generally well-meaning but not genuine addition of "If there's anything I can do to help, call me." By noon, I went out to Kammie's desk and told her, quietly, to let people know that I preferred not to talk about LaRissa's death and to please limit conversation to work-related topics.

Dr. Kahn was the only one who behaved normally. He came into my office and dropped a couple of grant announcements on my desk. "You're back. Good. We did receive news that we're being awarded a two-year grant to hire a social worker—something we've needed for a long time." Then he went on to criticize Kammie's management of the floor supplies and complain about the late delivery of prescription drugs and the confusion created by the board's decision to re-paint the examination rooms. After he left, I read the two new grant announcements and began outlining a response to the one due soonest. It made me feel normal. Normal felt good.

At home that evening, the smell of fresh paint overwhelmed me when I walked into the house. Don had finished painting

LaRissa's room. He left a note on the kitchen table saying he was going over to his folks' house for dinner and wouldn't be back till late. I busied myself preparing a large salad with eggs and ham chunks for Kyle and myself. When I took the food upstairs, Kyle wasn't in his room. There wasn't a note or any other indication of where he'd gone. To the Final Quest, I thought. Maybe he thought if I went back to work that he could. I knew the comic book and game store was his happy place, so it was a good sign.

I carried Kyle's food tray back downstairs, wrapped it in plastic wrap and put it in the refrigerator. I was finishing my salad when the doorbell rang.

Detective Simmons was on the doorstep when I opened the door. His face was somber. "Is your son here?"

"No, he's not. Shall I tell him to call you?"

"Yes. It's urgent that we talk to him. If he gets home soon, let me know. Otherwise, I want him at the sheriff's office at ten tomorrow morning." His eyes fixed on my face. "Do you understand?"

I didn't say anything. I closed the door in his face. I wished Sarah were here. She'd told me she had to be at the school board meeting tonight. I called and left a message for her to come over when she got home, whatever time it was.

Chapter 15

Thursday morning, April 19

Alphonse Simmons was reviewing the medical examiner's report when the duty officer called to say Kyle Spencer and his lawyer were waiting in the interrogation room. There were skin cells under the victim's nails—potentially useful DNA evidence. And there was evidence that the victim had had sexual intercourse shortly before her death, which meant more potentially useful DNA evidence. Unfortunately, the state lab would take at least six weeks to get results back to him.

The report also indicated that the bruises on the victim's face and neck weren't the cause of death. Instead, the medical examiner said that death had been from intracranial bleeding from a head injury. Simmons frowned. He'd assumed strangulation since he hadn't seen a head injury when he'd examined the body. He shrugged and rubbed his bad knee. "Okay, young Spencer, let's see what you can tell us." He picked up the folder with the medical examiner's report and stood up.

Don Spencer was sitting in the lobby. When he saw Simmons heading for the interrogation room, he leaped up. "About time you got here! I hope this is the last time you want to interview my son. Taking this time off work is losing me money—to say nothing of the expense of hiring a lawyer who's charging me by the minute. While you take your time." Don's face was red as he confronted Simmons, nose-to-nose.

"I'm sure you want us to find whoever did this to your daughter, Mr. Spencer. We want to do that, and we're tracking down a few leads. Your son may be able to fill in some gaps. He may remember more than he realized at first," Simmons said. "I know you're angry and frustrated. I would be too. But you need to let us do our jobs." He moved past Don and went down the hall and into the small interrogation room.

Kyle and James Barrow were sitting on one side of the small table. Barrow had one hand on Kyle's arm and stopped talking when Simmons entered. "Remember what I've told you," he whispered hurriedly.

"Thank you for coming in, Kyle," Simmons said. "I appreciate your cooperation, and I just have a few more questions. Could you go over your actions the night your sister disappeared for me?"

Barrow objected. "He's already told you what he did and where he was, Detective. Why does he have to repeat it?"

"Sometimes a witness remembers more details when he thinks back to the period in question, Mr. Barrow, as you well know." Simmons sat down and pressed the button to begin recording the session. "This is Detective Alphonse Simmons interviewing Kyle Spencer at ten-fifteen a.m. on Thursday, April 19, 2018. Mr. Spencer is accompanied by his lawyer, James Barrow. Now, Kyle, would you please tell me where you were and what you were doing on the night of Thursday, April 5?"

"Like I told you before, I went to the church social. My sister and her friends were there. I talked to my sister and told her Mom and Dad wanted me to drive her home. She laughed and told me to get lost. So I left. Then I walked around town for a couple hours, I think. I ended up at the park, the little one with the pond."

"Is that the park that's behind the high school?"

"Y-y-yes. That one."

"How long were you there?"

"I don't remember. Maybe an hour. And then I went home."

"Kyle, did you know there are surveillance cameras in the park? We've reviewed those videos for the entire evening that night, and there's no sign that you were there."

Barrow held up one hand. "Wait a minute. I want to talk to my client." He leaned over and whispered to Kyle. Kyle shook his head. More whispering. "My client chooses to terminate this interview, Detective."

Simmons grunted and turned off the recording. "You have a right to do that, Kyle. But it would be better for you if you just tell us where you were and what you may have seen. We all want to find whoever did this to your sister, and I'd think you'd want to help." He looked at Kyle, who was staring at the table. "One more thing. Are you willing to provide us with a DNA sample so we can exclude you if we find DNA on your sister's body?"

Kyle's face blanched. He leaned over and frantically whispered something to his lawyer. Barrow said, "No, my client isn't willing to provide a sample at this time. We will discuss it, and if he changes his mind, I'll call you to arrange it." He stood up. "We're leaving now. If you have anything further, please call me directly." Barrow looked at Kyle, who was still sitting. "Kyle, we're leaving." Kyle slowly rose, not looking at the detective, and followed Barrow from the room.

Don was waiting outside the interrogation room. Simmons stopped in front of him. "Your son isn't willing to answer any more questions, Mr. Spencer. Please talk to him and encourage him to cooperate."

"I think you have better things to do than harass my son. Find the person who did this!" Don turned to leave.

"Mr. Spencer," Simmons said. "I received the medical examiner's report this morning. I'm sorry to have to tell you this, but there's evidence that LaRissa had intercourse sometime the evening that she died."

Don whirled around. "My daughter was raped?" His voice broke. "Oh, my God. She was raped and murdered?" He staggered, and Simmons put out a hand to steady him.

"We don't know the circumstances, sir. It might have been consensual. Or it might have been rape," Simmons conceded. "The medical examiner also determined that her death was due to a blow to the head that caused a brain hemorrhage. If it's any consolation, she would have died within minutes of the blow." He waited as Don absorbed this information.

"One more thing. The medical examiner found DNA under her fingernails and . . . from the sexual activity. This may be the key to identifying a suspect, but we will need a DNA sample from you and your son to exclude you if more than one person's DNA is found on her body. Would you be willing to provide us with a DNA sample?"

"Of course. Anything. Just tell me what I have to do." Don was leaning against the hallway wall, shaken. "Right now?"

"If you're willing. I'll get a test kit and be right back."

Simmons strode rapidly through the lobby to the storage room on the other side of the building to retrieve the kit. He noticed that Kyle and Barrow were having what looked like a tense exchange in the parking lot. Simmons frowned. Something wasn't right, but he couldn't put the pieces together yet.

Don compliantly opened his mouth and let Simmons take a cheek swab. He seemed to have recovered his equilibrium for the moment. "Thank you, Detective. I'll talk to Kyle and see that he comes back and finishes the interview. I'm not sure what you're looking for from him, but he'll cooperate," Don stated. "I'll see to that." He shook Simmons' hand and walked quickly out the lobby door.

Simmons watched Don through the window as he joined his son and the lawyer in the parking lot. He grabbed Kyle's shoulder and shouted at him, then opened the car door and shoved the boy into the passenger seat. Simmons saw the lawyer say something to Don and walk away. Something isn't right here, Simmons thought again. A talk with the mother might be useful.

Chapter 16

Thursday evening, April 19

Don was shouting at Kyle when I got home from the clinic at six-thirty. I'd stopped at the grocery store to pick up bread and milk and a few other items on the way. And I'd left in tears when the checker smiled and asked where my pretty daughter was today. Often, in the past, LaRissa had made grocery runs with me after I picked her up from after-school activities. I froze at the cashier's question and then walked out of the store without taking the groceries. I guessed she didn't read newspapers or watch the local news. I sat in the car for a long time digesting the fact that there were people who didn't know LaRissa was dead. People who didn't have a cold center to their lives. People who were lucky enough to have their children with them.

I didn't have the strength to go upstairs and try to make peace. The kitchen beckoned, where I could be busy doing normal things in a normal way — and not have to think. I pulled hamburger from the refrigerator and began making meatballs: chopping onions, peeling garlic cloves, shaking out breadcrumbs, and mixing it all together with the hamburger, then rolling the meat into small balls and arranging them on the baking sheet. Mixed with prepared spaghetti sauce and served over zucchini pasta, it was a meal that even Kyle could eat without worrying about his carb load.

My phone rang as I popped the meatballs in the oven. I dug it out of my purse and swiped left. It was Sarah.

"Good, you're home." Sarah's voice sounded worried.

"Yeah, I just got here a few minutes ago."

"I could hear Don yelling at Kyle all the way over here. Is everything all right?"

I sighed. "Sarah, I don't know. He was shouting upstairs when I walked in. And he still is. I couldn't cope with another battle right this moment, so I'm in the kitchen making dinner."

"Well, it sounded serious. I've heard Don yelling at Kyle before, but never this loud and this long. Do you want me to come over?"

The shouting upstairs stopped. I heard a door slam, then footsteps on the stairs.

"No, it sounds like it's over. I'll talk to Don and try to figure out what's going on." Don walked into the kitchen as I said this. "Don's here. I'll call you later." I hung up and watched Don go to the coffeepot and pour a cup. He leaned against the counter and glared at me.

"Your son, it turns out, has refused to talk to the police any further. Detective Simmons seems to think he's holding back information." Don's voice was rising. "That damned lawyer told him he wasn't required to talk to the police. And Kyle refused to take a DNA test. For what reason, I don't know. But I gave them my DNA sample. If any of us touched LaRissa that night or kissed her goodbye or anything that might transfer our DNA to her, the police need our samples so they can rule us out as the contributors and focus on any foreign DNA they may find." He looked at me, helplessly. "Why in the world would Kyle refuse?" he asked. "I don't understand what's in his head."

Don's eyes filled with tears. "Oh, Jana. I can hardly tell you what the detective told me today." He sobbed once then pulled himself together. "The medical examiner found signs of . . . sexual intercourse. She was raped before she died." He buried his face in his hands. "I can't stand it. Knowing that." He was shaking.

I went to him and touched his shoulder. Angry as I'd been with him over the past weeks, his pain caused me to soften. "Come, sit down." He clutched the back of a chair, then sank into it.

"Fifteen years old, only fifteen, Jana. And some monster violated her. Before killing her." He looked up at me. "How can this happen?"

I bit my lip. I hadn't told him about Brenda's revelation. LaRissa telling her she wanted to get "fucked" the night of the social. Maybe she wasn't raped. Maybe she participated in the act willingly. And then maybe she got scared or angry and threatened to tell the police she was raped. Was that why he killed her? My mind was swirling. I wasn't sure what the laws were about age of consent. Was it even possible for a fifteen-year-old girl to consent to sex?

"Try not to think about it, Don. We don't know the circumstances yet. Hopefully, the police will find who she was with and learn what happened that led to . . ."

"Oh, for God's sake, shut up! You and your acceptance and belief that everything will return to normal if we just go through the normal motions!" He shoved the chair backward so hard that it crashed to the floor as he stood up. "You haven't cried for her since that first day! I cry every night, alone. I don't hear you crying or even see tears in your eyes when you talk about LaRissa. She's fucking gone, Jana! And I can't bear it, and I can't bear to be around you." He pushed past me. "I'm going out. I'm not sure when I'll be back. Or if I'm coming back." His tone was bitter. "As if you care." I heard the door to the garage open, then the sound of his car starting and tires squealing as he accelerated out of the garage.

I collapsed into a chair. Was Don right? Was I unfeeling, trying to maintain a normal routine in hopes that all this horror would go away? I rubbed my temples. The chaos of my life right now was too much for me. All I had was the illusion of normalcy, going through the motions and hoping that . . . eventually . . . a day would come when I wasn't overwhelmed. I stood up and went to the oven. The meatballs were burned, but not too badly. I took them out, put them in a bowl, poured the sauce over them, and put the bowl in the microwave.

The zucchini pasta was nearly done when Kyle appeared in the kitchen doorway. He glanced at me, nervous.

"Is he gone?"

"Your father? Yes. He didn't say when he'd be back. But dinner's almost ready, so put two plates and utensils on the table and we can eat." I drained the noodles, put them in a bowl, and set the microwave to two minutes to heat the sauce and meatballs. A caprese salad was prepared in the refrigerator, so I pulled that out and laid a set of tongs next to it. By the time everything was on the table, Kyle had completed his task, including folding the paper napkins and finding the Parmesan cheese shaker.

I was happy to see Kyle eating. He'd lost weight in the past two weeks, and I'd been worried about him. He polished off a second helping of the spaghetti then cleared the table while I rinsed the dishes and put them in the dishwasher.

"What was all the shouting about when I came in tonight?" I was tentative, not wanting to upset the rare pleasant mood.

"Dad was mad because I walked out of the interview with that policeman," Kyle said.

"Why did you walk out?"

"Mr. Barrow said I should stop talking and we should leave."

"He did?" I was confused. "Why would he recommend that? I don't understand."

"That detective kept pushing me on where I was that night. I'd told him I was at the park, but he said there were surveillance cameras that didn't show me there. Mr. Barrow stopped the interview then and told him I wasn't going to answer any more questions today. Then Mr. Barrow said he and I need to talk before we go back." Kyle stared fixedly at the table. "And he said I shouldn't talk to anybody about that night—not even you and Dad."

"Do they think you had something to do with LaRissa's death?" I was flabbergasted with this news. "The police? Or Mr. Barrow?"

Kyle shrugged. "I don't know. I don't think so. She went off with some guy, Brenda said. And I was already gone by then." He paused for a moment. "But Mr. Barrow wants to meet with me in a couple days."

"Your dad and I will make sure you get there. Are you okay, though? I'll talk to your father, try to get him to cool off." I studied Kyle's face. "Kyle, the reason the detective keeps asking you questions is he thinks you may know something that could help them find the person who hurt LaRissa."

"I don't know anything! I keep telling everyone that, and they don't believe me." Kyle's face was suffused with anger. For a moment, he looked like Don just before he burst into a rage.

78

I put my hand on his arm. "I believe you," I said quietly. "Maybe the issue is whether you've seen the boys LaRissa was with that night someplace before. Brenda said they looked rough. Are you afraid of them? If you tell the police what you know?"

He pushed me away. "I don't know them! If I did, I'd tell the police!" He ran out of the kitchen and up the stairs.

I sank into a chair and buried my head in my hands. Don was furious, Kyle was angry that I didn't trust him. I couldn't stand being around my husband of twenty years. My daughter was dead. Everything about my life was unraveling. I got up and finished loading the dishwasher. I decided to go for a drive. If Don could escape this house, so could I.

Chapter 17

Wednesday, May 2

LaRissa's sixteenth birthday. I'd planned a big party for her sixteenth birthday: eight of her friends, a special bakery cake, presents—including the new iPod that she'd been wanting for years—and dinner at her favorite Mexican restaurant. We'd taken her there every year since she was six, and the proprietor always welcomed us, arms wide with a big smile and *"Hola! Feliz cumpleanos!"* LaRissa would respond with *"Gracias, Senor Perez."* He would lead us to a festively decorated table in the private dining room and always place a yellow rose on her plate. The entire restaurant staff and all the customers would sing the happy birthday song to her as Mr. Perez brought the cake with candles lit and placed it in front of her.

I woke late that morning, with vague memories of dreams of LaRissa and happy times. On my way downstairs, I stopped at her bedroom and opened the door. There were no memories left there. I hadn't been able to stop Don from dismantling it and painting the formerly violet walls with a cream-colored paint that obliterated all traces of her. Her bedroom set was gone—picked up by the Salvation Army one day when I was at work—along with every personal item: clothes, pictures, makeup, books, and even the trophy she'd won at the sixth-grade spelling bee. I closed the door on the empty room.

The house was quiet. I hadn't heard Don, but remnants of scrambled eggs and sausage in the sink told me he'd eaten and left. We still weren't communicating about anything. He spent evenings either in the garage doing who-knows-what or was just gone. Sometimes I suspected he was gone all night. The odd thing was that I didn't care.

I poured a cup of coffee and went back upstairs to shower and get dressed. Kyle was coming out of his room as I passed in the hallway. "Morning, Kyle," I said. "I'm going to pick up Thai food for dinner tonight. Okay with you?"

He nodded.

"How's the schoolwork coming? It's only three weeks to graduation." Kyle's principal and teachers had agreed that he could finish the last weeks of school from home. A student dropped off his homework assignments every afternoon, and Kyle handed over the assignments he'd finished for the next day.

"It's okay. I'm passing everything. Principal Kumansky has told me I'll graduate." We'd reached the kitchen, and he opened the refrigerator to take out milk. "I told him I probably wouldn't come to graduation."

"Why not?"

"Because I don't want everyone watching me and thinking about LaRissa, that's why!" He poured Wheat Chex in a bowl and didn't look at me. "Besides, I don't have any friends, and I'm not invited to any graduation parties. I just want to get school over with."

"And then do what? Work at the comic bookstore the rest of your life?" My tone was harsh. I saw Kyle recoil, a hurt look on his face. He grabbed a spoon out of the drawer, picked up his cereal and headed for the stairs without responding.

I regretted my outburst. He got enough criticism from Don, who seemed unable to utter a kind word to him. I fixed breakfast for myself—a bagel with peanut butter—and turned on the radio. It was playing a country station and someone I didn't recognize was singing "You Are My Sunshine." I quickly changed the station to classic rock, but I knew that song would be in my head all day. Too sad on a day that I was already sad.

I went back upstairs and knocked on Kyle's door. "Kyle, can I come in?"

Hearing a muffled assent, I opened the door. Kyle was lying on his bed, one arm over his eyes. "What do you want?"

"I'm sorry about downstairs. You're young, and you have plenty of time to figure out what you want to do with your life," I said. He didn't say anything.

"Today is LaRissa's birthday. I'm going to take flowers to the cemetery. Would you want to go with me?"

He sat up in bed. "No! I don't want to go there. It's morbid to go there. Gross!"

"All right," I said. I was taken aback by his words. I found comfort in visiting LaRissa's grave. I talked to her there, told her what her friends were doing and how much everyone missed her. Was that morbid? I don't know. More like denial. But I'd gone there several times since the funeral. "Well, I'll be back in a couple hours. Do you need anything while I'm out?"

"No."

I closed the door gently and went downstairs. I had just picked up my purse and car keys when the doorbell rang. I went to the door and opened it. Detective Simmons was standing there.

"Do you have news, Detective?"

"No, we're still waiting for the state lab on the DNA analysis. But I do have a question for you." Simmons pulled a small plastic bag from his pocket. "Do you recognize this?" He held the bag up, running a thumb across the outside to better display the contents.

I stared at it, speechless. I did recognize it. It was a medallion of the Blades of Chaos from God of War. Kyle's favorite video games were PlayStation's God of War series, and he was eagerly awaiting the availability of the next game. He had bought the medallion last year at Final Quest, where he worked, and usually wore it on a black cord around his neck. "I'm not sure," I finally said. "What is it?"

"Our forensics people have been systematically going through all the debris that was collected near the dumpster where your daughter's body was found. This was in the gravel a few feet away from the dumpster. They investigated and found it was a representation from a video game. God of War. Have you heard of it?"

I frowned. "I think so. My son plays video games and may have mentioned it. I'll ask him if he knows anything about it."

"Don't bother. I'll ask him when he comes in next week for the follow-up interview we postponed." He turned to go.

"Wait, Detective," I blurted out. "What do you mean 'next week'? I haven't heard about an interview next week."

"His lawyer arranged it with our office, a couple days ago," Simmons said. "We just have a few more questions for him."

I nodded, thanked him, and closed the door. I turned and went back into the kitchen. Questions were racing through my mind. *Why did Simmons need to talk to Kyle? Why hadn't I asked Simmons about his interview with Brenda and whether he had identified the boy LaRissa had left the social with? Why did the detective have Kyle's medallion?* I was shaking as I poured a cup of coffee. And there was the question I didn't want to ask myself . . . *why was Kyle's medallion near where LaRissa died?*

Chapter 18

Wednesday afternoon, May 2

I couldn't think anymore. I grabbed my purse and car keys and headed to the florist shop. The woman at the counter saw me and turned around to take a small bouquet of yellow roses from the table behind her.

"Here's your order, Jana." Her face was sad as she handed them to me. Her daughter had been a friend of LaRissa's.

"Thank you, Ellen." I reached in my purse to retrieve my credit card. I paid and walked out. There was nothing else to say.

Dark clouds were gathering overhead as I reached the cemetery. The wind had turned cold, and I shivered as I walked to the gravesite. The marker still wasn't in place—the funeral director had told me it might be a month or more before it was completed: a simple pink granite stone with LaRissa's name and dates of birth and death. I'd wanted to add something that would say how much she was loved, but the right words hadn't found their way into my head. I sat down and laid the flowers on the grave. All I could think to say was "I miss you so much, Rissie." And "I'm sorry." Over and over.

Rain began to fall, striking me with force and soaking my hair and shoulders. The wind whipped up to near-gale speeds, and overhead the clouds had turned darker and raced across the sky. I shivered and stood up. The leaves and petals of the roses were being fragmented and blown away. Lightning flashed overhead, and thunder rolled and rolled and rolled. I bent and patted the dirt that covered LaRissa's grave. "I'll be back, sweetheart. I love you," I whispered. Then I ran through the rain to my car.

I still wasn't sure how to handle the information Detective Simmons had handed me that morning. Confront Kyle? Maybe . . . eventually? I started the car and drove around town aimlessly, thinking. When I saw the sign for Final Quest up ahead on South Street, I made up my mind. A parking place was open in front of the store, and I pulled into it and got out. Inside, Bob Harris, owner of the store, was talking to a customer. I browsed until he was free, then approached him.

"Bob? Do you have a minute?"

He looked up, brushed his long curly black hair from his eyes. He was at least my age—forty-two—but dressed in faded jeans worn at the knees and a T-shirt. It was black and said "I don't always play games. Sometimes I eat and sleep and once I even left my room."

"Hi, Jana. Kyle's in the back un-boxing. Do you want me to get him?"

"No. I actually wanted to ask you if you have any God of War items? Kyle's graduating soon, and I want to get him something he'd like as a gift."

"Oh, sure. I know he's into that." He motioned me over to a glass counter in the back of the room. "We have earrings, bracelets, and medallions on chains. Or were you thinking of T-shirts or jackets? Those are on the rack back there."

I bent over the counter and peered at the items inside. I didn't see the exact medallion Simmons had shown me with the Blades of Chaos imprint. "One of these might do," I said. "But I think he mentioned something about liking the Blades of Chaos. Anything with that?"

Bob studied the display. "We did have a couple, but we must have sold them." He looked up at me and frowned. "Actually, Kyle bought the last one. He said he'd lost the one he had and wanted a new one. So, I guess you're too late for that to be a graduation gift. You see anything else that might fit the bill? There's a new game that I don't think he has. You want to check that out?"

"Not really. I'm not the best person to pick out a game for him." I laughed. "The one time I did, he thanked me, put it under his bed, and never looked at it again." I glanced over at the T-shirts. "Maybe I'll get him a T-shirt and a gift card."

Back in the car, I tossed the bag on the back seat. A two-hundred-dollar gift card and a twenty-dollar T-shirt. Don would complain when he saw the credit card bill, but at least Kyle would like his graduation gift from me. Don could pick out his own gift. Not that I was feeling happy with what I'd found out. Kyle had replaced the medallion he'd always worn, and he'd bought the new one after LaRissa had died. That meant it was possible that the one Simmons had shown me was his. I should have asked Bob how many of those medallions he'd sold; maybe there were dozens of them around the necks of teen boys and girls in Fairview.

Don was working in the garage when I got home. I parked the car in the driveway and went in the house. I wasn't ready to talk to him about Simmons' visit and the medallion, so I plunked the bags of Thai food on the kitchen counter and slipped out the back door to Sarah's house.

"You look like a wet cat," she laughed, opening the door wide. "Come in. I have a pot of coffee on. Want some?"

I nodded and followed her into the kitchen. Sarah poured two cups of coffee, handed me one, and sat down across from me. The kitchen smelled of chocolate cake baking, she had a smudge of flour on her forehead, and wisps of her curly red hair had escaped her headband and were plastered to her cheek. Comforting. And normal.

"What have you been up to today?" She pushed the creamer and the sugar bowl toward me.

I poured cream and ladled two teaspoons of sugar into the cup and stirred before answering. "I took the day off from work." My eyes filled, and I angrily brushed the tears away. "It's LaRissa's sixteenth birthday today."

"I know, Jana." Sarah reached out and took my hand. "I know it's hard right now." She waited patiently.

"I took flowers to the cemetery and sat there, with her, for a while. Then I ran some errands." I paused, then burst out, "Sarah, I need to tell you something. But you have to promise you won't judge or repeat it to anyone."

She squeezed my hand. "You know you can say anything to me, and it's just between us. I'm here for you, whatever you need."

I told her about the detective showing up and the medallion that was found where LaRissa had died. "Kyle did have one just like it, Sarah. And Bob Harris told me Kyle had bought a replacement for it." My voice wavered, and I couldn't go on.

"Do you think Kyle killed LaRissa?" Sarah held my hand firmly.

"No!" I yanked my hand from hers. "No way! It's not possible! There must be dozens of those medallions sold."

"Right. It's just a strange coincidence. Maybe it being there doesn't even have anything to do with LaRissa. Who knows who left it and when?" Sarah leaned forward, re-capturing my hand. "What are you really worried about then?"

"I'm worried that the police will think Kyle's involved," I responded, rubbing my forehead. "They've already questioned him twice. The detective told Don he thinks Kyle isn't being honest about that night. Now they have this medallion, and they want him to come in again next week. What if they bully him into admitting something that's not true? What if he gets scared and breaks down and says something that makes them even more suspicious?" I was frantic by this time. I hadn't fully thought through the implications of the detective's suspicions and the medallion. "Then they won't keep looking for whoever killed her. And Kyle . . ." My voice broke. "Kyle won't ever recover from this . . . being accused, having people think he had something to do with . . ." I steadied myself. "I have to protect him, Sarah. But I don't know how."

Sarah was quiet for a few seconds, then she came around to sit next to me. I leaned into her and pressed my face to her shoulder. "I don't know what to do," I whispered.

She hugged me, then pushed me gently back to my chair. "Okay. Here's what I think. You need to talk to Kyle's lawyer and tell him all this. He needs to know, and Kyle probably isn't telling him what happened that night. If anything. Don't ask Kyle about it. Let his lawyer do that. You don't want to make your son think you suspect him of anything. Your job is to love him and do whatever you can to help him."

I nodded, feeling better. "And do I tell Don?"

She shook her head. "The two of you are going through something right now. He's angry with the world, and I don't know what he'd do. Remember, your job is to protect Kyle.

Telling Don would probably provoke a big confrontation, and Kyle doesn't need that."

"Thank you. I needed your clarity, Sarah." I swallowed the last of my coffee and stood up. "I brought Thai food home. I'd better go heat it up and be sure Kyle eats properly." I stood up and hugged her. "What would I ever do without you?"

She smiled and hugged me back. "You'd have worked it out. It would just have taken a little more time. Now go. My horde will be hitting the door any minute. I'll stop by tomorrow after school."

Chapter 19

Monday, May 7

I took Sarah's advice and called Kyle's lawyer first thing the next morning. He agreed to see me at four o'clock. His office was in Hinton, about fifteen miles from Fairview. Dr. Kahn had grudgingly agreed that I could leave work at three, after reminding me that there were two grant applications due in the next three days. I thanked him and headed out. The road linking the two towns was two lanes, winding through hills and forests. Some cows in the fields were the only signs of life. Fortunately, it was a pleasant day, and I drove with the windows open, enjoying the warm spring day and the early wildflowers that grew along the road.

When I reached Hinton, I turned on my cell phone and entered the address into the map app. Hinton was about twice as large as Fairview. The stores that lined Main Street featured espresso and patio dining, as well as bookstores and art galleries, reflecting the presence of a well-known writers' retreat on a former horse farm just outside the town limits. *In one hundred yards, turn right onto Third Street.* I made the turn and was immediately instructed by the impersonal voice that I'd arrived at my destination.

The law offices were in an old Victorian house that was painted a pale violet with pink and blue gingerbread trim. A porch ran the full length of the front, furnished with rocking chairs, a settee, and large planters already blooming with pink geraniums and purple petunias. The sidewalk leading up to the house was lined with lilac bushes that showed signs of flowering soon.

A small sign on the walnut door with leaded windows told me to come in. The entryway was small and paneled in dark wood. A directory indicated that several lawyers and accountants had offices in the building. James Barrow J.D.'s office was on the second floor. I climbed the staircase and walked to the end of the hallway. Barrow's office was on the left, and a young woman was working on a computer at the reception desk.

"I'm Jana Spencer," I announced. "I have an appointment at four with Mr. Barrow."

She looked up and smiled. "Of course, Mrs. Spencer. Mr. Barrow is at the courthouse but should be here soon. Can I get you a cup of coffee or some water?"

I declined and sat in one of the chairs across from her desk. It was five minutes till four, so I didn't expect a long wait. A half hour later, my expectations had been dashed. I stood and stretched and stepped over to face the receptionist. "Do you know whether he'll be here soon?"

"He was at an arraignment, Mrs. Spencer. He expected to be back before your meeting, but the court must have run late. I'm sorry. Are you sure I can't get you something to drink?" The distress on the girl's face appeased my irritation.

"No, thank you." I returned to the chair and checked my phone for messages. I'd hoped to be done with this meeting and home before Don finished work at five-thirty. I didn't want him to ask why I was late. Then again, he probably wouldn't even notice—or care—at this point. We'd spoken fewer than ten words to each other over the weekend.

Fifteen minutes later, I heard rushed footsteps outside the office and the door rattled a bit. Barrow pushed his way in with his shoulder, his hands full of a stack of papers. "I'm sorry to be late, Mrs. Spencer," he said hurriedly. His face was flushed, his rimless glasses were crooked, and his blond hair was tousled, making him look too young to be an experienced lawyer. "Let me give these things to my assistant here, and I'll be ready to meet with you." He hurried over to the young woman at the desk, set down the stack of papers, and talked quietly to her for a minute.

"All right. Please come into my office." He stood back and

motioned me toward the small hallway. "Judges make up their own rules," he said, opening the door to his office. "This one decided to put my client's case at the bottom of his pile." He gestured to the chair in front of his desk, then went around the desk and sat down. "Did Angela offer you coffee?"

"She did."

"Good, good. Well, how can I help you today?"

I took a deep breath. "I'm not sure how this works. If I tell you something that might affect my son, is that covered by privilege?"

He frowned and leaned back in his chair. "Client privilege means that I can't reveal anything that I learn from the client and others that is related to the client's case. So, yes. Anything you tell me about your son is covered by privilege." He waited for me to go on.

"Okay," I said. "I know that you've arranged for Kyle to meet again with the police on Thursday. I know the police are thinking he knows something or did something that might shed light on what happened that night. Mostly because he lied about where he was that night." I put up a hand to stop him interrupting. "Let me finish. I don't know where he was or why he lied. But Detective Simmons showed up at my house Friday and showed me a medallion that his evidence team found near where LaRissa's body was. He asked me if I recognized it. I said I wasn't sure. But I did recognize it. It was a God of War amulet, from a video game. And Kyle has one just like it." I took another deep breath. This was hard. But the lawyer needed to know.

"I didn't ask Kyle about it. Later that day, I went to the comic book and video game store where Kyle works and asked the owner about God of War items. I told him I was looking for a graduation gift for Kyle. He showed me some medallions. None of them were the same medallion. When I described the specific one I was looking for, Bob said that Kyle had bought the last one of those. Recently." My hands shook. "He's had one for a couple years, Mr. Barrow."

"I understand what you're implying, Mrs. Spencer—that Kyle must have lost the first one sometime before he bought the replacement," Barrow said. He pulled a pad of paper in front of him and made a note. "Which means that the one the police found might be his."

I nodded, unable to speak the words that might condemn my son.

"Look, there were probably hundreds of those medallions sold, so it could have been lost by anyone," Barrow said. "Would you send me a picture of the exact one that the detective showed you? I can check with the company who makes them to find out how many have been shipped to the Fairview and Hinton area since they were first sold. Assuming it's a large number, that would create a reasonable doubt that the one they found belonged to Kyle." Barrow leaned forward. "Even if they could prove it was his, which they could only do if it had a fingerprint or DNA on it, it still doesn't prove he was there at the time your daughter was killed. It might have been there for weeks before the event, after he legitimately lost it." Barrow frowned. "Are you worried that they might think your son was responsible for your daughter's death?"

His words hung in the air. I gasped and, finally, burst out with "No!" I felt faint and clutched the arms of the chair. "No," I repeated. "I'm worried that he was there and saw whoever did kill her. And that he's afraid of that person. Or even ashamed that he saw what happened and didn't try to stop it. I'm afraid for him—afraid the police will accuse him of a cover-up or obstruction of justice or something like that. I hadn't even thought about the police thinking Kyle was the . . ." I couldn't go on, couldn't finish.

Barrow came around and sat in the chair next to me. "Look, I don't believe the police will arrest Kyle for murder based on what I know at this point. Your providing this information is helpful. Kyle is supposed to meet me before the interview with the police. I'll talk to him, encourage him to tell me where he was that night and what happened to his first medallion. I can't reveal that information to the police, and I need to know the truth to give him the best representation possible."

I nodded in agreement. "Should I talk to him about it?"

"No, let me handle it," Barrow said. "Have you told anyone else about this? Your husband?"

"Not my husband," I smiled weakly. "We're mostly not talking to each other. But I did tell my best friend. She's the one who said I should tell you."

"Good advice. But you should talk to her and ask her not to mention any of this to anyone. We don't want there to be a lot of talk about the medallion and what it might mean."

"I will." I stood up. "Thank you. I feel better. Will you be able to talk to me, privately, after you and Kyle meet with the police? I'm so afraid for my son and knowing what's going on will help."

"Yes, though it's up to Kyle what I can reveal. But I can give you a general rundown on what happens in that meeting." He stood and shook my hand. "Feel free to call me if anything new happens or you have questions."

I left feeling better.

Chapter 20

Thursday, May 10

Detective Alphonse Simmons wasn't happy. He'd tracked down the young men who'd been at the church social. Allan Davis had been the one that LaRissa had left with, but his pals—and cell phone cameras—provided a solid alibi. Davis admitted he'd left the social with LaRissa and had sex with her under the bleachers at the high school. Simmons had wanted to slap him for the smug look on his face as he described how she'd begged him to "fuck" her. But two of his friends had videoed the interaction on their cell phones. After Davis finished, he'd pulled up his pants, laughed, and left LaRissa sitting under the bleachers. The group had then gone to a party. Simmons collected a DNA sample from Davis, but unless there was evidence that LaRissa had had sex with more than one man on the night of her death, all Davis' DNA results would do was confirm his story.

"I still feel like the brother is the key," Simmons said to his captain. "There's something off about him. He's coming in today for another interview, and I'm hoping that when I show him the medallion we found at the dumpster site, he'll finally tell me what he knows. I interviewed his boss at that comic bookstore. He confirmed that the kid had lost one just like it and bought a replacement a couple weeks ago."

Captain Hellman nodded. "The medallion isn't proof, though. Unless we find fingerprints or DNA on it, there's no way to confirm that it's the one the brother had. And likely there were others sold in the area." He looked at Simmons. "Are you thinking he actually murdered his sister?"

"Not really. But I do think he knows what happened and, maybe, who she was with after the incident under the bleachers. What I don't know is why the brother isn't telling what he knows. There might be someone he's afraid of, someone who threatened him. Or possibly a close friend or relative, and he doesn't want to be the one to finger him." Simmons groaned as he stood up. "He and his lawyer should be here any minute. I'll let you know how it goes."

Kyle, his lawyer, and his mother were waiting in the reception area as Simmons left to return to his office. Kyle was sitting on the bench, slumped over, his shoulders rounded and his head drooping. His mother said something to him and he glanced up at Simmons, then returned to his previous posture.

"I'll be with you in a minute, folks," Simmons said. "I'll send someone to escort you to the interview room." He proceeded to his office, sat down at his desk, and skimmed through his email for twenty minutes before finally heading to the interview room.

"Okay, let's get started," Simmons said, barging in.

Kyle started, jerking in his seat, his eyes wide. His lawyer put a hand on Kyle's arm, leaned toward him, and said something quietly to him.

"Same as before," Simmons said. "I'm going to record this interview." He pointed at a red light flashing over the door, then hit a button on the recorder on the table and the light flashed green. "Kyle, first question. Do you recognize this?" Simmons dropped a small plastic bag holding the medallion on the table and shoved it toward Kyle.

Barrow pulled it closer to Kyle, who leaned away from it. Barrow whispered to him.

"My client stipulates that he had a medallion like this. That he lost it a while ago and bought a replacement." Barrow nodded at Kyle, who pulled a medallion on a black cord out from under his shirt.

"May I see it more closely?" Simmons stretched out a hand. Kyle, hands shaking, slipped the cord over his head and handed the medallion to the detective, who held up his cell phone and took pictures of both sides of the medallion. He handed it back to Kyle. "Thank you. When did you first notice that you'd lost this?"

"A couple of months ago," Kyle answered, his voice cracking. He pulled the medallion over his head and tucked it back under his shirt.

"March? February?"

"Uh, I lost it sometime in March. I only take it off when I shower, and that's when I noticed."

Simmons leaned toward Kyle, fixing him with a piercing stare. "If it's so important to you, did you try to find it when you noticed you'd lost it?"

Kyle looked at his lawyer. Barrow nodded. "I did look for it. Went to all the places I remembered being the day before: school, the Final Quest where I work, Dunkin' Donuts where I bought lunch that day."

"Did you ask anybody at that time if they'd found it? Put up signs saying it was lost and offering a reward? Advertise in the newspaper?"

"No. I didn't think to do any of those things," Kyle stammered. "I just looked for it myself."

"And when did you buy the replacement one?"

"I-I-I don't remember exactly. Maybe a few weeks ago?" Kyle's hands were shaking, and he tucked them in his lap, under the table. Barrow again put a hand on his client's arm and left it there.

Simmons let Kyle's answer hang in the air for thirty seconds. "You bought it at the Final Quest five days after your sister died. I have a copy of the receipt from the store. Don't you think it's a little strange that you'd be worrying about replacing something as unimportant as a video game trinket when your family had just found out that your sister had been murdered?"

Kyle looked frantically at his lawyer. Barrow squeezed his arm again. "My client and I need to talk for a moment. Would you step out of the room and turn off the recording equipment, please?"

Simmons stood up. "Knock on the door when you're ready to resume." He hit the recorder button, and the red light came back on.

Five minutes had elapsed when Barrow knocked on the interrogation room door. Simmons re-entered the room, turned the recording device back on, and sat down.

"I'd asked you whether you thought it was strange that you were worried about replacing your medallion at a time when your whole family was grieving the death of your sister," Simmons said, addressing Kyle.

"The medallion means a lot to me," Kyle said, his voice low. "It's meant to protect the wearer from evil forces. I was upset about my sister and . . . and . . . just wanted it back." He slumped in his chair and buried his face in his hands.

"Sounds to me like you should have given the medallion to your sister . . . to protect her," Simmons retorted. "Is there a reason you felt you needed to be protected? Someone you're afraid of?"

Kyle shook his head, not looking up.

"You're harassing my client, Detective. He's answered your question. Go on to your other questions," Barrow sat forward in his chair, expectantly.

"All right, let's go back over where you were on the night your sister was murdered. You weren't at the arcade, and there's no confirmation on the surveillance cameras that you were at Green Park. Would you go over again for me exactly where you went after you left the church social and the time frame?"

After an hour of back and forth, Barrow called a halt. "My client has tried to answer your questions. It's clear that he doesn't remember what he was doing that night, no matter how many times you ask. Unless you have another avenue you want to explore, I think we're finished here."

Simmons grunted and stood up. "I'm done for now. But, as new information develops, I may need to talk to your client again. He shouldn't leave the area." He walked to the door of the interrogation room and held it open. Kyle slunk through, avoiding looking at the detective.

Jana saw Kyle and Barrow, followed by Detective Simmons, in the hallway. Kyle's posture and demeanor was defeated. She hurried to him, glaring at the detective as she took Kyle's arm. "Are you all right?" Jana whirled on Barrow as Simmons pushed by. "Two hours! I thought you said this would be a short interview!"

Barrow leaned toward her and whispered, "Outside. Not here."

Simmons watched as the three left. He shook his head. "What's going on in that kid's head? I know he's hiding something, but damned if I know what it is or how to get him to talk." He shook his head again and headed for his office.

Chapter 21

Thursday evening, May 10

I was furious with Kyle and with his lawyer. I needed to know what was going on. When we reached my car, I told Kyle to get in and Barrow that I wanted to talk to him. Kyle didn't say anything, he just climbed into the front passenger seat. Barrow looked at me, wary.

"What happened in there? Did he ask about the medallion? How did Kyle answer?" The questions poured out of me.

"I can't tell you anything much," Barrow responded. "Simmons did ask about the medallion, and he'd already talked with the owner of the shop where Kyle bought the replacement for the one he lost. Thank you for giving me a heads-up on that issue. I was able to prepare Kyle for it. Simmons also made Kyle go over, again, where he was and what he was doing the night your daughter died. Simmons did ask him if he was afraid of someone—or protecting someone—to make him so evasive. I called a halt to the interview after it was clear that it wasn't going anywhere."

I was frustrated. "So nothing's resolved. The police are still thinking Kyle knows something and won't talk. What's next?"

Barrow regarded me with a concerned look. "What's next? Unless some new evidence comes to light, I think Kyle's going to be okay. They may want to interview him again, but we don't need to cooperate." He turned toward his car. "I need to get back to the office. If anything else comes up, give me a call. And remind Kyle not to talk to anyone about this case."

I stared after him as he left. I understood his last words, but they worried me. Did Kyle's own lawyer think he was somehow involved? That he knew who murdered LaRissa but was afraid to tell? Or, even worse, that he knew and was protecting the person? My mind whirled, fuzzy with too much to contemplate. I got in the car and drove Kyle home.

Chapter 22

Saturday, May 19

The days passed quickly. At home, nothing changed. Don and I weren't talking or sleeping in the same bed. He went to work, fixed his own breakfast, sometimes ate a silent dinner with Kyle and me, and then either went out to the workshop in the garage or left the house and didn't return till late. Kyle spent most of his time in his room, only emerging to eat, hand over the homework his teachers sent home, and go to work at Final Quest. We didn't hear from Detective Simmons, which reassured me.

I also went to work. It was probably the most productive time of my professional life. I found I could immerse myself in writing grant applications. While I was writing, nothing else intruded—no thoughts or worries or images of LaRissa lying on the table in the morgue. The clinic was awarded two new grants during that period, which meant that Dr. Kahn was in a good mood and not charging into my office to demand I earn the pittance he was paying me.

Kyle's graduation from high school was scheduled for May 24, just before Memorial Day weekend. A call from my mother ended this numb-normal existence. She announced she was coming for Kyle's graduation and was planning to stay with me.

"Mom, Kyle isn't even sure he wants to walk in the graduation. The principal said they would mail the certificate to him if he doesn't," I protested.

"Of course he'll go to his graduation," Mom said, her voice emphatic. "These are the happiest days of his life coming to an end. It needs to be commemorated. Are you having a party for him?"

I stifled a sharp response. "No, Mom. No party. Kyle doesn't want one. And as for the happiest days of his life? I certainly hope that's not the case. We just buried LaRissa a few weeks ago. We're all still . . ." I couldn't go on.

"Jana, the best way to get over grief is to push forward with life," my mother said. "I don't want to criticize you right now, but you always were too sensitive, too emotional. And that's not going to help Kyle or Don or you move on. You need to be doing the normal things. Graduation and a party are exactly what your family needs." Her voice softened, and she added, "I'm not saying you forget LaRissa. I still think of your father every day. But returning life to normal gets you through this."

I couldn't respond.

"Well, in any case, I arrive next Wednesday night. Flight 520 on Delta gets in at seven-thirty p.m. I'll get my bag and wait for you at the curb." She hung up.

I dreaded my mother's presence in my house. She always criticized my housekeeping, décor, food, and appearance nonstop. In her eyes, I was an extension of herself, and it was essential that I never, ever embarrass her. She also didn't believe in taking "no" for an answer. That had been pretty much the story growing up and, according to my therapist, had contributed greatly to my retiring persona. As in, if you know you can't win, don't engage.

Her imminent arrival did pull me out of the fog I'd been existing in, replacing it with anxiety and dread. I went out to the garage where Don was making a kayak, his latest project. He raised one eyebrow when he saw me and turned off the sander.

"What's up?"

"My mother's coming for Kyle's graduation."

"And?"

"I need you to furnish LaRissa's room before tomorrow night, so she has a place to sleep."

Don shrugged. "No. I'm not going to rush around and do all that just so you can hide the fact that you're sleeping in a separate room. You figure it out." He turned the sander back on and bent to his woodworking.

Fuck you, I thought, startling myself. I never used that word, but there it was popping into my head. I left the garage and went upstairs to talk to Kyle.

He was huddled over his computer, wearing only pajama bottoms. His vertebrae stood out in stark relief, and when he looked up his face was drawn, dark circles under his eyes. I realized that I'd been derelict in monitoring his condition and resolved to get more focused. He might be legally an adult, but he obviously wasn't taking on the responsibility of self-monitoring.

"Kyle, your grandmother's coming for your graduation. We need to talk." I sat down on his bed. "Will you think about going? You know how she is."

He stared at me. "No."

I sighed. "What would it take to convince you to walk? I know you don't want to, but it would mean a lot to her."

He thought for a moment. "How about a one-way ticket to Germany and two thousand dollars?"

His answer shocked me. "Germany? One way? What are you talking about?"

"I want out. Out of this house, out of this town, and out of this country. There's nothing here for me."

"But why Germany?" My head was spinning. What had Kyle been thinking and doing these weeks in his room?

"Bob has relatives in Germany. His mother's family. He says I could stay with his cousin in Leipzig. I could take computer courses at the college." His face lit up. "I did okay in German classes. And if I was living there, I'd learn the language much faster."

I was reluctant to discourage him. This was the most animated and positive I'd seen him in months, going back long before LaRissa died. "I'll think about it and talk to your father. And to Bob. Wouldn't you need to apply for a student visa, though? There must be paperwork involved."

"Bob says I could go to Germany on a tourist visa, then apply for a student visa once the college approves me for study." Kyle had clearly worked this out, at least in his own mind. I was happy that he was even making plans for after high school, no matter what they were.

"All right. I can't promise anything, but you'll tell the school that you'll attend graduation, if I promise to talk to your dad and Bob?"

Kyle smiled broadly. "Yes. I'll call and tell them." He got up, came over to me, and gave me a quick hug. "Thanks. This is something I really want to do!"

I went downstairs and called Bob. He was at the Final Quest, and I could hear chatter and laughter in the background. Probably a D&D game or a video game competition. I explained why I was calling, and Bob confirmed what Kyle had said. He had a cousin in Leipzig who was willing to let Kyle live with him for at least a few months, and Bob had looked into visa requirements.

"Look, Jana, Kyle's had a rough year. You all have. He needs to go try something that challenges him, something that will give him confidence that he can make it on his own. He's a good kid, and I think this would be good for him. And Stefan will let us know if there are any problems while Kyle's there."

I thanked him, took a deep breath, and went looking for Don.

"Now what?" He turned off the sander.

"Kyle wants to go to Germany and study computer coding, or at least something to do with computers." The words rushed out of me. "Bob Harris has offered him a place to stay with one of his cousins."

"When would he go?"

Don's response surprised me. I was expecting a long, acrimonious discussion. "I'm not sure. Probably soon. He'll want to have time to immerse in German language before college starts in the winter semester."

"How much will it cost?"

"Airplane ticket, maybe two or three thousand dollars to cover living expenses and the first semester tuition."

"Okay."

"Really? You think it's a good idea?" I was caught completely off guard by Don's acquiescence.

Don shrugged. "Look, Jana. You and I are heading toward separation or divorce, it looks like. Kyle doesn't need to be here for that. He's got problems enough. So let him go and make his mistakes. We've done what we can." He reached over and turned on the sander.

I was staggered by his response. It took a long minute before I was able to breathe. I finally turned and walked out of the garage, through the kitchen, and across the yard to Sarah's house.

"Sarah . . ." I faltered. "Sarah."

My best friend led me to a chair at her kitchen table and gently pushed me into it. She sat down next to me. "What's wrong, Jana? What's happened?"

"My mother's coming, Kyle wants to go to Germany, and Don wants a divorce," I gasped out. My sobs were turning into wails.

Sarah put her arm around my shoulder and hugged tight. "Okay, this sounds bad. Start with your mother coming." She'd listened to my complaints about my mother since we'd become best friends in high school.

"For Kyle's graduation."

"Uh-huh," Sarah said calmly. "Did you tell her Kyle isn't going to walk in the graduation?"

"She didn't listen. She said these are the happiest days of his life ending and he needed to commemorate that." I glanced at her and saw the quirk of a beginning smile. I knew she was remembering when, in high school, my mother had told me the same thing—these were the happiest days of my life, and I should enjoy them while I could. I'd said to Sarah, at the time, that I might as well commit suicide then if these were the happiest days of my life.

I grinned back at her, through my tears. It *was* funny, in a sick sort of way. "Okay. But she doesn't know that Don and I are having problems. That's going to really make her go on a tear. I asked Don to get some furniture for LaRissa's room so she could sleep there, and he refused."

"No problem. I'll get Bill and the girls to move the sleeper couch and the chair from the rec room over there tomorrow. What else?"

"Kyle wants to go live in Germany and go to college there. And he said he'd walk in graduation if his dad and I agree." I was calming down. Sarah always had that effect on me.

"Sounds like a plan," Sarah said. "You probably are worried about how he'll do over there, but it might be good for him." She tightened her grip around my shoulders. "What else?"

"Don agreed to Kyle going to Germany." I stopped and couldn't go on.

"And?"

"And he said it was a good idea because if we were going to separate or divorce, it would be better if Kyle wasn't here for that." I sobbed and buried my face in my hands.

Sarah let me cry for a few minutes, then put her hand under my chin and raised my head. "Jana, you and Don have had serious problems, for a while, and the tragedy you're dealing with has brought it to the front. You know it, and you haven't been able to deal with it. Now what Don's thinking is finally out in the open. So, what do *you* want? Do you want a divorce? If not, then you need to sit down with Don and talk. Go to marriage counseling if you think the marriage is worth saving." She patted my arm. "Look, it's bad that this is all happening at once. Too much at once: LaRissa and not knowing who killed her. Don. Kyle planning on going away. And your mother coming. Wow! Way too much!"

We talked for another hour. Two glasses of wine and a cup of coffee later, I felt stronger. More able to cope. I went home, climbed the stairs, and slept the best I had in weeks.

Chapter 23

Thursday evening, May 24

Kyle was sullen but dressed in a new suit and tie under his graduation gown. The cap perched uneasily on his long hair, threatening to pop off into the air at any moment. When we arrived at the school gym, my mother pulled him to one side, spoke to him, and then gave him a quick hug. He looked bemused as he shuffled off to find the rows of seats where the alphabetical lines of graduates were to sit.

"What did you say to him, Mom?" I scanned the available seats to find good ones, near the center aisle, then led her to a row with four available seats. We sat down.

My mother laughed. "I just told him he looked handsome and was going to turn into a glorious man once he gets his full growth on him." Mom had been not-so-bad in the two days she'd been staying with us. While she had, as expected, spent time cleaning the house and rearranging the kitchen cabinets while I was at work, she hadn't remarked on the reasons she'd felt compelled to do it. And Sarah had made a point of entertaining her in the evenings, coming over after school, chatting with her, and talking my mom into sharing—and demonstrating the steps for—her "secret" recipe for genuine Italian gnocchi. She'd never shared it with me, but I didn't mind as long as Mom was busy and occupied and not commenting on the fact that I was sleeping in the guest room. We'd bumped into each other in the middle of the night on our way to the bathroom. Her lips pursed when she saw me come out of the guest room, but she nodded and ducked back into LaRissa's room.

Kyle had been in a cheerful mood since it'd been settled that he'd go to Germany for at least three months. Staying longer depended on whether he could get accepted at the college in Leipzig. He'd been studying and practicing German nonstop in the past week. I didn't know German—I'd studied French in school—and he sounded reasonably fluent to me. But I still had doubts about the whole idea. My mother had said, "You worry too much. He's a man, he needs to go off and learn what he can do. Besides, he'll have someone there to help, and what's the worst that could happen? If it doesn't work out, he'll come back here and enroll in college in Hinton next semester." I was surprised and reassured by her practicality.

Don and Bob Harris had parked the car and joined us just as the lights dimmed for the start of the ceremony. Mom was on the aisle, and I was next to her. Bob took the fourth seat in the row, leaving the seat next to me open. Don sat down, careful not to touch me. We'd talked some, but nothing was solved. I'd suggested to him the night before that we consider marriage counseling, and he'd been noncommittal.

The squawks of the horns and woodwinds tuning up provided a backdrop for the shuffling of people taking their seats. Behind the podium, the large screen came on displaying a picture of Fairview High School. *Déjà vu.* It had been twenty-four years since Don and I had sat in this gym, watched our friends' excitement, and felt the anticipation of going forth into the world as . . . adults. I hoped Kyle had that same feeling.

Principal Kumansky strode out onto the stage to a smattering of applause. The screen behind him read Welcome to Fairview High School's 55th Graduation. The color guard marched out and placed the flags, and we all stood and sang "The Star-Spangled Banner." Principal Kumansky said a few words of welcome and then introduced the school board chairwoman, who lauded the graduates, the teachers, the principal, and the board for their hard work. Then several teachers gave brief speeches, and the football coach narrated a video of the team's county championship year as it played on the large screen behind him. Kumansky then returned to the podium and introduced a video of other highlights of the year. Theater, band and orchestra, speech and debate awards, academic achievements, and other noteworthy events. At the end, a large picture of LaRissa flashed onto the screen. Kumansky spoke quietly of the loss to her family, friends, the school, and the whole community, ending with a request for a moment of silence to remember LaRissa. I was taken aback. No one had told me there would be a memorial at the graduation. My mother took my hand, tears running down her face.

"It'll be okay, Jana," she whispered. I'm not sure why she said that. It would never be okay. But I squeezed her hand.

The rest of the ceremony passed in a blur. Four more speakers—valedictorian, senior class president, two academic award winners—and then it was time for the presentation of the diplomas. The band began to play "Pomp and Circumstance," and, row by row, students stood, filed up the side stairs to the stage, and marched across to receive their diplomas. Despite pleas from Principal Kumansky to hold it all until the end, there was wild or polite applause for each graduate, plus whoops and whistles for popular kids. A few of the graduates danced across the stage after being handed their diploma. One did cartwheels. When Kyle finally reached the podium and was handed his, he nodded and shook the principal's hand. No display of happiness, but I hadn't expected him to do anything dramatic. The applause for him was scant, but Don and Bob did their best to make noise.

When it was over, the students were assembled behind the stage. Principal Kumansky made final remarks about pride and congratulations to the parents, then announced the Class of 2018. The graduates marched onto the stage and down the stairs and proceeded down the center aisle as the band played "Don't Stop Believing." As the last students left, the crowd began pushing to get up the aisle. I followed my mother, with Don and Bob behind us. Don hadn't spoken or touched me throughout the ceremony. I was preparing to say something congratulatory to him, share the positive experience, when I noticed he was no longer behind me. I scanned the crowd but couldn't find him. Bob saw me looking around and said, "Don's gone to the little boy's room. He said he'd meet us out front." I nodded and went on.

Outside the school, the parking lot was filled with happy, chattering students. A couple threw their caps in the air, touching off a hundred more caps flying. I didn't see Kyle.

"There he is," Mom said. She pointed to a figure walking toward the back of the parking lot. We hurried after him, catching up as he spotted our car in one of the back rows.

The drive home was quiet. Don and I in the front seat, not talking. Kyle and Mom in back. Bob had driven his own car and said he'd meet us at our house. Mom gave up asking Kyle how he felt and what he wanted to do to celebrate. Kyle's answers were brief: "Good" and "Pizza."

"What the hell?" The first words from Don on the drive from the school were uttered as we pulled up to our house. A patrol car, blue and red lights flashing, was parked in our driveway. James Barrow, Kyle's lawyer, was standing beside his car parked on the street.

As we got out, two deputies came toward us, grabbed Kyle, and spun him around to cuff his hands behind his back. Detective Simmons joined them, stopping in front of Kyle.

"Kyle Spencer, you're under arrest for the murder of LaRissa Spencer. You have the right . . ."

I began to run toward Kyle, but his lawyer stepped in front of me. "You can't interfere right now, Jana. I'll go with him to the station and see if they'll release him on bond. I'll call you when I know something."

I tried to push past Barrow, but he held fast, not letting me move toward Kyle. "Why are they arresting him?" I screamed, frantic, as the deputy placed a hand on Kyle's head and pushed him into the back seat of the cruiser.

"They have an arrest warrant charging him with second-degree murder in LaRissa's death," Barrow said. "They notified me an hour ago. I knew graduation was tonight, so I asked that they wait and take him into custody when you got home." The police were driving away. "Look, I have to go. I'll call you."

Don had joined us and put a restraining hand on my arm. "Jana, calm down. This must be a mistake. Let's go inside and wait to hear from Barrow."

I shook off his hand. "I can't wait, I need to go to the police station. Kyle needs me."

Sarah, who had come out of her house when she saw the flashing lights, wrapped an arm around my waist. "You can't go, Jana. They won't let you in. His lawyer is with him and will handle things." I bit back a hot response and let her lead me to the house.

Chapter 24

Tuesday, May 29

Kyle's arraignment was scheduled for Tuesday morning. He'd been in jail for over four days. The Memorial Day weekend had delayed the arraignment, but Barrow had gotten his initial court appearance on the docket for the day after the holiday. Don, my mother, and I arrived at the courthouse in Hinton at nine-thirty. Over my protests, Mom had insisted on changing her plane reservations to stay with me through the arraignment.

Barrow met us on the other side of the screening area and escorted us to the courtroom. The room was packed. I recognized several of our neighbors and a few students who'd just graduated with Kyle. Murder is a rare occurrence in our small county.

"I met with Kyle this morning and went over what would happen today," Barrow said once we were seated. "The charges against Kyle will be presented to the judge, and Kyle will have to respond. I've told him not to say anything in court except 'Not guilty' when the judge asks how he pleads."

"Will we be able to take him home after that?" I was horrified at the thought of Kyle remaining in jail. Don and I had seen him on Sunday during visiting hours. He'd looked defeated, dressed in a faded gray coverall, his hair lank, and his eyes shadowed. I was terrified that they weren't feeding him properly or allowing him to monitor his diabetes, but he claimed he'd been seen by the medical staff and they were providing insulin on schedule. His affect, though, was dull, almost indifferent to our presence. He stared at his hands the whole hour we were there.

"It's a murder charge, Jana," Barrow said. "The judge is unlikely to decide whether he should be released on bail today. I've requested a preliminary hearing where the prosecution will present an overview of the evidence against Kyle. Depending on what happens then, the judge will either deny bail or set an amount. The preliminary hearing will also give me a chance to learn what the evidence is and whether there are weaknesses in it we can use to defend Kyle."

"How soon will the preliminary hearing be?" I asked. I couldn't bear the thought of Kyle remaining in jail for an extended time. "And how much is bail likely to be?"

Barrow shook his head. "I know it's hard to have so many things uncertain. We won't know whether he'll get bail or how much until the preliminary. I'll try to get it set as soon as possible."

The bailiff appeared at the back of the courtroom and escorted Kyle to the table in front of the railing that divided the spectators from the court. "I'll talk to you later," Barrow said. He went through the swinging gate in the railing and sat down next to Kyle, who was hunched over, head in his hands. I returned to the seat Mom was holding for me.

"Kyle looks terrible," my mother whispered as I sat down. "Are they taking proper care of him in that place?" I nodded as Don shushed her. He was sitting on the other side of her, a grim expression on his face.

The arraignment went quickly. The prosecutor presented the charges. Kyle and his lawyer stood when the judge asked how he wanted to plead. Kyle said "not guilty" in a low voice. Barrow then asked that a preliminary hearing be scheduled. The judge studied her calendar and set it for thirteen days later. My heart sank. Kyle would be incarcerated for nearly two more weeks.

The judge then ended the arraignment, and Kyle was led out by the bailiff. Barrow joined us outside the courtroom minutes later. "I asked the prosecutor to send me discovery as soon as possible, but I doubt he'll do that until after the preliminary hearing. You all just need to sit tight and be patient while the process works. I'll do my best to persuade the judge that Kyle should be released on bond until the trial." He shrugged his shoulders and added, "No guarantees on that, but I'll try. The fact that he's charged with murder means that the judge may not want to release him, even with electronic monitoring. This is a big case, and she may be concerned that he'll try to flee the country."

I flinched and looked at Don. Kyle's plans to go to Germany. Had he come up with them because he knew he might be charged? I felt guilty even thinking that. Don avoided my eyes and walked away. I turned to Mom and asked her to go back to the car, saying that I needed to talk to the lawyer in private. She frowned but went.

"Is everything I tell you protected by confidentiality?" I asked Barrow once Mom was out of earshot.

"If it's about Kyle's case, then yes. What are you thinking?"

I quickly told him about Kyle's plan to go to Germany and enroll in college there. "I don't think there's any way that the police could know about it," I added. "But would the judge be likely to refuse bail if she knew about it?"

Barrow rubbed his forehead, a worried expression on his face. "It might affect the judge's decision. How many people know about Kyle's plan?"

"I think just me and Don, our friend Bob Harris, my friend Sarah, and my mother. And anyone they may have mentioned it to. Kyle doesn't have any real friends, so I doubt he'll have told anyone else."

"But he might have," Barrow said. "I'll ask him. In the meantime, you might want to mention to the people who know that they shouldn't discuss Kyle's plans with anyone else."

I agreed and thanked him for his help, then joined Don and my mother in the car. It was a quiet ride home.

Chapter 25

Monday morning, June 11

I hadn't slept the previous night. Mostly because I was anxious about the preliminary hearing. Barrow said the prosecutor will have to present convincing evidence for the judge to let the case go to trial. She could decide that the evidence is too weak to justify a trial, but Barrow said that almost never happens. The main reason he requested the preliminary was to learn the major details of the prosecution's case and begin to prepare Kyle's defense.

The other reason I didn't sleep, though, is that Don had told me last night that he wanted out of our marriage. I'd tried to talk to him, to convince him that we need to go to marriage counseling, but he'd refused to consider it. Then he had told me he wouldn't be able to take off from work for the preliminary hearing.

My mother had finally gone back to Florida the previous morning. Even though she'd tried her best to be supportive, I was happy to see her go. Her unspoken criticisms of everything I did were hard to deal with while I was struggling with Kyle's situation and deep depression over LaRissa's death. I was relieved to drop her at the airport. If I'd been feeling charitable, I might have thought that Don had been considerate enough to wait till she was gone to tell me he was leaving, so I wouldn't have to deal with her reaction. But probably not.

After Don left, I had had a couple glasses of wine, took a Shakespeare play—*Hamlet*— from the bookshelf, and tucked myself into bed, intending to read till I fell asleep. Shakespeare was usually good for that. Not this time. I tossed and turned, turned the bedside light off and on, read a page or two— lather, rinse, repeat. I was relieved to see the sky lightening at dawn.

I drove to the courthouse in Hinton early to be sure I got a seat right behind where Kyle and his lawyer would be sitting. But no such luck. The front rows were already full, an hour before the hearing. I found an aisle seat on the fourth row and waited for Barrow to arrive.

He appeared just as the bailiff was announcing "All rise!" for the entry of the judge. He strode up to the front and stood at the defendant's table. After everyone was seated, Kyle was brought in through the door at the back. He was handcuffed in front and had shackles on his ankles. His neck was bent, so I couldn't see his face as he shuffled to his seat.

The preliminary hearing was intended to present evidence to the judge so she could decide whether the prosecution's case warranted the charges against Kyle. Barrow had warned me not to react to anything I heard and that he would not be defending Kyle at this hearing. "Defense doesn't present at the preliminary," he'd told me. "Our only role will be to learn what the prosecution has and use that to prepare our defense at trial."

I listened as the witnesses appeared, one by one. Detective Simmons was first. He detailed his efforts to learn where Kyle had been the night LaRissa was murdered and said that Kyle had lied repeatedly about his whereabouts. He also gave testimony about the medallion found at the site where her body had been, the steps he'd taken to ascertain that Kyle had had a similar medallion, and that Kyle had purchased a replacement for it shortly after LaRissa's death. The prosecution then called the medical examiner who described the autopsy findings and the cause of death —a blow to the head. He then told the court that DNA evidence had been found under LaRissa's fingernails. The prosecutor had obtained a subpoena for Kyle's DNA after his arrest, and it had been found to match what was under LaRissa's nails.

I gasped when I heard that testimony. Could LaRissa and Kyle's argument at the church social have gotten physical? I didn't remember seeing any scratches on Kyle at the time, but he always wore long-sleeved shirts to cover the insulin injection marks. My head was whirling, and I couldn't focus on the next two prosecution witnesses.

It was all over in less than an hour. Barrow asked the judge to rule that there was insufficient evidence to proceed, the judge denied his request, and she set a date for the trial in three months' time. Barrow then requested that Kyle be released on bail, but the judge denied the request. The guards appeared and escorted Kyle out of the courtroom. He had stared at the floor through the entire hearing.

I waited for Barrow to gather his papers and followed him out of the courtroom. He shook his head as I started to ask a question. "Not here, Jana. Meet me at my office in twenty minutes." He hurried to the parking lot.

I was shaking as I drove the three blocks to his office. The DNA evidence was devastating. The horrifying thought that Kyle had killed his sister—killed my daughter—raged through my head. I sat in the car outside Barrow's office for fifteen minutes, unable to move, almost unable to breathe. Finally, I pulled myself together, took four deep breaths, muttered a mantra that was supposed to relax me, and got out of the car.

Barrow was waiting in the reception area of his office. "Come in my office, Jana. Where's Don?"

"He couldn't make it today," I said tersely as we walked to his office. It wasn't his job to think about our personal issues. "Tell me, honestly, what's your assessment of Kyle's situation?" I sat down.

Barrow fixed me with a level gaze. "What's your take from what you heard today?"

"It sounds like he might be found guilty." My voice caught in my throat. I swallowed and went on. "They seem to have convincing evidence, though there might be other explanations for the DNA under her fingernails. They lived in the same house. She might have accidentally scratched him sometime during the day. There are hundreds of those medallions. They can't prove the one they found is Kyle's." I looked at him, hopeful he'd agree with me.

"Jana, they have other evidence. At a preliminary hearing, the prosecution only has to present enough to convince the judge there's sufficient reason to go to trial. I do know, though

I can't tell you my source, that they found Kyle's fingerprints on the dumpster. That means that, at some point, he was at the dumpster where her body was found." He looked at me for a long minute. "You may need to come to terms with the fact that Kyle may have been involved somehow."

I bolted to my feet. "Are you out of your mind?" I leaned over the desk, poking a finger at the lawyer. "If you think he's guilty, we need to find a different lawyer. Kyle would never . . . never hurt his sister!"

"Sit down and listen to me. I said Kyle was most probably there when LaRissa was killed. He may know who did it and be afraid to tell anyone."

I sputtered. "Who? Who would he be afraid of? Some bullies at school? That kid who she ostensibly had sex with that night? Kyle knows we would protect him. We agreed he could go to Germany before all this came out." I sank back into the chair, still furious with Barrow. "I don't believe he knows who it is and isn't willing to tell us."

"All right. Is it possible that Kyle and LaRissa encountered each other sometime that evening and got into an argument about something? An argument that got out of control and Kyle shoved LaRissa. She fell and hit her head?"

I shook my head. "No, I don't believe that would happen! And if it did, Kyle would have called 9-1-1 and tried to help her." All these speculations were making my head hurt. "Besides, that would make Kyle still responsible for her death, wouldn't it?"

"It would," Barrow said. "But he wouldn't be charged with second-degree murder. It'd probably be a lesser charge like involuntary manslaughter. It's a difference between thirty years or more in prison and up to twenty years."

I couldn't think anymore. I had to get out of there. I picked up my purse and fished out my keys. "I need to go, Jim. We can come up with scenarios all day, but it doesn't help if we don't really know what happened. If Kyle was there—and you say the evidence is that he was—he's the only one who can tell us what happened. I can talk to him when I visit him."

"No! Anything he tells you there could be used against him at trial. I'll talk to him and lay this all out so he knows what he may be facing. Tell Don to call me. I'll discuss the options with both of you when I have more information," Barrow said. He walked me to the stairs. "It doesn't look good right now, but there's months till the trial. There's time to figure this out and produce the best outcome for your son."

I stared bleakly at him and then started down the stairs. I drove home in silence. What should I tell Don if he called tonight? I was angry with him, but he had a right to be involved in Kyle's defense. I pulled into the driveway and got out. A young man rushed up and shoved a manila envelope at me.

"You've been served," he said before dashing down the driveway and jumping into his car.

Confusion muddled my thinking. I stared at the envelope and went into the house. Inside was a petition for divorce. Don hadn't wasted any time. I collapsed onto the sofa and started laughing. Today it looked like my son might end up in prison for years, and this was the day that my husband of twenty-four years decided to serve me with divorce papers? I laughed and laughed, tears rolling down my cheeks, then got up and poured a glass of wine. What else, I said to myself, could go wrong today?

Chapter 26

Monday evening, June 11

I was on my fourth glass of wine when Sarah knocked on the kitchen door and came in. She watched me warily as she sat down on the sofa.

"Have you eaten anything today?" Sarah finally asked.

"Umm, not sure. I don't think so." I hadn't had the stomach for breakfast before the hearing. Afterward, my stomach had felt like acid, so I'd swallowed a couple Tums. "Had some Tums, does that count?" I grinned and raised my glass to her.

Sarah stood up. "We need coffee, and I'm going to scramble some eggs and make some toast. Then we'll talk."

I grinned again and stood, wobbly. "Great idea! You always have such good ideas. I don't know what I'd do without you." I staggered a little, but I caught myself and followed her into the kitchen. "How about a glass of wine to celebrate?" I plunked myself down on the kitchen chair and waved the bottle I'd carried from the living room at her.

Sarah sighed. "It's four o'clock in the afternoon, Jana. A little early for wine, at least for me." She made coffee, popped toast in the toaster, and got the frying pan, butter, and eggs from the refrigerator. "What happened at the preliminary hearing?"

I gulped down the last inch of wine in my glass. "It was bad, Sarah. They have a lot of evidence, and Kyle's lawyer said they probably have more that they'll present at the trial." Tears began leaking down my cheeks. I sobbed. "Kyle couldn't have done this. I know him. He doesn't have a violent bone in his body." I buried my face in my hands. "He's just a boy, always been a little different, but good-hearted."

Sarah set the bowl of eggs down and came over to me. "It'll be okay, Jana. No one at school believes Kyle could have done this." She stroked my hair, causing me to cry even harder. "Right now, you need to eat something." She poured a cup of coffee and set it in front of me. "Drink this, and I'll finish the eggs and toast."

I'd finished about half the cup of coffee when Sarah slid a plate in front of me. And after another cup and a full stomach, things didn't seem quite as hopeless. I told Sarah about the evidence presented by the prosecution, and she agreed that it looked damning for Kyle. "But, Jana, it's circumstantial. There are other explanations for why Kyle was confused about what he did that night. He was upset when LaRissa's friends laughed at him. And the medallion isn't proof. There are probably dozens of kids who have exactly the same thing, so anyone could have lost it."

"And what about the DNA under LaRissa's fingernails?" That was the one thing that had truly shaken me at the hearing. How could Kyle's DNA have gotten under my girl's fingernails?

"I don't know," Sarah admitted. "But there must be an explanation. They lived in the same house, maybe DNA could have transferred from a bar of soap they both used or something. Your lawyer will find expert witnesses who know about things like this. We don't have that kind of knowledge. But we know Kyle isn't guilty, so there must be some explanation." She got up and poured us each another cup of coffee. "Not to change the subject, but Bill told me that Don packed his bags and left this morning while you were gone. A couple of his buddies from the firehouse were playing horse in the driveway when Don came out of your house. They yelled at him to come join them, and Don said he was done with this house and this neighborhood. Even gave them the finger as he got in the car and left. Really? The jerk left you during your son's preliminary hearing?"

Her words hit me hard. "Does everyone in the neighborhood know?"

"Probably. I expect everybody who was there went home and told their wives. It's okay, though. I wouldn't have said this before, but Don's never been very popular around here. How do you feel about his leaving? Were you expecting it?"

I shook my head. "No. Well, not till last night when he told me he was going to move out. I mean I know we have problems. But I thought it was the stress over LaRissa and Kyle's situation and we'd work things out eventually. We always did before." I wrapped my hands tight around my coffee mug. "I've read enough psychology to know that a high proportion of couples separate after the death of a child. A while back, you know, we went to marriage counseling and really worked on getting our marriage back. And I thought we had. He stood by me when I had cancer—he did everything for me and the kids and was patient and loving through all of it."

Sarah's face scrunched into a frown. "I don't know how you forgave him for what he did back then. I'd just take a shotgun to Bill if I caught him with an eighteen-year-old in my bed!" She squeezed my hand. "You're a saint, is all I can say."

"I love . . . loved him, and he's the father of my children, Sarah. And you know how women are always tempting him." I took a deep breath. "I don't know how I feel right now. But I do know that Kyle needs us. The fact that Don didn't even bother to show up at the preliminary hearing bothers me a lot. Maybe he's washed his hands of Kyle and me. I just have to deal with that and do what I can for Kyle."

"You're very brave, Jana. If there's anything you need, I'm here for you." She stood up. "I need to start dinner. The horde will be wanting to eat soon. Do you want me to come over later?"

"No, that's okay," I said. "I missed work today, and there's a grant due in three days. I'm going to work on that and then, hopefully, get a full night's sleep." I walked her to the door.

The house seemed deadly quiet after she left. I put a John Denver CD on and sat on the sofa, computer in my lap. The divorce papers were sitting on the end table. I'd completely forgotten about them when Sarah was here. I pushed the thought of divorce aside and turned on the computer. Oddly, the writing totally absorbed me, and it was after midnight when I finally trudged up to bed.

Chapter 27

Wednesday, June 20

I went to the jail twice a week to visit Kyle. It hurt, but I knew he needed me. Our conversation today, though, was worrisome. He stared blankly past me for the first fifteen minutes as I talked about seeing Bob at the Final Quest and Bob's certainty that Kyle was innocent.

"Bob knows you and knows you couldn't possibly have hurt LaRissa," I told him. "And he says everyone he talks to says the same thing: your teachers, your friends at the store, everyone. He's willing to be a character witness for you and said to tell you to hang in there. This will all work out, and his cousin is looking forward to your visit to Germany once this is over."

"Kyle," I said softly, "you know we're all supporting you. Your lawyer says there's a good chance you'll be found not guilty. All the evidence is circumstantial. No one can testify that they saw you with LaRissa that night, and there's reasonable explanations for the rest of their evidence."

Kyle leaped to his feet. Rage contorted his face, and he banged his fists on the table. "Cut it out! I've had it with you trying to make me feel better. Just get out of here. Don't come back." He pushed back off the table, knocking over the chair he'd jumped up from. A guard came hurrying over, one hand on his baton. "I'm done here," Kyle told him. "Take me back to my cell."

I watched as the guard led him away. For the first time in my life, I'd been almost afraid of my son. The way he'd lunged at me was terrifying. What had this whole experience done to him? I blinked back tears, and then fury at Don swept over me. What kind of father leaves his son alone in this hell?

After I left the jail, I stopped at Safeway on my way home. I was leaning into the Lean Cuisine freezer when Florence, Brenda's mother, swept up to me.

"I'm surprised to see you out in public, Jana," Florence said to me. The smug look on her face gave me an unexpected urge to smack her.

"Just buying groceries, Flo. What most people do at the supermarket. How's Brenda?" I pulled out two packages of Lean Cuisine and faced her.

"My daughter's none of your business. She isn't going to associate with a family like yours. Your son's a murderer. And your husband? Well, don't get me started on him."

"What are you talking about?" I could feel myself flushing red. Apparently, she'd heard through the grapevine that Don and I had separated, but I wasn't giving her the satisfaction of acknowledging that.

"He's shacked up with that twenty-year-old girl, that's what I'm talking about. Her parents are devastated, and I can't blame them. Who would want their daughter living with a man twice her age and the father of a murderer?" Florence stepped back a pace as I moved toward her. "And you're no better."

My thoughts were whirling. *Don had texted me that he was staying with a friend from work.* "What are you talking about?" I repeated, my voice shrill. I could see several people stopping to stare at us.

"I'm talking about Joelly Pearson, as if you didn't know. She moved out of her parents' house, and she and your husband are shacking up in an apartment over on Cleveland Street." Florence smirked as she registered the shock on my face. "Half his age and a college student. But no surprise there. Everyone knows your husband's been on the prowl for years. He nearly broke up the Cartwrights' marriage two years ago. And most folks think that 'surprise' baby of Patricia Smith's is his."

"You seem to enjoy being a gossip, Flo. Not a saintly trait in someone who claims to be God-fearing." I somehow held my voice level, tossed the Lean Cuisines in my cart, and turned away from her. The small crowd that was watching avoided my eyes as I headed toward the checkout stand.

I held it together as I paid and carried my bags of groceries to the car. I held it together until I got inside my house. Then I dropped the bags of groceries on the floor, screamed, and threw a vase of flowers across the living room, scattering blossoms and water across the sofa and chairs. I sank to the floor, clutching my head. *Helen Cartwright? I'd worked with her on the middle-school graduation arrangements and after-party. And Pat Smith, one of my book club members? We'd gone out for drinks several times awhile back.* She'd had a baby boy three years ago, and I'd heard she'd moved to Chicago to be close to her parents. I rubbed my temples, hoping to ward off a migraine, picked up the bags of groceries, and went in the kitchen. "Put away the groceries, pour a glass of wine," I mumbled out loud. "That'll help." Three glasses of wine later, I collapsed into bed.

Chapter 28

The sun was shining, and the temperature was seventy degrees at eight-thirty on Friday morning. The beauty of the day raised my spirits. Flowers lined the driveway—geraniums, salvia, and beds of multi-colored moss roses all in full bloom. I bent to snip off a few dead heads on my way to the car. Kyle's lawyer had emailed me at eight o'clock last night and asked me to meet him at his office at nine. Could there be good news? He didn't say so, but the trial was still over two months away. I could hope the police had finally found the real guilty party.

I needed some good news. Since Flo's revelations of the previous day, I'd done a lot of thinking. And the more I thought, the more the reality stood out. Even when we were in high school, friends—and sometimes people who weren't friends— had hinted that Don was fooling around with other girls. I'd been steadfast in denial. I was sure they were just jealous of me, of the fact that I'd snared the best-looking, most charming boy in school. Don was always loving, solicitous of me, generous as a lover. It wasn't possible that he was cheating. When I got phone calls where someone hung up when I answered, I wrote it off to wrong numbers. When a woman showed up on our doorstep and insisted that Don was her lover and had promised he'd divorce me and marry her, I'd believed Don when he told me that she was someone whose car he'd fixed twice at the shop and who'd become obsessed with him. Even Sarah had hinted

126

once that Don might be too charming for his own good. It was one of the only times we'd ever argued, and she'd finally agreed with me that there was nothing there.

And now? Now I felt like a fool. But I'd come to terms with it. Don was gone, LaRissa was gone, and Kyle needed me to help him through this—whether he recognized it or not. Florence's revelation had steeled my resolve, I'd realized. I had to get through this. For Kyle.

Today would be a better day, I told myself as I started the car. The drive to Hinton to meet with Jim Barrow was pleasant. I made it in twenty minutes and sat out front, windows down, slight breeze wafting through the car. At precisely eight fifty-five I went into the building.

Barrow was chatting with his receptionist when I came in. "Jana, thank you for coming," he greeted me. "Please, come into my office." The serious look on his face raised my anxiety level. I followed him and sat down on a chair in front of his desk.

Barrow took his seat and cleared his throat. "There's no way to make this easy. Kyle has admitted to me that he did kill LaRissa. He asked me to be the one to tell you."

I surged up out of the chair. "No!" I shouted, leaning over the desk and pointing a finger at him. "No! That's not true. It can't be true. He's just saying that because you've convinced him that he's going to be found guilty." I was trembling all over, almost unable to breathe. "You tell him that's a lie and this will all work out." I got to my feet, staring daggers at him. "He didn't do it, and it's your job to make sure the jury knows that."

Barrow came around his desk and took my arm. "Please sit down, Jana."

I shook off his hand and sat, glaring at him.

"Here's where things stand. Kyle was convincing when he admitted this. He had details that he wouldn't have had unless he'd been there. He did say it was an accident. He was furious with LaRissa. He'd seen her under the bleachers having sex with the guy she'd left the social with. He hid until she was alone, then he came out from behind the bleachers, grabbed her, and started yelling at her. She fought back and began running away from him. He caught up with her by the dumpsters and grabbed her by the neck. She clawed his arms and broke the cord on his medallion. He said he was in a rage and started pressing harder on her neck. She pushed away from him, hard, fell backwards, and hit her head on the metal edge of the dumpster. He tried to save her, tried CPR, but when the bleeding stopped, he realized she was dead."

I stared at Barrow. "No," I whimpered. "No."

"I think it's true, Jana. What he told me. The question is what do we do now? There's a high likelihood that if this goes to a jury, they'll find him guilty. He might get life in prison if he's convicted of second-degree murder."

"What's the alternative?" I whispered. My eyes were dry, scratchy.

"I can work on a plea deal with the prosecutor and maybe get them to agree to reduce the charge to involuntary manslaughter. That has a penalty of up to twenty years. With good behavior, he might be out in ten years. He'd be on parole, but he'd would still have a chance for a life." Barrow's sympathy was evident. "I know this is hard. But I've talked to Kyle, and he's willing to plead guilty in return for the lesser charge."

My head was shaking back and forth. Denial. "I have to think about this. I can't make a decision right now." I grabbed my purse and stood up.

"Jana, it's not your decision to make. Kyle is legally an adult at eighteen. He's authorized me to proceed to negotiation with the prosecutor." Barrow's voice was kind, but firm. "And Kyle has taken your name off his visitor list for now. He doesn't want to talk to you or see you until this is finished."

I left his office, slammed the door, and rushed outside. This made no sense. Why would Kyle do this? To LaRissa? To me? I sat in the car and wept for all that could have been, all that I had dreamed for my son, and for LaRissa.

Chapter 29

Thursday, July 26

On Thursday, July 26, 2018, my son, Kyle Alan Spencer, was sentenced to twenty years in prison. The guards led him away in shackles, and he didn't look at me as he shuffled between them.

Chapter 30

Thursday evening, July 26

I'd taken the day off work so I could recover from the moment when the judge announced the sentence. Sarah had gone with me to the hearing, held my hand, and led me out of the courtroom after it was over. Barrow tried to talk to me, but I'd waved him away.

After Sarah drove me home, she'd asked if I wanted her to come in and stay with me overnight. I'd shook my head and fumbled my way out of the car. I was in shock, I think. Somehow this had never seemed real. But the last image I had of Kyle—head hanging, in a too-large jumpsuit, his hands cuffed, and with shackles on his ankles—was seared into my memory. I made it to the sofa and sat down.

What was I supposed to do now? kept running through my head. *What do people do when their older child is in prison for killing their younger child? When their husband deserted them and disowned his son? What? What? What?*

It was nearly dark when I emerged from my mental fog. I went in the kitchen and made a cup of tea, then pulled out a pad of paper and a pen. I wrote "What do I do next?" on the top of the page, then wrote bulleted items. "Keep working" was first. I needed to work, both for the money and to keep myself sane.

The next item on the list was "Visit Kyle in prison." The Greyson State Prison was over two hours away by car. I needed to call and find out about visiting hours. And whether Kyle had put me on his visitors list.

I paused, trying to think. What was the third item? I finally wrote down "Finalize divorce." I'd had the divorce papers a month, and they were still lying on the kitchen counter. I got up and went over, picked them up, and read them. I nodded slowly as I read. No fault, equal division of assets, no surprises. I scrawled my signature on the pages where his lawyer had placed yellow tags. I put the pages in the addressed and stamped envelope provided. Then I put a check mark by the third item on my list. Done.

What else? Item four was obvious. "Contact real estate agent." I couldn't afford the mortgage, and I doubted that Don wanted to live here. I'd ask Sarah to recommend someone.

I couldn't think of a fifth item for my list. I finally wrote "Eat dinner" and put the list on the counter. It was a start. A start to my new life.

Chapter 31

Sunday, August 5

Sarah and her daughters showed up at eleven a.m. to help me with the packing and throwing out tasks. The real estate agent had been firm that the house would sell more quickly and at a higher price if I emptied it and she could do some staging. Don had come over last weekend to remove all the items he wanted. I'd spent that afternoon at a movie. I still hadn't seen him since he'd moved out of the house. All our communications had been through texts. Even those limited, non-emotional exchanges had often roused me to anger. I was no longer angry about his leaving me, now that I finally knew what he was. I was angry about his indifference to Kyle's situation. He'd not asked even once about Kyle—where he was, how he was. He'd never expressed any feelings about him. It was as if, for him, he'd never had a son. He'd taken one picture of LaRissa from the house, but none of Kyle. The movie I chose was a revenge flick. It was satisfying, as was the large, buttered popcorn I'd eaten my way through while cheering on the good guy as he cut a swath through the evildoers.

"Where do you want us to start?" Sarah was cheerful, as always, and had brought a bucket full of cleaning products and equipment. She'd come prepared to clean and pack, dressed in old sweatpants with holes in the knees. Her curly red hair escaped from the edges of the bandana she'd tried to wrap it in. Her daughters Bridget, Siobhan, and Mary—thinner versions of their mother—were in jeans and T-shirts, and they didn't look as cheerful as Sarah. I was sure they'd rather be most anyplace else, but I was equally sure Sarah hadn't given them a choice.

"How about the kitchen? Throw out any food products that've passed their expiration date. Pack up the dishes, silverware, and pans. I've already boxed up the things for Salvation Army. And I'm keeping that pile there," I pointed at a tray on the counter, "so I have a couple plates and silverware to use till I find a new place." Then I pointed at the moving boxes and newspapers piled in the corner. "Just pack everything away and mark the boxes 'Kitchen.' The tape is in that drawer."

"Can do! Let's get to work, girls." Sarah threw open a cupboard door and started taking out plates. The girls picked up two boxes and some newspapers and began wrapping the plates.

"I really appreciate this, all of you," I said. "I've been working on clearing, but it just seems overwhelming. Twenty years in a house, so much accumulates." I watched them for a minute. "Okay, I'm going upstairs to tackle the guest room."

Sarah waved at me, grinning. "Yep, the repository of everything there's no other place for. Have fun."

I carried tape, a few medium boxes, one large clothing box, and several large trash bags up the stairs. I'd stopped sleeping in the guest room after Don moved out. The bed in our old bedroom was much more comfortable than the pull-out sofa. But I'd removed all traces of Don—pictures, magazines, clothes he hadn't taken, and the bowling awards he'd won. I'd thrown it all in the trash. If he didn't want it enough to take it, I certainly didn't need to look at it.

The floor-to-ceiling bookcase that covered one wall loomed before me. I unfolded and taped four boxes. Where to start. Classics that I'd kept from college? LaRissa's childhood books? Kyle's baseball magazines, science fiction books, and video games?

I slid my fingers over LaRissa's books. I'd planned to save them for when she had children of her own. My throat tightened, and I sat down on the sofa. LaRissa wouldn't have children. Should I keep the books? Maybe Kyle would have children someday. He'd only be in his late twenties or thirties when he got out of prison. I nodded and stood up. It took only minutes to pack all the children's books—assorted Dr. Seuss, *Mog the Forgetful Cat,* all the Laura Ingalls Wilder and Louisa May Alcott series, *Wind in the Willows,* all the wonderful books I'd read to LaRissa. I marked the box "Kids' Books-Keep" and turned to Kyle's shelf. I'd read to him too. Different books— Robert Heinlein, Isaac Asimov, Arthur C. Clarke—classic science fiction. I packed them all, plus his baseball magazines and video games in a box marked "Keep-Kyle."

Don hadn't taken any of his engineering and mechanics books and manuals. Those I tossed in a trash bag, in keeping with my mantra "If he didn't take them, he doesn't want them." My classics next. Those I kept. I did toss the textbooks; twenty-year-old science, economics, and history books were outdated. I hadn't looked at them in all the time they'd sat on these shelves. When I finished, I sat down on the sofa again, catching my breath before tackling the closet. It was stuffed with old clothes and things we almost never used—most of which I'd send on to the Salvation Army.

Sarah stuck her head in the doorway. "How're you doing? We're almost finished in the kitchen. What would you like us to do next?"

"How about the master bedroom and bathroom? Would you and the girls want to tackle that? Don cleared out most of his stuff. Take down the curtains too. I want to take them with me." I thought for a minute. "Put everything in the closet in boxes, except my clothes. I'll sort through those."

"Sure, we'll get right to it. You need any help in the guest room?"

"No, I'm making good progress. Once I finish in here, we'll order pizza—whatever kind you and the girls want." I heard them go into the master bedroom and turned back to my task in the guest room. I decided to tackle the closet that was stuffed full of outgrown, old, and seasonal clothes. I pulled open a couple trash bags and began loading clothes to take to Salvation Army, checking the pockets of each item. Items that I or Kyle might use someday, I hung in the garment box.

The gray coat with the white buffalo pattern stopped me. I'd bought it on a family trip to Yellowstone. I stroked its furry texture, remembering the expressions on LaRissa and Kyle's faces when a herd of buffalo had strolled onto the road and surrounded our car. LaRissa had shrieked in excitement, and Kyle had shoved himself backward on the seat when a bull had pressed his nose against the back window and *huffed* at them. They'd only been ten and seven at the time, but Don had swatted Kyle for being scared. There was something heavy in the left pocket of the coat. I frowned and pulled out a composition book.

My mind was fuzzy, but I recalled finding the composition book between the mattress and box spring in LaRissa's room the night Sarah and I were searching for clues when she was missing. I vaguely remembered that the first page was a drawing of a girl that had frightened me and made me want to hide it from Sarah. I laid the coat on top of the garment box and sat down on the sofa bed.

The first page of the book was even more disturbing than I'd recalled. LaRissa had been a talented artist. The child she'd drawn was huddled in a corner, wearing a white nightdress, her knees drawn up to her chest, head down with her hair covering her face. The drawing radiated fear, despair, and desolation— reinforced by jagged black lines that surrounded the girl.

A wave of near-terror engulfed me. *Who was this child? Why had LaRissa depicted a child so devastated?* I was afraid to turn the page. When I did, I moaned. LaRissa had written, in shaky capital letters: **Why? Why is he doing this? I don't know what to do.**

I flipped through the pages, and my hands trembled as I read:

I don't understand what's happening. He came in my bedroom when I was asleep. When he touched me, I woke up. He was in bed with me and put his hand on my stomach under my nightgown. I pushed him away and got out of bed and said I had to go to the bathroom. I stayed there a long time and he was gone when I got back.

Several pages later, she'd written:

Mom's going to be away this weekend at some stupid conference. I asked Brenda to ask her mother if I could spend the weekend at her house. I'm glad she said yes. I'm afraid and …

135

I flipped through the pages, unable to absorb what I was reading. On the final page, LaRissa had written:

> *He says he wants to be my first so he can teach me to enjoy it. No, no, no!! I won't let him! I'll do it with someone else and then laugh and tell him he's not the first. I'm afraid of him and I don't know what to do to stop him. He says if I tell anyone, they won't believe me and accuse me of making things up. I don't know what to do.*

That final entry was dated a week before LaRissa died.

I couldn't read anymore. Inside my head I was screaming. I slammed the book shut. But I knew something terrible had happened to LaRissa. I didn't know when or how or who, but I knew. Her words to her friend, Brenda, on the night she'd disappeared— "I want to get fucked"—had upset me. They didn't sound like my happy, popular daughter who'd never even had a serious boyfriend. But I'd put those words out of my mind when they'd found her body. Now I heard them in my head, repeating over and over, and I knew. Someone had sexually abused my daughter. I had to know who it was. He— that man—was responsible for LaRissa's death. I knew it, and I wanted to kill him.

There was a knock on the door that made me jump. I leaped up, my heart pounding, and slipped the composition book into the garment box as Sarah opened the door.

"We're done in the master bedroom. Are you ready for a break? What kind of pizza do you want me to order?" She stared at me. "Are you all right, Jana? You're white as a sheet." She stepped into the room, a concerned look on her face.

My voice was shaky as I answered her. "I'm okay. It's just hard to go through these things." I reached into the garment box and lifted the skirt of LaRissa's Homecoming prom dress. "Remembering happy times and knowing . . ."

Sarah rushed over to me. She wrapped her arms around me and held me tight as I sobbed. We stood that way for minutes, Sarah patting and rubbing my back and murmuring comforting words. I finally pulled myself together and disentangled myself.

"Really, I'll be okay. Sometimes I'm just . . . overwhelmed."

"Of course you are. Anyone would be," Sarah said. "The girls and I can finish up in here. Right now, you need food. Everything pizza work for you?" She smiled at me. "And I think we all . . . even the girls . . . need a glass of wine to go with it. I kept out a bottle of Chardonnay when we packed up the kitchen."

"Thanks, Sarah," I said, wiping my eyes. "You go order the pizza, and I'll wash my face and be down in a minute. Pour a glass for me."

When Sarah left, I fished the composition book out of the garment box and went into the master bedroom. I looked around, trying to think of a hiding spot that would be safe from visitors and prospective real estate buyers. I did what LaRissa had done and slid it between the mattress and box springs of my bed. Then I went in the bathroom, washed my face, and went downstairs.

Chapter 32

Tuesday night, August 7

I hadn't been able to think about LaRissa's composition book Sunday night. Or Monday night. I knew I would, eventually, but it was too overwhelming, too horrific, for me to take in at once. For the first time, work wasn't a refuge. It couldn't distract me from the thoughts that had invaded my mind . . . the image of the child on the first page and the word on the second page: *WHY?*

Dr. Kahn had been on a rampage when I arrived at the clinic on Tuesday morning. We'd not received funding for a grant he'd been counting on, and I hadn't submitted all the information required for another grant. He was watching the door and strode out to meet me as I entered the clinic.

"Jana, we need to talk!" Not words anyone wants to hear at eight o'clock in the morning. I nodded and proceeded to my office with him breathing down my neck. He loomed over me as I sat down at my desk.

He glared at me as he announced my failures, ticking them off on his fingers. "We can't stay in business without grants. You need to get it together soon, or I'll need to find another grant writer. One who can produce."

I was too tired to respond. After all that had happened over the past six months, why not lose my job too? I half-smiled as a mental image of me huddling under a cardboard box shelter under the highway overpass flitted through my head.

"You find this amusing?" Kahn's face flushed a deep red. "I'm putting you on notice. If your performance doesn't improve in the next two weeks, you're out!" He turned on his heels and abruptly left my office.

I tried to switch my focus back to the grant announcement in front of me. It would provide funding for a health care ombudsman, a person who would help patients with chronic conditions coordinate care among multiple doctors—a worthy cause, as many of our patients were poor, uneducated, and homeless. And nearly all of them had chronic health problems and faced barriers to managing their health. I pulled the application form up on my computer screen. The words blurred in front of my eyes, and I shut off the computer. Dr. Kahn was right. I wasn't up to the job today.

LaRissa's composition book had thrown me back into the foggy, depressed state I'd been in after she died. Worse was my inability to communicate with Kyle and know whether he was getting proper care for his diabetes. The state corrections agency had sent me a letter about visiting procedures. They didn't permit any visits to a new inmate for the first two months of incarceration. After that, there were visiting hours on Saturdays from ten in the morning until four in the afternoon, and visitors had to be on the inmate's approved list. Kyle had taken me off his list at the local jail awaiting trial, and I hadn't seen him for two months. My son, in prison with big, evil, men who had committed horrendous crimes and who had no conscience. I was terrified that he was their prey, that the prison guards weren't watching out for him, and that the prison medical staff wouldn't ensure that Kyle's diabetes was managed.

How could a grant application compete with those worries? I looked around my dismal office with the battered desk and file cabinet, stacks of papers on the floor, and dangling bare 40-watt lightbulb. I'd taken this job ten years ago because I wanted to do some good in the world, to help people who had few resources, faced discrimination, and had few opportunities to improve their lives and the lives of their children. Dr. Kahn's free clinic was, for most of them, the only available source of health care. Despite his abrasive manner, I respected the doctor who'd founded the clinic, and I knew he wanted to help people.

But I no longer believed I was making a difference in the world by bringing in money to pay for supplies and services. There were more patients every year as the economy worsened, poverty increased, and politicians became increasingly disinterested in addressing the social and economic problems that created this permanent underclass. My tiny contributions to these patients didn't really make a difference. Nor did my worry about Kyle make a difference.

It's all hopeless. Everything. My life. My lost family. The country. The world. Hopelessness, sadness, and depression swept through me, and I couldn't face another grant, another exchange with Dr. Kahn, or another sad story. I stood up, grabbed my purse, and walked into the hall. Kammie, my one friend at the clinic, was coming out of the supply room as I passed.

"Hey, Jana. Are you going somewhere?" She was smiling and happy, her blue hair in braids with daisy ties at the ends. She was wearing jeans with holes in the knees and a T-shirt with a picture of a grinning alpaca on it.

Her bright young face depressed me. I knew she was still unaware of what life would do to her. "Tell Dr. Kahn that I quit, will you? He can mail my final paycheck to me." I stroked her shoulder as I moved past her.

Kammie's mouth dropped open. "What? You can't quit. We need you here!" Her eyes were round with surprise, and her hands reached out as if to stop me from leaving.

I didn't answer. Seconds later I was in my car, driving home. *What am I doing? I need to work. How will I pay the bills, buy groceries, gas?* Despite the dire thoughts running through my head, I felt as though a weight had been lifted from my shoulders. My life was in tatters, but I'd taken action. I wasn't just coping or reacting to things outside my control. I didn't know where I'd go from here, but it had to be better. *Didn't it?*

When I got home, I finished clearing out the house and garage, stacked boxes for donation items and a half-dozen boxes I wanted to keep, and filled a dozen trash bags with things to throw away. It took hours, but it was done—ready for the movers and Salvation Army pickup. My clothes, toiletries, coffeepot, and grocery staples were all that was left. There were no pictures on the wall and no personal items visible, and the house was no longer our family home. I set the ivy and violet plants I'd nurtured for years on the kitchen table. Sarah would find homes for them if she didn't have space herself.

At six o'clock, I collapsed into a kitchen chair, clutching a glass of wine. My cell phone had rung several times while I was in my "finish it" frenzy. I hadn't answered, but the dings told me there were voicemails and text messages. Caller ID said the calls were from Dr. Kahn, Kammie, and my mother—none of whom I wanted to talk to.

I was rummaging in the near-empty refrigerator when Sarah knocked on the door and opened it. I smiled widely at her and lifted a container of cottage cheese. "Dinner! Garnished with a glass of wine."

She laughed. "Not much of a dinner. Come over and have Chinese with us? Hot and sour soup, Kung Pao chicken, House Supreme fried rice, and lo mein. Plus egg rolls, and I don't know what else for sure. Bridget ordered way more than we'll eat."

I put the cottage cheese back in the fridge. "Sounds good, though I'll bring the wine. Red or white?" I grabbed both bottles on the counter. "Or both! Definitely both." I picked up my keys and followed her out of the house, across the yard, and through the gate in the fence between our two houses.

"You seem cheerful today, Jana," Sarah said as she opened the back door into her kitchen. "Something good happen today?"

I giggled. "Yup, very good. I quit my job. I'm footloose, fancy free, and soon to be living in a cardboard box under the overpass."

Sarah frowned and took the wine from me. "I'm thinking you may already have had more than enough wine. How about some coffee?" She set about making a pot and waved me into a chair. "Did you really quit your job?"

"I did," I told her. "It was meaningless, it didn't pay much, and Dr. Kahn threatened to fire me. So, I quit. Better to say I quit due to poor working conditions than to say I was fired, right?"

Sarah frowned. "I guess that's right, but most people look for another job before they quit the one they have." She set a cup of coffee in front of me and sat down across from me. "Have you thought about what you're going to do, work-wise? And what you're going to live on until then?"

"I didn't think about anything. I just quit." I leaned toward her. "Sarah, I need a fresh start. This life is over for me. The house will sell, I get half of the payoff. I can live on that for months if I have to."

"What kind of job do you want next?" Sarah was her usual organized self, trying to get me to think rationally, make lists, make plans. I was too giddy follow her down that logical pathway.

"Pole dancer? Jiffy Lube oil changer? You can't take your work home with those jobs. For the last ten years, I've come home, made dinner, helped the kids with homework or school activities, and then worked for a couple hours before falling into bed." I saluted her with my cup, sloshing coffee on the table. "I'm sorry, I'll clean it up," I said, standing up.

"Don't worry about it, Jana." She grabbed paper towels and mopped up the spill. "I think you need to get something in your stomach. Bill and Bridget just pulled up with the food. Come in the dining room and help me dish it up. Table's already set."

I followed her, a bit unsteadily, into the dining room as Bill and Bridget came in carrying two full bags from the China House restaurant. They plunked them on the table and greeted me, then went into the kitchen to wash their hands. I unloaded the cartons, opening and placing a serving spoon in each. Two eggrolls on each plate and hot and sour soup in each bowl finished my job.

Sarah's daughters came into the dining room, took their places at the table, and began passing around the white cartons. Bill and Sarah sat at each end of the table, looking on fondly. I loaded my plate with Kung Pao chicken and lo mein. "You're right, Sarah. I'm absolutely starving!" I dipped my spoon in the hot and sour soup and slurped, dribbling a little down my chin. I looked up from my bowl in time to see Sarah looking at Bill and raising her eyebrows.

"How are things going, Jana?" Bill glanced at me as he began scooping food on his plate. "Sarah says the house is nearly ready to go on the market."

"I finished the last of the packing and sorting today. Tomorrow, Salvation Army is coming to pick up. I'm only looking at furnished apartments, so I have movers coming to take the furniture to a storage unit," I told him. "The agent said she'd get the listing up on Saturday."

"At least you don't need to paint before you list," Bill said. "Don and I painted the whole house last year. He was supposed to help me do the same over here this year, but I guess that's not on his agenda now."

I think Sarah kicked him under the table, because he flinched and went back to eating his soup. "Doubtful," I said. "I think he's kind of busy with that girl he's living with." I tried to keep the bitterness from my voice but didn't quite succeed. "Anyway, how are things at school? Is the football team going to be a contender for state again this year?"

We talked about the economy, what the girls were up to, and Mary's upcoming tennis match for the rest of the meal. By the time I finished the last of the lo mein, I was stuffed. I rubbed my midsection and burped. "That's a compliment on the food in Japan, right? Thank you for inviting me. I may need help fitting through the door on my way out."

"Not yet, Mrs. Spencer," Bridget said. She held up a bag. "We all have to have fortune cookies and read the fortune out loud." She took one and passed the bag to her sisters. After everyone had pulled out a cookie, Bridget broke hers and read the fortune inside. "Love will find a way." She laughed. "Sure it will. Maybe in twenty years or so."

Mary read hers next: *Your dream will come true.* She blushed and crumpled it up. "Who are you dreaming about, Mary? That cute boy in band?" her sisters teased. "Shut up," Mary muttered, sliding down in her chair.

Siobhan's fortune said, *Stand firm.* She laughed. "Yeah, Mom. I'm going to stand firm on it not being my turn to do the dishes, okay?"

Sarah just smiled. "Not many to do today. I can live with it."

Bill's fortune created a flutter of interest in the group: "The greatest risk you don't take is not taking one." He waved it in the air. "I have my answer! I'll go ahead and apply for the coaching position at Hinton College!" Sarah and the girls applauded, adding positive comments. She nudged me and said Bill had been dithering on the decision and she hoped now he'd go ahead.

Sarah's fortune was *Let your deeds speak.*

"They always do, Sarah," I said. "You're the best person I've ever known. Thank you for being my friend."

"Open yours, Mrs. Spencer," Mary said. "Maybe it's something good!"

I broke open the fortune cookie, read it, and burst into tears. Sarah took it from my fingers. She read it and frowned.

"Jana, why are you crying? This is a good fortune. It says, 'All is not yet lost.' That's hopeful! There's still a lot of good things ahead of you."

I gulped and my voice got caught in my throat. Eventually, I raised my eyes. "That's not what it means to me, Sarah. What it means is, 'You think you've lost everything, but there's more for you to lose.'" I grimaced. "What can it be? My cancer comes back? The house burns down? A car accident? Don fathers a new son with that Joelly and he's nice to that one?" I laughed, my voice a little hysterical. "What's next?"

Sarah shooed her girls and Bill out of the dining room and sat down next to me. "Stop it! I know you've been through hell this past year, but you're going to be okay. It'll be okay. But you might want to think about finding a therapist." She put up a hand as I opened my mouth to protest. "Not long-term therapy. Just someone to listen and help you make sense of everything and help you think about where you want to go from here." She stood up. "Come on, help me clean up. Routine is good for pulling yourself together."

As always, Sarah's sense and compassion helped. I loaded the dishwasher, wiped the counters, and didn't drink any more wine. When I got home, I was barely able to get to the bed before falling asleep. But I smoothed out the crumpled fortune and tucked it between pages of the book I'd been reading.

Chapter 33

Wednesday, August 8

I slept till ten in the morning. It felt wonderful, and I woke feeling better than I had in months. I pulled on jeans and a T-shirt. Not going to work anymore seemed increasingly attractive as an option. I'd left my phone turned off overnight, and there were calls that I chose not to return and voicemails I didn't bother checking. A couple cups of coffee and a piece of toast with cheese and I was ready for the Salvation Army folks when they arrived a little before noon. The house seemed bare and uncluttered with nothing left but the furniture and the few boxes I was going to take to wherever I landed. It felt good to be dismantling my old life. Maybe the optimistic interpretation of my fortune cookie was the right one after all.

It was a beautiful day, so I decided to do yard work. The real estate agent had said curb appeal was important. I mowed, edged, and then started weeding the flower beds that lined the driveway and walk that led to the front porch. By the time I was done, sweat soaked my clothes and there were grass stains and tiny blades of grass coating my jeans. The August sun was broiling, and, despite the bottle of water I'd been sipping at, I felt dizzy from dehydration. I went in the house and turned the air conditioner down a couple degrees. A cool shower, change of clothes, and a peanut butter and strawberry jam sandwich revived me.

It was nearly four o'clock. My "to do" list had two things checked off. The third item was groceries. I hadn't been to the grocery store since my encounter with Florence weeks ago. Seven-Eleven carried milk, bread, eggs, coffee, and the few other items I normally used. It wasn't that I feared running into Florence again, though that would be unpleasant. It was that most of the people that I'd known either pretended not to see me or tried to make awkward conversation with me.

Thank heaven for Sarah and her family, I reflected as I picked up my purse. *What would I do without her?* I decided to pick up a thoroughly gooey dessert and a bottle of wine for her at the store. The six-block drive to the grocery store was a little unreal. Over the past month I'd gone nowhere except to work, the gas station, and C-store, all of which were in the opposite direction. The neighborhood looked both familiar and unreal. I realized that this place, where I'd lived for twenty years and raised my children and went to church, wasn't my neighborhood anymore. It wasn't the comfortable, familiar place where I'd envisioned Don and I living out our lives. The thought saddened me, but at the same time, I felt a twinge of excitement. What would my new life be?

My excursion was successful. I didn't meet anyone I knew and came home with four bags of groceries—enough to tide me over for a month. I'd just finished putting the groceries away when Sarah knocked and came in the kitchen.

"Hey! I have a couple presents for you," I announced. The chocolate trifle cake and a bottle of Chardonnay were sitting on the counter. I waved at them. "For you! And your family. Thank you so much for dinner last night and for talking me through my meltdown. I slept and slept last night, and I feel so much better. To hell with Don, right?"

Sarah laughed. She hoisted the bottle of wine and repeated, "To hell with Don! He'll get his when his little girlfriend leaves him for a good-looking college boy who wants to take her partying every night." She sat down. "You know, they can't have anything in common. He likes fixing cars and playing with wood. What do they talk about, do you think? She doesn't even remember the Clinton administration, and I bet she's never even heard of the Eagles."

"Uh, I suspect they don't spend a lot of time talking, Sarah. 'The attraction is purely physical,' per Rod Stewart."

Sarah giggled. "I bet that little girl doesn't know who Rod Stewart is either. Or know that that song was about soccer! Should we open the wine?"

I dug out the corkscrew and handed it to her. "You do the honors." I got out the two remaining wine glasses and sat down. "Anything new at school?"

We drank a glass of wine and then had a second as she filled me in on the insanity of the school board and the new requirements for English and math that parents were protesting. "Same old, same old." Sarah sipped her wine. "I'm glad you're feeling better. I was a little worried last night. Have you given any thought to where you want to live once the house sells?"

"I'm thinking of moving to Hinton. There's a new apartment complex there that looks good. It has an indoor swimming pool and a fitness center, as well as a small convenience store." I smiled. "Probably single and divorced men too. Not that I'm thinking about dating."

Sarah's face fell. "I was hoping you'd stay in Fairview. Hinton is twenty miles away."

"I know. And I'll miss having you right next door. But living here? This is a family place—a place to raise your children and grow old gracefully. That's not my life anymore. I need to break with it and start over." I leaned over and patted her hand. "Don't worry, we'll see each other often. And email and talk on the phone."

Sarah nodded. "We will! Let's make a resolution that we'll get together for lunch or dinner at least once a week. There are a couple new restaurants in Hinton that I've been wanting to try out too. Zorba's, especially. I love Greek food, and Bill really hates it. It'll be fun." She didn't say anything for a few minutes. From the pensive expression on her face, I thought she was reminiscing about all the good times—and bad times—we'd shared over the decades we'd been best friends and neighbors. She surprised me though. "Jana, you quit your job. Have you thought about what you're going to do next?"

"I really haven't. I know I don't want to do grant writing anymore. But I don't really have any other experience to market. My college degree was in English with a minor in psychology. What does that equip me to do? A forty-two-year-old woman with limited computer skills and who writes well about health services?" I wrinkled my forehead and looked at her. "I'll have enough money from the sale of the house for a year or so to figure it out. Maybe I'll go back to school and learn computer programming?"

Sarah laughed out loud. "Somehow, I don't see you sitting in a dark basement room, hovering over a computer and sharing tips with a bunch of young guys who have tattoos and nose rings. Why don't you get a copy of the college catalog and spend some time figuring out what really appeals to you? This is the rest of your working life you're talking about."

"Maybe." My mood plummeted. "I don't think I'm a very good judge of what's right for me anymore. I mean, I fooled myself about Don for twenty-five years. And I didn't protect Kyle from Don, and I didn't notice that LaRissa was in trouble when she clearly was." I'd told Sarah about LaRissa's statement to Brenda the night of the church social about wanting to get fucked. We'd talked about it and tried to figure out what might have happened that caused LaRissa to behave so oddly. But I hadn't told her about LaRissa's composition book and what it seemed to suggest. I couldn't. "Anyway, I haven't had a good track record as either a wife or a mother, have I?"

Sarah stood up. "Stop it! Stop thinking everything is your fault. What happened to you wasn't your fault. You were an excellent wife married to a sleazy man. The fault is his! And we never know whether we're doing everything we can for our children. My mother said she didn't realize she'd done okay as a mother until I was in my thirties." A little smile drifted across her face. "I was a real handful and never, ever told her anything I was thinking or scared of or doing. I should have, but I didn't. Last year for Mother's Day I gave her a coffee cup that said 'Mom, thank you for giving me life and for not taking it back when I was a teenager.'" She laughed, but I knew she agreed with the sentiment. "Look, I tell my girls that I promise not to take credit for anything good they accomplish in life, and, in return, I refuse to take the blame when things don't turn out however they wish. I do the best I can. You did the best you could, and you were . . . are . . . a good mother. All we can do is our best and hope for our children to know we love and support them."

I heard her, but I wasn't convinced. Somehow, I should have done more. Found a way to prevent what had happened.

Realized that LaRissa was in trouble and done something. Sarah's earnestness, though, made me nod and give her a tremulous smile. "Thank you for saying that. And I'll figure out what I want to do. Just not today, right? I have time."

"Good. Now, do you want to come over for dinner tonight? I have a lasagna in the oven."

I shook my head. "No, not tonight. But thank you. I'm reading a good book, and I'm going to bed early again. The movers will be here early for the furniture tomorrow, and Ann James, your agent friend, is coming to stage the house for prospective buyers. I'll be fine. You go and enjoy the lasagna and the cake."

After she left, I realized I hadn't taken the mail from the mailbox. As I walked to the end of the driveway, I admired how neat and attractive the front lawn looked after all my work. *Definitely has curb appeal. Ann will be pleased.* I opened the mailbox and pulled out a packet of flyers, catalogs, and letters. I flipped through the mail as I walked back into the house. Two bills and a letter with a handwritten address. Kyle! His handwriting was more like printing, all in capitals. I threw the other mail on the sofa and ripped his letter open.

The letter was short. Kyle asked if I'd visit him sometime. He added that he'd put me on his approved visitors list and listed the days and hours of visiting times. He'd signed it "Your son, Kyle." Tears ran down my cheeks. The next visiting day was this coming Saturday—three days away.

Chapter 34

The house listing went live on Thursday, and it sold in twelve hours. I knew the real estate market was hot, but I wasn't expecting a cash offer $15,000 over asking price and a closing within four weeks. The real estate agent was enthusiastic. As she should have been— hardly any work or investment for an immediate sale that would net her close to $6,000.

I hadn't even looked at places to live. The day after the contract was signed, I scrambled to make appointments to view apartments in Hinton. Several looked promising, but only two had units available as soon as I needed one. By Friday evening, I'd signed a rental agreement for a furnished one-bedroom apartment in the complex with the swimming pool, fitness center, and convenience store. The manager promised to repaint the olive-green living room and bathroom before I moved in.

The flurry of real estate activity had distracted me for a couple days, but I'd remembered to call and get on the list to visit Kyle. The person at the prison had given me a detailed set of instructions for visitors: cell phones and purses left at the entry, nothing that might be used as a weapon carried through security, pat-down, walk through metal detector, and no touch contact with the prisoner. If a siren went off, all visitors must leave immediately. My appointment was at one p.m. With all the rules to be followed, I headed out at nine a.m. for the drive to Greyson where the prison was.

I played loud classic rock music on the drive to keep from letting my anxiety overwhelm me. It had been months since I'd seen Kyle and longer than that since I'd talked to him. *What if he refused to see me once I was there? Or looked injured? The prison set movies and TV shows I'd seen painted a horrific picture of what life behind bars entailed. What if he seemed sick? Could I talk to the prison medical staff if I thought they weren't managing his diabetes properly?* Those were the thoughts I was trying to avoid on the drive there. Those, and what I would even say. And what he would say. I'd heard Kyle recite what had happened to the court when he had pleaded guilty. But was there more to the story? I wasn't sure I was ready to hear anything more.

A nagging thought penetrated my concern for Kyle—I still hadn't pulled LaRissa's composition book out from where I'd hidden it under the mattress. It was like there was a blank spot in my brain that refused to remember it was there. I'd think about it and plan to read it again, but then the thought would evaporate. I resolved that I would do that tomorrow. If there was information on who had been sexually abusing LaRissa, I needed to know and to report it to the police.

Greyson State Prison loomed ahead of me, finally. High concrete walls with razor wire lining the top surrounded the castle-like sandstone building. Kyle's attorney had told me it was a Level Two security prison, one that housed prisoners who were low-risk and offered more opportunities for rehabilitation. It also meant it didn't have the most dangerous and violent prisoners, but that didn't mean it was safe. He'd counseled Kyle to keep his head down, follow all the rules, and try to avoid interactions with other prisoners until he was acclimated. Barrow had also told me that the prison offered vocational training and college-level classes for prisoners in good standing.

The entry process was depressing. I stood in a long line waiting to reach security. Most of the visitors appeared to be women, some holding the hands of small children. I surrendered my cell phone and purse at the front desk and received a ticket to retrieve them. The pat-down process was much more thorough than I'd experienced with TSA guards at the airport. It made me feel uncomfortable, even though it was a woman guard who searched me. Once I was through the metal detector, a guard escorted me and other visitors to a large open room with nailed-down tables and benches. Prisoners expecting visitors would be brought to the room at exactly one o'clock.

The tables were more than half-filled with other visitors. Only a few men were among them, but the ones who were there intimidated me. Most had tattoos and facial hair and were dressed in rough clothes. The women, with a few exceptions, were young and dressed in tight jeans and T-shirts. Two women looked to be in their sixties or older. *Grandmothers, maybe, or mothers of older prisoners*, I thought. Their faces were careworn, and their eyes were sad. *Is that what I'll look like here in a few years?*

A bell rang, and a door on the far side of the room opened. Two guards entered, followed by men dressed in orange jumpsuits with numbers on their chests. The room rustled as visitors spotted their loved ones. Kyle was next to last in the line of twenty-some men. I stood up and waved at him. The guards closed the door and posted themselves at each end of the visiting room.

Kyle slowly walked through the room and sat down opposite me. I reached out a hand to touch him, but he pulled back. "No touching," he said. "You have to follow the rules, or they'll make you leave." His voice was low and hoarse. I studied his face. He was thinner than I remembered, and either the prison or he had decided on a buzzcut. The long hair to his shoulders was gone, making his sharp cheekbones stand out. The lack of bruises or cuts on his face and arms was reassuring.

We sat in silence for a few minutes, Kyle with his eyes fixed on the table. Finally, I said, "How are you?"

He raised his head and looked at me. "I'm okay, Mom. The medical people here are good. I get my insulin shots on schedule."

"Tell me about what your days are like. Do you have a job? Do they let you go outside for a while every day?" I was struggling to figure out what to say. There was so much I wanted to ask, but I didn't want to alienate him or make him sad.

He sighed. "Yes, they gave me a job in the prison cafeteria—washing dishes, cleaning up. They put ten cents an hour in my account for every hour I work. It's usually just four or five hours a day."

"And what do you do the rest of the day?"

152

"We get an hour a day outside in the yard. There's basketball hoops and soccer goals, so a lot of the guys here play those. I mostly just walk around the outside to get some exercise. I read in my cell a lot and watch TV in the afternoon and evenings." He shrugged. "It's pretty boring, actually. But the social worker says I can sign up for vocational training or college courses once I've been here three months."

"That's good. What are you thinking of signing up for?"

"Not sure. Maybe computer programming would be good. Or I might try auto mechanics. Both are things I could get a job with after I get out." His eyes focused again on the table. "But that's not for a long time. And people tell me it's hard to find someone who wants to hire a convict."

"I'm glad you're thinking about preparing for the future, Kyle," I said, clutching my hands together to prevent reaching out to comfort him. "That's important. You'll still be young even if you serve the full time they gave you."

He shrugged again. "Maybe. How are you doing? And Dad?"

I had a hard time deciding what to tell him about his father and me, but he deserved to know. "Your father and I have separated, Kyle. It's been coming a long time." I didn't want to have him think our separation was his fault. "And I've sold the house. I'll be moving to Hinton in a couple weeks. Can I give you my new address?"

"Send me a letter with it, okay? They don't allow us to bring paper or pens in here," he answered. "Why Hinton? And what did you do with all my things?"

"I packed up your room, put your name on the boxes, and have them in a storage facility. Your bedroom furniture, pictures, and clothes are stored for you. For when you come home. And Hinton because I quit my job. I couldn't take being harassed and disrespected all the time by Dr. Kahn." I swallowed and added, "And I need a new beginning. Start over. I may take some classes at the college. If I can figure out what I want to do with my life." I smiled. "Like you."

He smiled at that. He'd heard me complain at least a hundred times over the ten years I'd worked at the clinic. "That's good! You should have done it years ago." His voice dropped. "I'm glad you're moving on, Mom. I was afraid that what happened—what I did—would cause you to . . . I don't know . . . give up? It's good that you're making a new life." He paused, and his eyes dropped again to the table. Finally, he looked up at me. "And Dad? How is he doing?"

"I honestly don't know. He hasn't talked to me except through lawyers since before your trial. I don't know what he's doing, though I think he's still working at the body shop." Kyle didn't need to know his father was living with a girl close to his son's age. Or anything else about the situation.

The rest of the hour passed quickly. We talked about Bob and Final Quest and his friends there, and what Sarah and Bill and their girls were doing, and my new apartment. Just chatting about nothing—something we hadn't done for a long time. It was comfortable and reassured me that future visits would be tolerable, despite the circumstances. The bell announcing the end of visiting hour startled me, and I reached out again for Kyle's hands. He yanked them back and laughed. "Nope. Not going to get you banned from visiting." He looked at me, anxious. "You are going to come back?"

"Of course I am!" I thought for a second. "I'll try to make it every two weeks, okay? And Bob asked if you'd put him on your visitor list. He wants to come too."

Kyle's face lit up. "That would be great. I'll do it today. Tell him I'd like that, would you?"

The guards began motioning to the prisoners to stand and get in line. I watched as Kyle was escorted back through the door to the interior of the prison. Then I followed the other visitors out of the room. I didn't realize that tears were leaking from my eyes until one of the older women visitors spoke. "It's hard, isn't it? But you get used to it. Was that your son?"

I nodded.

"Well, it's hard. I know. My son's been in for seventeen years now and has at least ten more to go. But I visit him every week and put money in his commissary account. You can do that, you know. Up to ten dollars a month for your boy to buy snacks and stuff like toothpaste and soap."

"Really? How do I do that?" Kyle had mentioned they paid him a nominal amount for working, but he hadn't mentioned that I could contribute to his account. I couldn't do much for him, but at least I could give him some money to buy whatever he wanted.

"Just stop at the front desk. They'll accept the money and mark it for his account. Do you know his inmate number?" I shook my head. "Well, they'll look it up for you. I'm Rose, by the way. Maybe I'll see you next week." She went through security and waved as she opened the door to the outside.

I went through security and then headed to the front desk. The woman there accepted the ten-dollar bill I handed her and assured me that it would be placed in Kyle's account. I was feeling happier when I left than when I'd arrived. Kyle appeared well and seemed to be adjusting. And I had been able to do something to make his time there a little better.

Chapter 35

Saturday night, August 11

My mother had called four times while I was visiting Kyle. I kicked off my shoes, fixed a Lean Cuisine, read the newspaper, and finally called her back. She wanted to know how Kyle was, and I was able to reassure her that he was injury-free and getting adequate medical care. Mom had always favored Kyle over LaRissa. Maybe because he was the first boy child in her family for three generations. I finally hung up after convincing her that she didn't want to fly here and visit him herself. "Wait a few months," I told her. "Give him a chance to get settled in." If I'd thought that Kyle would welcome a visit from his grandmother, my answer would have been different. But my mother had a knack for saying that one thing that would most upset anyone she talked to, especially me.

Sarah was attending a fundraising dinner-dance with Bill that night, so she wasn't available to talk to about my visit to Kyle. I called Bob at the Final Quest and told him Kyle would love to see him. Bob said he planned to go next weekend and was happy to hear that Kyle seemed to be doing okay. "I was worried, honestly," he admitted to me. "Kyle's a quiet kid, and I wasn't sure he'd have an easy time of it in there." I reassured him again and thanked him for his devotion to Kyle. Bob was the one person I could count on to support my son.

The rest of the evening I watched mindless television. Nothing seemed amusing, and the news, as usual, was grim.

I went to bed early and fell asleep quickly. A nightmare woke me at three a.m. I couldn't recall the details, but the feelings stayed with me, and I couldn't fall back asleep. An hour later, I got out of bed and went downstairs to make cocoa, which is always good for helping me sleep. By the time I realized that cocoa wasn't going to work, the sky was lightening, and some birds were singing. I took a shower and dressed.

What should I do today? The packing was done for my move to the new apartment, the house was clean, the yard work was done. I was at a loss. There wasn't anything I had to do and, really, nothing I wanted to do. I found a pad of paper and began making a list of things I could do. Take a drive? Not after yesterday's six-hour round-trip drive to the prison. Go to church? My faith hadn't ever been strong. Church was one of those things I did because others—my mother, my friends— expected me to do. The past year hadn't increased my belief in a benevolent God. So, no, not church.

The nagging thought that there was one thing I was avoiding penetrated finally. I needed to look at LaRissa's composition book again to see if I'd missed anything that could reveal the truth about who had abused her. I dreaded re-reading it. I went upstairs to retrieve the composition book from under my mattress. I steeled myself and resolved to read for information and clues—not to wallow in self-blame for not recognizing the trauma that my daughter had experienced. I opened the composition book to the first page I'd already read. Those words were seared in my brain. The next page said, *"I hate him!"* The pen she used had ripped the page. The page after that was longer. *"Is there something wrong with me? That makes men think that I'm only good for sex? I'm more than that! I get good grades and I work at the homeless shelter sometimes. I think I'm a good person. Why is this happening? Again. I never told anyone about the man who trapped me in the bathroom at the movie theater when I was seven. He touched me in places that weren't right, but I was able to get away. And now this is happening. Is it some way I behave or dress? I'm not eating anymore, maybe if I'm really skinny they'll stay away from me, know that's not what I want."*

A moan emerged from my center. This had happened before to LaRissa? When she was seven? I thought back. There had been a movie I'd taken her to when she went to the bathroom by herself and was crying when she came back and said her stomach hurt. Was that when this happened? I slammed the palm of my hand against my head twice to stop the pain. Was I so oblivious that I'd been irritated with her for wanting to leave in the middle of the movie? The bigger question was, why hadn't she told me what happened? And worse: Why wasn't I the mother a young girl could confide in? Tears rolled down my cheeks. It was an hour or more before I could bring myself to read more.

The next entry in the composition book was confusing. LaRissa wrote *"I got away from him. Good for me."* Then there were several blank pages, followed by one that said *"I hate Mom's job. She's always going away to overnight conferences. I'm staying at Brenda's tonight."*

That was her last entry before the final one I'd read earlier. The one that said *"He says he wants to be my first so he can teach me to enjoy it. No, no, no!! I won't let him! I'll do it with someone else and then laugh and tell him he's not the first. I'm afraid of him and I don't know what to do to stop him. He says if I tell anyone, they won't believe me and accuse me of making things up. I don't know what to do.* The date on the page was a week before she died.

I flipped through the rest of the composition book. She hadn't written anything else. Were there clues that I was missing? Was Brenda's father the molester? I knew that LaRissa and Brenda often spent the night at each other's homes, so maybe that next to last entry was just a comment with no important meaning. I closed the composition book and slid it back under the mattress. *I have to talk to Brenda. If LaRissa told anyone about this, it would be Brenda.*

Chapter 36

Tuesday, August 14

Getting Brenda alone wouldn't be easy. Florence felt it was her duty to protect her daughter from bad influences, and I was now one of those bad influences. But the school year had just started yesterday. For the second day in a row, I was sitting in my car across from the high school at three-thirty when classes let out in hopes of spotting Brenda. I planned to follow her for a few days and learn her after-school schedule, so I could identify the best time and place to approach her. Yesterday, she'd gone straight home. Since Florence didn't work and her car was in the driveway, I'd determined to shadow LaRissa's friend for as long as necessary.

A sharp knock on the passenger window startled me. Florence was peering in the window, a grim expression on her face. She circled her hand, telling me to roll down the window. I did, with some trepidation.

"What are you doing here? Brenda told me she thought she saw you yesterday sitting here." She glowered at me, her mouth set in a tight line.

"Nice to see you, too, Florence. Is there a law against parking across from the school?" I kept my voice calm.

"Are you stalking my daughter? One of the other students?" Florence grated out. "There's a law against stalking. And if I see you here again, I'll notify the police."

"Go ahead," I said. "I haven't approached anyone. I'm just sitting here and enjoying the sight of young people enjoying themselves. Not doing anyone any harm. What are you going to report?"

"If I see you here again, I'll think of something," she sputtered. Florence turned and stomped away, her heavy body looking as though it should be making holes in the asphalt. She saw Brenda coming down the front steps of the school and waved at her, motioning her daughter to her car.

I knew that Florence would definitely call the police if I was here tomorrow, so my plan to surveil Brenda and find a time when I could talk to her wasn't going to work.

My backup plan was talking to Sarah about what I'd found and asking for her help, but I really didn't want to do that. Somehow, telling someone else would make it real, and one part of me was still in denial, thinking maybe I was misinterpreting LaRissa's composition book. But if I showed it to Sarah and she was horrified, it would confirm the reality. I didn't have an alternative plan, though. I started the car and drove home.

Sarah often stayed at school to meet with students, so I didn't expect her home until at least five. Then she rushed around to make dinner for her family. I waited till seven o'clock to call her.

"Hi, Sarah. Any chance you could come over for an hour or so?"

"Sure. Should I bring cupcakes?" Sarah's cheerful acquiescence raised my spirits. If anyone could reassure me that I was misinterpreting LaRissa's composition book, Sarah could. And if she didn't? I stammered out an answer, and she said she'd be right over.

I went upstairs and pulled the composition book back out from under the mattress and carried it downstairs. I poured two glasses of wine and sat down at the kitchen table, waiting.

When Sarah knocked, I stood up. She opened the door, stared at me, then pulled it closed. "What's wrong?" She came into the kitchen. "Sit down and tell me what's going on." She sat down next to me.

I pushed the composition book toward her, my hands shaking. "Read this and tell me what you think."

Sarah bent over the composition book and opened the cover. I heard her suck in a breath as she examined the artwork—the girl huddled in a corner in abject misery. She slowly turned the pages, reading, and then closed it. Her eyes, brimming with tears, met mine.

"Oh, Jana. I'm so sorry. How terrible for LaRissa, and for you. You didn't have any idea?" She put up a hand to stop what she started to say. "No, of course you didn't." Sarah reached out and squeezed my hand. "How can I help? What do you want to do?"

"I want to find out who it was that was doing this," I said, my voice steady. "Then I want to kill him. He's the reason LaRissa is dead." I had told Sarah what LaRissa had said to Brenda the night of the social. "She would never have gone off with that boy, and Kyle wouldn't have seen what happened, and . . ." My voice broke. "It's all that terrible man's fault, and I need to know who he is." I buried my head in my arms and sobbed.

"You couldn't have known, Jana. Teens are always hiding things from their parents. And something like this? No one ever suspects that someone in a position of trust would . . ." Sarah was trying to comfort me, but I knew I should have suspected something was wrong when she stopped eating much and lost weight. Had there been other signs? Had I been too busy worrying about Kyle's problems to notice that my daughter was in serious trouble?

I raised my head. "I need to know who it is, Sarah. I have to know."

"You don't really intend to kill him, do you?" The concern on her face was real.

I shook my head. "No, but I'll turn him in to the police. He won't have a chance to do this to another young girl. And he'll be on the sex offender registry, right? So everyone will know what he is."

"That's a good plan. Do you have any suspects? All I could tell was it's someone who had the opportunity to be alone with her. Privacy. Maybe a teacher?" Sarah frowned. "I can't think of any male teachers at school who might have . . . But, of course, pedophiles don't wear a big 'P' on their foreheads. I think they usually seem like normal people."

"I don't know, Sarah. Brenda's father? She often spent the night there. But if it were him, LaRissa wouldn't want to be there. A teacher, maybe? She was running track and had a lot of after-school practices, so the track coach, maybe?" I looked at her.

"Seems doubtful," she responded. "Mr. Handlespoon has been at the school for over forty years, and everyone assumes he's gay. Never married, very fussy about his clothes. That could be wrong, though."

"The thing is, I think Brenda is the key to this. If LaRissa talked to anyone about it, it would have been Brenda. But Florence won't let me near her. I parked outside the school at quitting time yesterday and today, hoping to catch Brenda when Florence wasn't with her. But Brenda must have seen me yesterday and told her mother. Florence was there today and came over to my car. She said she'd call the police if she saw me parked outside the school again."

"That holier-than-thou Florence," Sarah said. "She only reads the parts of the Bible that she agrees with, and Christian kindness and charity aren't in those parts. Do you want me to talk to Brenda? She's not in my classes, but I could try to talk to her over lunch."

"No, I need to talk to her myself. If I write a letter to her, though, could you give it to her?"

Sarah agreed she would, and I promised to have the letter ready for her in the morning. We chatted for another half hour or so about nothing, and then she left, promising to stop by in the morning to pick up the letter.

Chapter 37

A week passed with no response from Brenda, but I was too busy to obsess over her silence. I had to be out of the house by the end of the next week so the new owners could move in. Over the past week, I'd weeded out the last of the detritus in the house I'd lived in for twenty years. All that was left were kitchen supplies I was taking with me, my clothes, and personal items. The movers showed up at ten, loaded, and left. They had another load to pick up and deliver, so I stayed behind to do a final sweep to be sure nothing was forgotten. By noon, I was done. I left the keys and the garage door opener on the kitchen counter and drove away. I thought I'd feel sad to be leaving the place where my children had grown up and there were so many memories. But I wasn't. I didn't feel anything except tired.

The furnished apartment in Hinton was empty except for the bland furniture, a couple boxes I hadn't trusted the movers to handle, and two plants. One was an ugly cactus that was at least seven feet high. I'd bought it when I'd first moved into our house, so it was twenty years old, at least, and still thriving with almost no assistance from me other than erratic watering and ensuring that it had a sunny spot to live in. My kids used to laugh at it and decorate it with Christmas ornaments and put an angel on top every year. The other plant was a supposed-to-be bonsai tree. LaRissa had given me a bonsai tree kit as a birthday present five years ago. I'd planted the seeds and nurtured it for months before it started to grow . . . and grow . . . and grow. I'd never had the discipline to prune it and trim the roots like the instructions said, so now it was the world's largest bonsai tree—three feet tall and still growing. LaRissa and Kyle had found it hilarious and teased me unmercifully about my super-green thumb. I didn't remember what the kit was supposed to grow, but I liked my little tree, whatever it was. I set both plants near a sunny window on the east side of the apartment.

The movers showed up an hour after I arrived. It took them only twenty minutes to unload and place the boxes where I directed. Once they left, I made a pot of coffee and sank down on the sofa to think about all that needed to be done. Unpack the kitchen boxes and my bedroom boxes first, I decided. Two hours later, the kitchen was done with dishes on the shelves, a few staples in the small pantry, and pots, pans, and utensils tucked away. The bedroom took even less time. I hung up my clothes in the closet and made the bed. LaRissa's book had traveled here with me in a bag of breakable items. I slipped it back under the mattress.

The building manager had given me written instructions for moving in. Cutting down the boxes and taking them out to the dumpster behind the building was next on my list. I'd made my second trip down and placed a stack of boxes in the dumpster when my cell phone rang.

The number wasn't one I recognized. I swiped Accept and said hello.

"Mrs. Spencer?" The voice on the other end of the line was young and nervous.

"Yes, who is this?"

"It's Brenda."

I leaned against the dumpster, shaking. "Oh. Thank you for calling, Brenda. Are you where you can talk?"

"I just finished cheerleading practice, and my mom will be waiting out front in a couple minutes," Brenda said.

I swallowed and went on. "Brenda, I know that someone was . . . that LaRissa was afraid of someone." I didn't want to say the word "molesting." I didn't know for sure that Brenda knew what was going on.

"I don't know who it is, Mrs. Spencer. I know she was upset and scared. Anytime you were going to be gone overnight, she begged me to let her sleep at my house. Sometimes my mom would say no, and Rissa would get this scared look on her face. I asked her, but she wouldn't tell me what was going on. When I asked her, she just said it was too disgusting to talk about."

I could hear the noise of kids leaving the gym. "I've got to go," Brenda said, her voice panicky. "If my mom finds out I called you, I'll be in a lot of trouble."

"If you think of anything else, will you call me? I just want to find out what caused LaRissa to do what she did." The words came out abruptly. I was afraid she'd hang up any second. "Please, Brenda. LaRissa would want whoever was hurting her to be punished."

There was silence on the other end of the line for a moment. Then Brenda said, "I think the person who killed her *is* being punished, isn't he?" She ended the call, and I stood, looking at the words "Call Ended." Had Brenda told me anything useful? I had wanted her to know the answer, but she didn't know much more than I already did.

I walked back to the stairs and up to my new second-floor apartment. My mind blank, I went in the kitchen, opened the pantry, and pulled out a bottle of wine. The corkscrew was in the third drawer I checked. After pouring a large glass of wine, I sat down at the kitchen table and thought. *I need to make a list of what I know. Organize and see if I can figure out something more.* I got up and searched the apartment for a pad of paper and a pen. I couldn't find either, not in my desk, not in my purse. Frustrated, I grabbed my purse and raced down the stairs, past the pool where a half dozen residents were enjoying the late afternoon sunshine, and into the convenience store. The clerk looked up as I barged in. I must have looked odd because he had a worried expression on his face as he asked, "Can I help you with something?" He looked about sixteen years old, a bit of peach fuzz above his lip, overweight, with long blond hair pulled back in a man-bun. His eyes widened. "Are you Kyle's mother? I think I saw you at the Final Quest a couple times."

I froze. Moving to Hinton had been a way to get away from everyone who knew me and my children . . . my old life. And here was someone recognizing me on the first day of what I thought of as new beginnings. I nodded, finally. "Yes, do you know Kyle?"

"Yeah. He and I played in a couple tournaments at the Quest. He was really good." His face fell. "But . . ." His mouth moved, but no words came out.

"I know," I said, my voice flat.

"I didn't believe it when I heard, ma'am. Really. Kyle was always quiet and kind. When I started going there, he helped me learn how to play the games and gave me advice. Some kids there made fun of me because I'm sort of . . . overweight and nervous. But he always slammed them down. I don't know what happened, but I know he'd never hurt anyone on purpose." The last words he said emphatically, adding, "Never."

"Well, thank you," I said. "I wish other people could believe that. But most people seem to think the worst of others. I'll tell Kyle I saw you."

He flushed, flustered. "Yeah, do that! Tell him Eddie G says hi, okay? And . . ." He couldn't seem to think of anything else to add.

"I will. What I need right now, though, is to buy a pad of paper and a couple pens. Do you have them here?"

Eddie came out from behind the counter and lumbered down the second aisle. He bent and stood up holding a pad of white lined paper and two ballpoint pens. "This what you want?"

I paid and thanked him again. Back in my apartment, I realized I was smiling. Finding out that someone in the world, besides me and Bob, thought Kyle was a good person was the first positive thing that had happened in months. I sat down at the kitchen table, laid the pad of paper in front of me, and picked up a pen. *What do I know for sure?*

- LaRissa was molested by a man in the movie theater bathroom when she was seven. The man touched her, but she got away from him.
- That incident is unrelated to what happened to her later but may have affected her feelings and response.
- There are dates on the entries in her composition book. Check the dates for patterns. Where was I?
- She begged to stay at Brenda's house when I was going to be away overnight.
- She told Brenda what was going on was disgusting and didn't want to talk about it.

- Her last entry said she wouldn't let "him" be the first, and she told Brenda she wanted to have sex the night of the social.

I went to my desk and pulled out the calendar I kept of my appointments to see if there was any pattern that linked LaRissa's dates to my schedule. I'd been away at conferences on two of the nights when she'd made entries. Kyle had been with me on one of those trips. It was to Orlando, a reward for improving his grades. I'd gone to evening functions on the other nights, including on the last night she'd written in her composition book. As I reviewed my notes, my stomach roiled. A horrendous glimmer of acknowledgement pushed its way into my thoughts.

Could it be Kyle? I pushed the thought away. No! I rejected that possibility out of hand. He'd been away with me on one of the occasions, and LaRissa wouldn't have hesitated to punch Kyle in the face . . . more likely the groin . . . if he'd ever even tried . . . No. She wasn't afraid of him. She'd dominated him even when she was small. He was socially awkward and shy, while she had always been outgoing, personable, had lots of friends, and had been confident. *Until the last few months of her life.*

My mind was refusing to go on to the other possibility. There was only one other male who had access to LaRissa in our house, at night, when I was away. I sat, shaking my head, and a low moan emerged uncontrolled from my throat. No. It couldn't be. *But who else could it be?* My rational mind refused to let me ignore the evidence. Don, my husband of twenty years, LaRissa's father, had molested her. Had told her that he wanted to be her "first." And she'd died because she refused to let that happen. She'd decided to have sex with someone else, anyone else, to prevent her father from being her first sexual experience.

I slumped over the table and pounded my forehead with my fists. *How could I not have known? How could I have married someone who could do this to his own daughter?* I sat there for hours thinking about the horror that LaRissa had faced and my role—my stupid, ridiculous delusions about Don and his behaviors. If I'd left him years ago, instead of refusing to believe he was unfaithful, would that have protected LaRissa? Somehow, I knew this was my fault. It had to be. I was the mother, the one who was supposed to protect her children against evil. I hadn't protected LaRissa or Kyle from their father. Don's disdain and harsh criticisms had cowed my boy and turned him into a person who could erupt and attack LaRissa when he saw her in a sexual situation.

Finally, I realized it was dark outside. I looked at the clock. Nearly ten. I slowly stood, picked up the empty wine glass, and threw it at the wall. It shattered into a thousand pieces. *Why did I do that? Now I have to clean it up.* I felt like I was moving through water, slowly, pushing through weight, as I walked to the broom closet, picked up the broom and a waste pan, and began sweeping. Then I got out the sponge mop, wet it, and damp mopped the floor to get up all the shards.

When the floor was clean, I sat back down. *What am I going to do now? What can I do?* The thought of Don living with Joelly, a twenty-year-old girl—only five years older than LaRissa had been—made bile rise in my throat. *Am I sure?*

I thought back to earlier times. Memories of Don pulling LaRissa into his lap and kissing her, even when she tried to evade him. He'd always been excessively physically affectionate with her. He liked to give her a bath at night—daddy time, he'd called it. When she'd been a child, she'd liked it and even encouraged it. But since she'd reached her teens, she'd avoided her father's attempts to hug and kiss her. Don had taken to walking into her room without knocking, sometimes catching her undressed, and had laughed and told her he'd changed her diapers so she shouldn't mind. Should I have noticed and been suspicious? At the time, it had seemed like the normal distancing behavior of a young teen. And it never, ever flickered through my mind that Don was overly obsessive about LaRissa—or that his obsessiveness could be a sign of something as evil, as immoral, as disgusting as this.

My body was rigid with tension. With trembling hands, I poured myself another glass of wine, and then another. I went to bed, finally, and tossed and turned. My dreams were terror-filled and woke me in a panic. As the sun came up, I lay there, thinking. *Am I sure? And, if I am, what am I going to do?*

Chapter 38

Friday, August 24

The next three days were a blur. In retrospect, I was in shock, unable to think or make decisions about what to do next. Part of me was still in denial. The refrain *Am I sure?* kept running through my head. I slept a lot, and it was a heavy sleep—as though I were drugged. I went through the motions of eating and drinking but have no memory of those activities. Everything was silent. I hadn't called the satellite company to hook up the TV, and I hadn't brought a radio. My cell phone rang several times, and I ignored it, not even checking to see who was calling me.

Friday afternoon I was startled out of my fog by pounding on my door. I ignored the noise at first, but when I heard keys rattling at the lock, I finally roused. The door opened, slowly, and the building manager peeked in. When he saw me, he opened the door fully and stepped back to reveal Sarah. She thanked him, told him she'd take it from there, and closed the door in his face.

She looked at me. I was sitting on the sofa, my legs tucked up under a blanket. Her nose wrinkled. "You smell. How long has it been since you took a shower?"

I didn't answer, just stared at the wall.

"Jana! Get up off your keister and go take a shower!"

My eyes focused on her. I knew it was Sarah but didn't know how she'd gotten here. "What? What are you doing here?" The words were strangled, my voice weak.

Sarah marched over to the sofa, bent, grabbed my legs, and pulled my feet to the floor. "Stand up!"

I struggled up off the sofa and stood swaying in front of her. "What?"

Sarah slapped me. Hard. The brain fog lifted. The slap hurt! I shook my head. "Sarah, what are you doing here?"

She pulled me over to the large mirror on the living room wall. "Look at yourself!"

My reflection in the mirror stared back at me. My hair was tangled and matted. Dark circles surrounded my eyes. Food stains and crumbs littered the gray sweatshirt I was wearing. I stepped backward, treading on her foot. "I'm sorry," I said, turning to face her.

Sarah lifted my right arm. "Smell yourself."

I bent my head and sniffed. The odor was pungent and disgusting. "I don't understand," I whispered. "What's happened? Why am I here? Have I been sick?" I looked around the apartment. "When did I move here?" It was starting to come back to me. The movers, the trip to the convenience store in the complex, talking to Brenda, and . . . I started to cry. "It was him. I know it was."

Sarah hugged me—a true act of friendship, given the state I was in. "You're going to be all right. Let's get you cleaned up and then we'll figure this out." She took my hand and led me into the bathroom. She turned on the shower, pointing the head at the far wall since I hadn't hung the shower curtain. She felt the water temperature. "Okay, this is ready. Do you think you can manage to take your clothes off by yourself?" I nodded. "I'll go find soap and a washcloth and towel."

I pulled down my sweatpants, wrinkling my nose at the smell, and kicked them toward the toilet. Getting the sweatshirt off was harder. Something I'd spilled had been sticky, and the front was glued to my skin. By the time I was naked and stepping into the shower, Sarah was back. She knocked once and extended one arm around the door.

"Here's the soap and washcloth. I'm putting them on the sink. Can you reach them?"

I leaned out of the shower and retrieved them. "I have them. Thanks."

Sarah tossed a towel on the toilet lid. "Okay, I'm going to stay here, outside the door, until you're done in case you need anything." She closed the door.

The steaming hot water cascaded over me. I scrubbed and scrubbed every bit of my body, turning my skin bright pink. I used the soap to wash my hair since there wasn't any shampoo. When the soap suds were washed away, I turned off the hot faucet, and icy water ran over me until I was shivering and goosebumps appeared on my arms. I turned off the water, stepped out of the shower, and wrapped the towel around me.

"All done! Coming out," I said. My mind was clear for the first time in days.

Sarah was waiting for me on the other side of the door. "Feel better?" She smiled as I nodded emphatically. "I checked the bedroom. It looks like you did unpack your clothes before whatever this is happened. Get dressed. I have a pot of coffee on."

I put on white jeans, a red sweater, and blue socks with basset hounds. I blow-dried and brushed my hair, carefully arranging it to highlight the white streak at the hairline. When I was done, I looked in the mirror and decided a touch of mascara and eyeliner was warranted. Satisfied, I went to the kitchen.

"Hallelujah, you look better than you have in months. Sit down. I'll pour us some coffee, and you'll tell me what's going on." Sarah grabbed the coffeepot, poured, and sat it down on a trivet. She looked at me expectantly.

"Well," I started. "First, thank you. I don't know what I'd have done if you hadn't broken in here."

"Oh, you would have pulled out of it eventually," Sarah said. "You're a strong person, but even strong people have their breaking points. You would have gotten through whatever has happened, but I just couldn't wait." She smiled. "And I'm very persuasive, as your building manager will tell you."

"I have no doubt that he'll hide in his office if he ever sees you coming again," I grinned and took a sip of coffee. I could feel the caffeine coursing through my system.

Sarah's face went serious. "What happened, Jana? Whatever it is, it'll help if you put it in words."

I looked down at the table, my hands clutching the coffee cup. "Do you remember when I asked you to give a letter to

Brenda?" Sarah nodded. "She called me the day I moved here. She didn't know who the man was that LaRissa was afraid of, but she told me a few things that made me think." I took a deep breath. "Brenda said LaRissa begged to stay at her house whenever I was going to be away overnight." Sarah frowned. "I went back to my calendar and compared my schedule with the dates on her entries. They match."

"What are you thinking, Jana?" Sarah's voice was gentle.

"There were only two possibilities: Don or Kyle. And LaRissa would've kicked Kyle's ass if he ever tried anything. She's dominated him since she was two years old."

Sarah's eyes widened. They reflected the horror I was feeling, but she didn't say anything.

"It must have been Don. Her own father." My voice broke, and I could hardly speak for the lump in my throat. "My husband. The man I . . ." I forced myself to go on. "I was so blind. I refused to see him for what he is, all these years. I look back and realize the clues were always there. Rumors that I dismissed, his weak explanations when women showed up at the house, and when the phone rang and whoever was calling hung up when I answered. He had to leave me before I opened my eyes. Then Florence hit me with it that day, and I finally knew. But even now, how can I believe that the man I married, the man I bore two children for, would molest his own daughter. My daughter!" My voice rose. "I did this, Sarah. I let that man . . . that pervert . . . into our lives, and now he's living happily with a twenty-year-old girl, going on his merry way, disowning his son, and not suffering any consequences."

"It's not your fault," Sarah said finally. "Men like Don are good at fooling people. I never told you this, but there was an incident with Don and Bridget, when she was thirteen. She told Bill that she didn't want to come to dinner at your house one time. Bill asked her why and she said that Don had touched her breasts and told her he bet they were pretty. Bill was ready to charge over to your house with a baseball bat. I calmed him down and told him to talk to Don about it. I couldn't believe Don would do something like that, and I thought Bridget misinterpreted something he'd said. Bill did talk to Don, and Don told him that he remembered telling Bridget she was pretty. But he swore he never would have touched her or said anything inappropriate. Bill said Don had tears in his eyes as he denied it and begged Bill to believe him. Bill finally did accept that Bridget had misinterpreted or read more than intended into something Don had said. He talked to Bridget later and told her it was right of her to tell us about something that made her uncomfortable and that he'd talked to Don and Don had promised he wouldn't ever say or do anything that would upset Bridget again."

I thought back to when Bridget was thirteen. "That was about when we stopped having family dinners every week. That was the reason?"

Sarah nodded, her face miserable. "Even though Bridget accepted that she'd misinterpreted Don, she still felt uncomfortable around him. Bill and I thought it would be better not to force her to go where she didn't want to go, so we begged off after that. I'm so sorry. I should have said something at the time. But it seemed so unbelievable, and I knew you would be upset that we even thought for a moment that Don could do something like that."

I rubbed my temples. My anger at Don rose. He'd done this to my best friend's daughter—or tried to. How many other young girls had he abused? "He's not going to get away with this! We can't let him. He'll go on and on, as long as he's alive, destroying other girls, ruining their lives," I said, fiercely. "I want to destroy him."

"How?"

"I'll go to the police. I'll tell them everything and ask them to investigate him as a pedophile." I held Sarah's eyes with mine. "Will you go with me? Tell them about what happened with Bridget?"

Sarah agreed. We made a list of the points we would raise with the police. Evidence.

Chapter 39

Detective Alphonse Simmons was back at work after a three-day weekend. He was sunburned, and his knees hurt from taking his grandsons fishing and playing two-on-one basketball the past two days. He'd offered to take the kids so his daughter and son-in-law could go to Vegas for a brief vacation. It had been a fun weekend for his grandsons, and he valued the time he spent with them, but today he was reaping the negative rewards of his good deed. He lumbered to his desk and dropped into the swivel chair. There was a stack of pink slips staring at him. He leafed through them, discarding some, and laying out those that he had to deal with immediately.

The next to last message stopped him: "Jana Spencer requests meeting. Will arrive 4:30 p.m." He rose, holding the message, and went to find the receptionist who'd taken the call. Rosa was sitting at her desk, filing her nails, and looked up as Simmons approached.

"What's up, Detective?" The receptionist continued to attend to her nails.

"What's this from Mrs. Spencer?" Simmons waved the pink message at Rosa.

"She seemed nervous and asked for you. I told her you wouldn't be in until afternoon today, and she asked to meet with you at four-thirty," Rosa responded. She yawned. "I told her you were free then. You don't have anything else on your schedule for today."

"She didn't say what this was about?"

"No." Rosa returned to filing her nails.

Simmons walked back to his office. *Her son confessed. It was cut and dried. What could she want?* He recalled feeling sorry for the woman. She was young, attractive in a near-middle-aged way, and quiet. She wasn't the typical mother of a kid who was charged with a crime. Those usually came at him tooth and nail, accusing him of lying or police brutality. He shrugged and dropped into his chair. He spent the next three hours reviewing his current cases and items that needed to be tracked down for the prosecutors. It was a never-ending list, and he was only halfway through when his intercom buzzed announcing Jana's arrival.

She knocked lightly on his door and walked into his office. Another woman accompanied her—older and heavier, with bright red hair in a bun. Simmons stood up.

"Mrs. Spencer. I was surprised to see that you wanted to meet with me. How can I help you?" He waved the two women to the chairs in front of his desk.

"I . . . we . . . want to talk to you about a crime," Jana said. Her voice was shaky, and Simmons saw her face flush. "This is my neighbor, Sarah Sullivan. She has information too."

The detective sat down and pulled a pad of paper in front of him. He picked up a pen, prepared to take notes. "We always appreciate citizens who come forward. Please, continue."

Jana looked at Sarah, who reached out and pressed her hand. "We believe that my husband . . . my *ex*-husband . . . is a pedophile," Jana blurted out. She bent and retrieved a composition book from her purse. "I found this in my daughter's bedroom." Jana laid it on Simmons' desk and shoved it toward him.

The detective nodded and opened the composition book. He stopped on the first page, struck by the drawing of the young girl huddled in a corner, head down and knees drawn up. *Something had traumatized this child. I can understand why Mrs. Spencer believes something had happened to her daughter.* He turned the pages slowly. When he reached the final entry, he closed it.

"Your daughter was most likely being abused by someone, Mrs. Spencer." Simmons' voice was compassionate. "But she never says who it was. Why do you think it was your husband?

Is he your daughter's biological father?" Simmons knew stepfathers were a risk for sexual abuse, but it was rarer for biological fathers.

"Yes, he's her real father," Jana retorted. "And I have evidence. My calendar shows that I was either away overnight or out for an evening on the dates in LaRissa's composition book when she said these things were happening. Also, I talked to a friend of hers who said that LaRissa asked to spend the night at the friend's house when I was going to be away."

The other woman sitting in front of Simmons raised her hand. "Detective, I want to support what Jana is saying. My oldest daughter, Bridget, told us that Don Spencer touched her breasts and said inappropriate things to her when she was thirteen." Her eyes filled. "My husband accused Don and threatened him at the time, but Don managed to convince us that Bridget had misunderstood. He appeared distraught and apologized for anything he may have said that upset our daughter. My husband came back and told me he believed Don hadn't intended what Bridget had thought, but he still had reservations. We made sure that none of our girls were ever alone with Don again."

"It was him. I'm sure of it!" Jana's voice rose. "And now he's living with a twenty-year-old girl. Since our divorce I've learned that he's always been a predator, seducing women— friends of mine and others. But how could he do this to his own daughter? It's his fault that she's dead, and he's still out prowling and enjoying life. While his son is in prison." She broke down, covered her face with her hands, and sobbed.

Simmons waited to give her time to recover. When she raised her head and looked at him again, he said, "Mrs. Spencer, I know this has been a terrible time for you. And you may be right that he's guilty of sexually abusing your daughter. But, with what evidence you've given me, there isn't a case we can investigate. We would need a victim who could testify that he abused her before we could go forward." He turned to Sarah. "Your daughter's experience, if he did touch her inappropriately, also isn't sufficient, even if she would testify against him. It could have been a misunderstanding, as you and your husband initially believed. Any decent defense attorney would assert that."

"You're saying there's nothing you can do? He just gets away with it," Jana said. Her shoulders slumped.

"I could go talk to him," Simmons said. "If I did, though, he would deny it and possibly come after you in some way—sue you for slander, for making a false statement that damages his reputation. Or even threaten you physically. I'm sorry." He stood up. "I'll take this information to the attorneys to ask if they think there's enough here to at least open an investigation, but I doubt very much that they will authorize me to do anything else."

Jana was crying, and Simmons wasn't certain she had heard what he said. He looked at Sarah helplessly. She nodded and helped Jana up, an arm wrapped around the other woman's shoulder.

"Thank you for listening, Detective Simmons," Sarah said. "If we discover any other evidence that might support our concerns, I'm assuming we can come back and present it to you?"

"Of course," Simmons said. He came around his desk and escorted the two women to the door.

After they were gone, Simmons sat down and ran his hands through his unkempt hair. *That poor woman. I don't know if her suspicions are correct, but if they are . . . no one should have to go through what she has.*

Chapter 40

The sun streaming through my bedroom window woke me early on Friday. I lay in bed thinking about what Detective Simmons had said. The police couldn't do anything about Don unless there was evidence—a victim or a witness. Yesterday I'd sat in my apartment in despair. He was going to get away with it: LaRissa was dead and couldn't support my allegations, and Simmons said Bridget's experience wasn't sufficient for an investigation. I knew there had to be someone out there that Don had victimized but finding that person was the problem.

Don had often made me uncomfortable with his remarks about women. Times he'd grinned and said things about a young girl's body, her breasts, how the boys must be wanting to "hit that." I recalled my embarrassment at those incidents and how I'd hissed at him to stop, fearful that someone would overhear him. The signs had been there, and I'd ignored them. It was clear, though, in retrospect that he'd had a thing for girls in the twelve- to sixteen-year age range.

There had to be a way I could find evidence that Simmons could pursue. *Maybe I should confront Don and secretly record his response!* I sat up in bed, a wave of determination coursing through me. I would go to Don's work and accost him as he was leaving, force him to admit what he'd done. And record it, so there would be proof.

After a shower and two cups of coffee, my resolve strengthened. I hadn't seen Don since he'd moved out, and the thought of a meeting filled me with trepidation. He'd always been able to get around me, to ignore what I was saying or twist it to convince me that I was overreacting. My inability to change his disdain for Kyle was proof of that. Kyle's lack of confidence and dispirited view of the world, despite my love and concern for him, was the direct result of Don's behavior. He'd harmed both of my children, and I hadn't been able to help either of them. *But I will make him pay. Somehow.*

I went grocery shopping, then did housework to work off the nervous energy that my decision had raised. Keeping busy until time to go to the auto body shop where Don worked was essential. After lunch, I drove to the mall and bought curtains for the bedroom window, then came home and hung them. I followed up by hanging pictures in the living room and bedroom. At four-thirty, my new apartment looked lived-in—a basket of fruit decorated the kitchen table, spices were arranged alphabetically in the spice rack, and a meatloaf ready for the oven was in the refrigerator. I looked around in satisfaction. This was my apartment, the start of my new life, and I was ready to do battle.

I parked across the street from the auto body shop. I could see Don working on a truck in the first bay. At five o'clock, I watched him put his tools away and go into the bathroom to clean up. When he emerged and strolled out of the open bay, he hollered back to his boss, "See you tomorrow."

I got out of my car and met him as he was reaching to open the door of his truck. "Don, we need to talk," I said, my voice loud and strong, as I pressed the Record icon on my phone and dropped it into my pocket.

Don turned and looked at me. He was still handsome, thick black hair a bit too long and curling around his face. I'd forgotten how piercing his blue eyes were, the work scent of him, and the tanned muscles of his arms. My resolve wavered for a moment.

"What the fuck are you doing here?" Don's irritation strengthened me. If he'd said something welcoming or kind, it would have been harder to continue.

"We need to talk," I repeated. "I found LaRissa's diary."

Don's face flushed, deep red under his tan. "What are you talking about?"

"Do you really want to talk about this here?" I said. "Where people can hear us?"

He grabbed my arm, his fingers pressing hard enough to leave red marks. "I don't want to talk to you anywhere. Leave me alone!"

"Oh, so you want me to announce to your boss and pals here that you were molesting our daughter?" I yanked away from him and took a step toward the open bay door where several men were watching our interaction.

Don stepped in front of me, blocking my way. "Stop it! Have you finally gone crazy? I always knew you were weak in the head, but this is going too far. Meet me at the school athletic field and we'll have this out." He motioned with his head toward the empty playing field at the middle school a block away.

I nodded. "But if you don't show up there, I'm coming to your apartment. I'm sure your little girlfriend will find what I have to say interesting." I could feel him glaring at me as I crossed the street and got in my car. He was climbing into his truck as I drove away.

A dozen boys and a couple men—football coaches, I guessed—were on the field when I parked. The presence of other people was reassuring; Don wouldn't risk any physical violence with witnesses. His truck pulled up a minute later and parked next to me. I pressed the Record icon again, got out of my car, and walked past him to the bleachers on the edge of the field, close enough for the people on the field to hear me if I screamed or shouted, but far enough away to have some privacy for the conversation I was about to initiate.

"Now, what's this craziness you're talking about?" Don asked, sitting down near me. "Something about a diary?" He looked calm.

"This is what I'm talking about." I handed him copies I'd made of two of the entries in LaRissa's composition book.

Don read them and shoved them back at me. "So, someone was molesting my daughter? That's terrible . . . horrible . . . but what does it have to do with me?"

"The dates that she wrote those are also dates that I was out of town for conferences. And Brenda told me that LaRissa begged to stay over at her house whenever I was gone." I fixed him with an accusing stare. "Who else could it be? It's not like there was anyone else who had access to her."

Don scowled. "Only your precious son who murdered her, have you thought of that?"

The bile in my stomach rose into my throat, and I coughed. "Kyle was with me in Orlando on one of those dates. And you know how LaRissa treated Kyle. If he'd ever approached her like that, she would have kicked his butt and then told me . . . or you, more likely ... what he'd done." I tucked LaRissa's pages back in my purse. "I talked to Sarah about this last week too. She told me about your little incident with Bridget a few years ago. That Bill wanted to come after you with a baseball bat, but you convinced him Bridget must have misheard or misunderstood something you said. And then I thought back about all the times you made comments about underage girls and their sexual attributes. It's a pattern, Don. You like young girls. This Joelly girl—I've seen her. She looks about fifteen, slender, small breasts, and talks in a little girl voice." I raised my hand as he started to protest. "No, shut up! I won't listen to you. Unless you want to admit how you destroyed our daughter's life. And our son's, not that you care!"

Don stood up. "I don't have to listen to this. You're a bitter old woman . . . yes, old. You hate that I've moved on and have someone who's younger and prettier than you." He half-smiled as he added, "And a whole lot better in bed than you ever were. You don't even have breasts anymore. How could you ever expect to have a man want you?" He held up a hand with the middle finger extended. "Well, fuck you. If you come close to me again, or Joelly, I'll file a restraining order against you. Stay away from me, my work, and my friends."

I was shaking as he walked away. My heart was racing, and I could hardly breathe. I tried to remember the steps my therapist gave me to control panic attacks—slow deep breaths, tense muscles and relax, ground myself. I breathed deeply and grasped the edge of the bleacher tight, then tensed and relaxed, tensed and relaxed, for minutes. The panic finally receded, and I could breathe normally. Don's words had struck me hard. He knew how to hit where it hurt the most. Breast cancer had robbed me of my breasts and, also, my confidence in myself as a sexual being. *He's an evil person.* I repeated it out loud and then shook myself and walked to my car.

Sarah called while I was driving home. I pulled over to talk to her.

After I explained what I'd done, she was horrified. "You didn't! Did he admit it?"

"No, he verbally attacked me and said he'd get a restraining order if I ever came near him again," I told her. "And he accused Kyle of being the person LaRissa was afraid of."

"That bastard!" Sarah's indignation matched mine. "Kyle couldn't hurt a fly." She stopped, abruptly, aware of what she'd just said. "I'm sorry, Jana. But it's still true. Kyle wouldn't even think of his sister that way. And if he did, LaRissa would have broadcast it across the school and beyond."

I laughed, bitterly. We knew Kyle was innocent because he was her intimidated brother. But her father? Him, we could envision doing something this vile. "Do you think there's any chance we're wrong, Sarah? Any chance at all?"

Sarah paused before answering. "I think you're right about Don. But proving it may be impossible. I'm sorry." When I didn't say anything, she asked, "Do you want me to come over? Stay with you tonight?"

Tempting as it was to have a warm, reassuring friend to commiserate with, I said no. I needed to think, to come up with a strategy. There had to be some way to make Don pay for his behavior and its consequences.

Chapter 41

Sunday, September 2

I had made the round-trip drive to Greyson State Prison on Saturday to visit Kyle. He looked good, much better than I expected. He'd gained weight in the two weeks since my last visit, and he said he was working out with weights every day. "There's not a lot to keep me busy here," Kyle had said. "But I'm trying to do things that will help me improve. A couple of the guys in here with me meet in the library and talk about books we've read too," he said. "It's bad here, but not as bad as I thought. And soon I can start taking a college course." He smiled when he said that, and I was relieved. *Maybe he'll get through this all right,* had flickered through my mind. My worries about him becoming hard and embittered lessened.

The long drive home gave me time to go back to considering how I could bring Don to justice. I finally decided I needed to learn more about the pathology that would permit a father to sexually molest his own daughter. My job—my former job—required strong research skills, and I resolved to spend Sunday doing research on the topic, unpleasant as it was. Understanding the behavior might provide me with clues on what to do next.

Sunday morning, I woke up and, after a leisurely breakfast and a look at the news on TV, I sat down at my computer and began the task I'd set for myself. Google Scholar was my go-to site for research. It contained hundreds of thousands of professional journal citations and articles on any topic. The search terms

"Pedophile characteristics" yielded over 20,000 hits. I began wading through the abstracts that summarized the purpose and key findings of the research articles. When I refined the search criteria to "Pedophiles attracted to young teens," I discovered there were special names for men (and women) who were primarily attracted to children between the ages of eleven and seventeen—*hebephiles* and *ephebophiles*. The literature suggested that these men targeted young teens by appealing to their desire to be cool, attractive, mature, and accepted, grooming them sometimes over a long time. Grooming behavior included moving from appropriate physical touching to more intimate touching over time, as the child came to depend on and trust that the groomer was a friend and advocate. I nodded to myself. Don had often told LaRissa how attractive and popular she was and that he admired her maturity. He had always been very physically affectionate with her too—hugging her, pulling her into his lap, and stroking her arms and back. *How could I not have seen the signs?* I recalled times when I had thought he was too affectionate with her, but I'd never called him on it.

Understanding how Don had evolved to sexually abuse LaRissa wasn't going to help me find a strategy for stopping him from hurting other young girls. I focused on the characteristics of pedophiles who targeted teen girls. The literature was all over the place. Contrary to my expectations, there wasn't much consistent evidence that the hebephile/ephebophile had been abused himself as a child. And men who commit incest come from the full range of socioeconomic backgrounds—white collar, blue collar, intermittently employed, rich, and poor. The offenders also weren't often diagnosed psychopaths or sociopaths. That surprised me because I had thought that those characteristics might be essential to abusers who were unable to comprehend or didn't care about the harm they were doing. Two factors that struck me as relevant for my purpose were a correlation between drug and alcohol use and abuse and a similar correlation with low impulse control. Don wasn't a drug user, but it wasn't unusual for him to consume a six-pack of beer in the evenings. And impulse control had always been a problem for him. There were times when we argued about his impulsive decisions about major purchases and when I had to talk him down from physically attacking someone he felt had disrespected him. But I came away from hours of reading about these sick men with little to guide me in plotting Don's downfall.

The most useful information I gleaned was that most pedophiles had a "type" that they targeted. They had sexual preferences for females that they had been attracted to when they themselves hit puberty because they had never developed more mature and appropriate sexual preferences. That fit with Don. The two girls I knew he had abused were between thirteen and fifteen, were slender with small breasts, and were outgoing. His current girlfriend, Joelly, was older but looked much younger. I was certain that he had abused other young girls and, if I could find them and they would talk, I'd have something solid to take to the police.

How to find other victims was the question I wrestled with. Don had coached LaRissa's softball team and spent a lot of time at the school observing and assisting with the girls' track team. Those were possible sources of potential victims. There were probably others that I didn't know about. I thought about calling mothers of teen girls and asking them, flat out, if their daughters had ever had bad or uncomfortable interactions with Don, but I doubted that would produce any useful results. There were dozens of people I'd have to call and delicately raise an issue that would rouse strong feelings. Besides, I doubted that Don had abused or tried to groom a lot of girls over the past twenty years. More likely the number was small and calling parents at random wouldn't produce much other than to have a bunch of parents think I was a crazy lady.

I took a break from the computer and went in the kitchen to grab something to eat. It was already late afternoon, and I was tired of immersing myself in evil pathology. After I ate a corned beef sandwich with horseradish mustard, I decided to go down to the pool and enjoy the sunshine for an hour. A change of surroundings might help me come up with new ideas.

Eddie, the convenience store clerk, was cleaning up discarded paper cups and cigarette butts around the pool area. Otherwise, it was deserted. I guessed that all the young people who lived in the complex had gone to their apartments to prepare for dates or whatever it is that young people do on a Sunday night.

"Hi, Mrs. Spencer," Eddie greeted me. "How are you liking living here?"

"It's fine," I said. "I think I must be the oldest person in the complex, though. All the people I see are a lot younger than me."

Eddie laughed. "Not even close. Mrs. Schultz, on the first floor, is ninety-four. And Mr. Thomas, up on three—he's seventy-eight." He wrinkled his forehead. "But except for them I guess you're right." He winked at me, a strange gesture in his round, acne-scarred face. "You don't look like you're old, though. No one would guess you're old."

I took the compliment with a smile, despite the implication that, indeed, I was old. "Do you work just here, Eddie? Or do you have another job or go to school too?"

He sat down on the chair next to me. "I'm taking a class at the community college. My dad died a couple of years ago, and my mother works as a manager at McDonald's. We don't have enough money for me to go to school full-time, but I'll get there. It'll just take me longer to graduate. This job isn't bad. I work from three till ten. There's not much activity at the store during most of those hours, so I get a lot of studying done."

"What are you studying?" I was interested in what someone close to Kyle's age was doing—what Kyle might have been doing if he weren't in prison.

"Computer science. I've always been pretty good at computing, and one of my professors says he can probably get me a programming job at the college after I finish this semester. It'll pay more and give me experience." He grinned. "I really enjoy what I'm learning. One of my classes is on creating computer games! I'm working on one that I think might be a big seller. It's sort of a Dungeons & Dragons quest."

"That sounds interesting," I said with a smile. "Though I don't know anything about gaming or, really, Dungeons & Dragons. But Kyle is into all that. He told me when I visited him that the prison offers college courses in computer programming, and he's looking forward to signing up for them."

"Oh, yeah, he'd be really good at it. He was always helping me with tech things when we were together at the Final Quest. How is he doing?"

"He's doing okay, Eddie. I worry about him, but so far he seems okay in there. He did say to tell you hi and said he'd like to hear from you. I'll give you his address if you want to write to him." Eddie nodded emphatically, and I got a pen from my purse and wrote Kyle's address on the back of an empty envelope.

"Thanks! I'll write to him. It's really bad what happened to him, but he was always nice to me." Eddie got up. "I better get back to work. See you."

I watched Eddie walk back to the convenience store. A half hour later, I was sweaty and ready to go back to my air-conditioned apartment. The complex bulletin board near the stairway stopped me. It was covered with dozens of announcements: activities, items for sale, and two posters featuring lost cats. One had a full-color picture of a tortoise shell cat with the headline "Have you seen me?" Under the picture, it read "Lost August 30. Reward. Call 555-8888, if you see her." I studied the picture for a moment, thinking. Then it hit me. I could post pictures of Don—around the school, the mall, and any other places young people hang out—and offer a reward to anyone who had information about his pedophile activities!

Excited, I ran up the stairs to my second-floor apartment and dug out the box of family pictures I'd put away in my bedroom closet. There weren't any of Don, it turned out. I'd been so angry with him over deserting Kyle and divorcing me that I'd either thrown away or defaced pictures of him with me or the kids. *I'll have to call Sarah, maybe she has one.*

"Hi, Sarah," I said when she answered the phone. "I have a strange request for you."

She laughed. "Sure, anything."

"Do you have a picture of Don? One that shows his face clearly?"

I heard Sarah take a deep breath before answering. "Why?"

"You don't want to know," I said brightly.

"I do want to know. I'm sure I can find a picture, but first I want to know what you're planning to do with it." Her tone was serious.

"I'm going to make a flyer and distribute it around Fairview, asking people to contact me if they have had a bad experience with him. It's the only way I can think of to find other girls that he may have abused," I blurted out. "Detective Simmons said there had to be a victim who'd testify before he could do anything about Don."

"Are you sure this is a good idea? That detective said Don could sue you if you went around accusing him of molesting girls. If you say in your flyer that he's an abuser, hitting on young girls, I think that's libel unless you can back it up. With evidence." She paused for a moment and then said, "You need to be very careful what you say or imply on this flyer."

"I will be careful. I'll work on it tomorrow. Maybe you can come over—or I'll come to your house after school tomorrow and run the wording past you. How about that?"

"Tomorrow's Labor Day, and we're going on a family picnic. We'll be back around six, so I'll come to your place after that. Don't do anything in the meantime. We really need to think this through."

"Thanks, Sarah. Don't forget to bring the picture." I hung up, relieved that Sarah was going to help, or try to keep me from getting in trouble, at least. I sat down at my computer and began working on what the flyer would say.

Chapter 42

Monday, September 3

Sarah arrived with a couple of pictures of Don. I chose one where he's smiling, dressed in tennis clothes, his black hair slightly disheveled, blue eyes crinkling, and looking charming. He had one arm around LaRissa in the picture, and that nauseated me.

"You can cut the picture in half," Sarah said. She held up scissors.

I took them and carefully excised LaRissa from the photo and then trimmed the edges. "That should do it," I said. I stared at the picture of LaRissa that I'd laid on the kitchen table. "She was so beautiful, wasn't she? I look at her picture now, and it makes me think how sad and scared she must have been. This was taken just a couple months before she died."

"I know," Sarah said softly. She touched my shoulder. "But let's focus on what you're going to do next. My cousin, Justin, is a lawyer. He said he'd look at what you write on the flyer and tell you if it leaves you open to a libel suit."

I thanked her and went to my bedroom to get my laptop. I put it on the kitchen table and fired it up. "I've been working on the wording. Tell me what you think."

Not all my drafts had been serious. The first one read "PEDOPHILE ON THE LOOSE" over the space for the picture. Under where the picture would go, I'd written "This man lusts after teenage girls. If you run into him, stay away! If he's molested you, call or text 555-0225 and we'll help you get revenge!"

Sarah looked up at me, after reading it. "I hope you're not serious about this one. Legal action without a doubt!"

I laughed. "No, not serious. Just what I wish I could say on it. Read down for the ones that I think would do the job without getting me in trouble."

"I'm not sure there's anything you can say that won't get you in some sort of trouble," Sarah responded, frowning. "You do know that Don's going to go ballistic when he sees these? He may not have legal cause, but I don't doubt he'll come after you some way."

I shrugged. "Last of my concerns. Read the other options and tell me which you think would work."

Sarah read, frowned, and read again. "Okay, I think the third one works best. But this isn't your phone number, and what's this email address?"

"I bought a pre-paid burner phone and a hundred minutes. And the email address is one I created on a free-mail site. I didn't want to have crazies who might respond be able to identify me."

"Good thinking," Sarah said. "Anyway, I think your wording is good. It hints at pedophilia but isn't explicit and asks to talk to anyone who may have had unpleasant encounters with him. Let me email it to Justin, and we'll see what he says." She copied the text into an email and sent it off.

We turned to importing Don's picture into a Word document. The document read "Have you seen this man" at the top and, under the picture, read "If you have had unpleasant experiences with this man, call or text to 999-555-0225 or email us at justice666@mmail.net and tell us about what happened. We're here to help."

It took Sarah's cousin over an hour to get back to her. He signed off on the wording but cautioned that it could provoke physical or verbal reactions from the target of the flyer. "Just be careful," he wrote. His warning didn't deter me. I doubted Don would try to beat me to a pulp or kill me, and anything else I'd take to find justice for LaRissa.

I printed out fifty copies of the flyer and laid them on the kitchen table. "Done. Tonight I'm going to tack them up around Fairview."

"Where are you thinking?" Sarah still looked doubtful

about the wisdom of my plan.

I handed her the list I'd prepared. "Around the middle and high school, in the parks, on the bulletin board at the community college annex, on the campus here in Hinton, and near the Fairview Rec Center. I'll put a couple up on Main Street close to the Green Grill where high school students hang out." I grinned. "And I think I'll post one on a telephone pole outside his apartment building and another outside his workplace."

Sarah raised her eyebrows. "Really? You want to get in his face with this right off? If you post them at the schools and parks and on Main Street, it might be a few days before Don learns about it. Put them up at his home and work and he'll come after you tomorrow."

"I don't care, Sarah! I really don't care. He's the reason that LaRissa is dead — the reason she was scared and anxious and did what she did that night. And the reason that Kyle is in prison for twenty years. He has to pay a price for destroying their lives!" My voice rose as I said these final words.

Sarah stared at me, her eyes filling. "I understand but, like Justin said, be careful. Don't be alone with Don. Does he know you've moved to Hinton? If he does, don't let him in your apartment. In fact, stay away from Fairview. He'll probably call you when he finds out about this and try to threaten you. Don't answer if he does." She leaned over and hugged me. "I don't want anything to happen to you, Jana."

"I'll be all right." I was grateful for Sarah, grateful that she cared when most of my so-called friends and acquaintances had avoided me since Kyle had confessed. I hugged her back. "It'll be fine."

"I hope so," Sara said. She wiped her eyes and got up. "I'd better get home. Bill said he'd take the girls out for dinner, but I have papers to grade tonight."

After she left, I poured myself a glass of wine and went in the living room. There were four hours to kill before I'd head to Fairview and distribute the flyers around town.

Chapter 43

The only phone calls I received after posting the flyers were from Don. He was furious, threatening, and more extreme with each of the three voicemails he left on my cell phone. I saved the messages in case he did attack me. The police would want to have evidence. It was clear, though, that he didn't know where I had moved to, and I was staying away from Fairview for the near future.

But no calls came in on my burner phone. I kept it with me twenty-four/seven, not wanting to miss a call that would, I hoped, provide what I needed. By Friday, I was giving up hope, though, and told Sarah that when she made her daily check-in call.

"Don't give up yet, Jana. You're trying to persuade someone—maybe multiple someones—to call and tell you about a traumatic experience. They might have to think about it for a while before they decide to call." As always, Sarah was the practical and sensible one. If it had been me reacting to the flyer, I'd want to accuse him right away. But maybe these women had kept their experiences secret for some reason—and for some time.

"You're probably right," I said with a sigh. "But I wish they'd hurry up and decide. Waiting is painful."

"What have you been doing this week?" Sarah changed the subject. "Any thoughts about finding a job?"

"Not yet. Selling the house gave me a nice nest egg, so I don't have to worry about money for a while. I went to the college yesterday and picked up a catalog. Maybe I'll take a couple classes next semester. I had a psychology minor in college and thought about getting a master's degree in counseling." I laughed. "But then I got pregnant with Kyle and decided to be a stay-at-home mom for ten years."

Sarah's surprise was evident, but not in a bad way. "What a great idea! I've often wished I could go back to school. I love teaching, but home economics is a field that schools are phasing out in favor of STEM, which I'm completely unprepared to teach. What are you thinking of doing with a master's?"

"Maybe counsel girls who were sexually abused by their fathers?" Truthfully, I hadn't thought that far ahead. My interest in psychology was mostly because I wanted to understand what had happened to my daughter and how it had affected her. "I don't know, Sarah. I'm still thinking about it."

There was a long pause, then Sarah replied, "I don't know whether that's an area you should immerse yourself in, Jana. It's too close, I think." She stopped again and finally said, "But taking classes is a good idea. I'd be nervous to even start. I don't know if I could keep up with a bunch of twenty-year-old kids. But you've been doing research and writing grants for the past ten years. You won't have any problems."

"Maybe. We'll see," I said. "Hey, I meant to ask you something. Would you drive by the schools and the parks and see if the flyers are still posted? Don's left me voice mails, and I'm worried that he may be finding and destroying them. If I need to, I'll print out a bunch more and repost them."

"Sure, I'll do that tomorrow while I'm grocery shopping and getting gas. I do know there are some posted near the high school. I pass by two of them on my way there."

We chatted for a bit longer and hung up after promising to get together for brunch on Sunday. Sarah was coming to Hinton for our brunch date, agreeing with me that Fairview should be off limits, with Don breathing fire and threatening me.

I was sitting at the kitchen table Saturday afternoon, filling out the online application to attend Hinton College, when the burner phone rang. I was so startled that I nearly dropped it when I snatched it off the kitchen table.

"Hello."

No one said anything, but I could hear breathing.

"Are you calling about the flyer that was posted? About the man?"

There was no response, and then whoever was on the line hung up. My heart was pounding. I checked caller ID, but it said "Restricted." There was no way to call back or identify the caller.

I poured myself a glass of wine and collapsed on the sofa. My thoughts were whirling. *There IS someone out there who has been Don's victim before. Why didn't she say something? Will she call back?* I gulped down my wine and went in the kitchen and poured another glass. I just hoped—prayed—she'd call back.

By ten o'clock I gave up waiting for the call. I went into my bedroom, brushed my teeth, put on pajamas, and lay down in the bed. Despite the four glasses of wine I'd consumed, I didn't expect to fall asleep, but I did. I'd put the burner phone on the night stand next to the bed, and when it rang, it took me a minute to realize I wasn't dreaming. Then I sat straight up in bed and grabbed the phone.

"Hello," I said breathlessly. "Please talk to me. I'm here to help you."

There was silence on the other end of the line.

"He hurt my daughter too. He's an evil person, and whatever he did to you, he should be punished."

A strangled sob came through the line. "He did. He hurt me." The voice was young and anguished.

"I'm so sorry, dear. I'm sorry that happened to you. It wasn't your fault, and you didn't do anything to deserve that." I tried to remember what LaRissa had written. She'd been confused, hurt, and thought there was something wrong with her that caused the abuse. "It's him," I added. "He's a sick, sick man. And I want to make it so he can't hurt any other girls like you."

"That would be good," the girl said in a whisper.

"Can you talk about it? Tell me what happened?" She didn't respond. I added, "I know it's hard to talk about or even think about."

The caller took a deep breath. "I don't know. It happened two years ago. I've just wanted to forget it, but I can't." She started crying. "I'll call you back, maybe." The line went dead.

Chapter 44

Monday, September 10

Despite my resolve not to go to Fairview, risking an encounter with Don, Sarah had checked the status of the flyers I'd posted around town and reported that the majority had been torn down. She was only able to spot three remaining. "Don must have scoured the town and removed them," she told me. "What do you want to do?"

"I'll print off some more and come over tonight and put them up," I said. "Don't worry. I'll wait till near midnight. No way Don will be watching for me then. He gets up for work at six."

"About that," Sarah said. "Bill ran into Don a couple days ago, and Don told him that his boss had let him go. Customers had recognized Don from the flyers and decided to take their business elsewhere. So be careful if you do come over. Don asked Bill if he knew where you moved to. Bill denied knowing, but Don's looking for you. And I imagine he's even angrier than when he called you."

I promised to be careful. And I was. I wore black jeans, a black T-shirt, and a black knit cap and stayed inside the car with the doors locked while I scanned the streets and sidewalks before getting out and tacking up a flyer. The full moon reassured me that I'd be able to see anyone coming and have time to get back to the car before they reached me.

He caught me outside the middle school.

"I knew you'd be back here to put more up," he growled, coming out from behind the Fairview Middle School sign on the lawn. He lurched at me and knocked me down. I scrambled to hands and knees and tried to crawl toward the car. "No, you don't! You and I are going to have a talk." He grabbed me by one arm and hauled me up, then pulled me face-to-face with him. I could smell the beer on his breath.

He held me too tightly by the upper arms to get away. I struggled, but that only made him grip me harder. I looked at his face, shadowed by the bright moon, and couldn't see the man I had been married to. His face was contorted in a scowl, his hair was disheveled, and hatred was in his eyes. I realized that this was the true Don, the one I'd refused to believe in, the one I'd been kowtowing to for twenty years. Don was a bully who counted on his size and muscles to intimidate. I spit in his face.

"You bitch!" He yelled and slapped me hard in the face. I kicked his shins, which wasn't effective in the soft-soled shoes I was wearing. I saw him make a fist and tried to duck but couldn't evade the punch. On the ground, I screamed and tried again to scramble away. He kicked me in the ribs. I curled up in a ball to protect myself. In the distance I could hear a siren. Don raised his foot to stomp me as the siren drew near, but a spotlight turned on. He turned and ran.

The cruiser pulled up and two deputies got out—a man and a woman. The woman rushed to me and knelt down. "Are you hurt?"

I pulled myself to a sitting position. My ribs were sore, but nothing felt broken. My jaw hurt; I'd probably have a major bruise there. I probed my teeth with my tongue and found a wobbly one. *I'll have to go to the dentist.* A mundane thought, given my situation. "I think I'll be okay. Just some bruises," I told her. She helped me to my feet.

"If you need to go to the hospital, we can take you there. Have yourself checked out to be sure?" She led me toward the cruiser and settled me in the back seat. "We'll want to get a statement from you once you've seen the doctor. But do you know who attacked you? Would you recognize him again?"

My broad smile surprised her and made my sore face hurt. "You bet I know who it was. My ex-husband, Don Spencer."

I settled back in the seat. "Would you mind getting my purse from my car?" I pointed to my white Toyota parked next to a tree. "It's that one."

As she jogged to my car, the male deputy walked over to the open door. He had two flyers in his hand. "Are these yours?"

"They are, and that's who attacked me," I told him. "My ex-husband."

He muttered something and closed the cruiser door. I watched him motion to his partner, and the two stood talking for a minute. When they returned to their vehicle, the woman opened the back door again.

"We'll take you to the hospital, but we do have questions that you'll need to answer. These flyers? I'm not sure they're legal. Your ex-husband might claim harassment or defamation, my partner says. Of course, that's no excuse for beating you up, but we'll have to pass this on to a detective and see what he says."

"Contact Detective Alphonse Simmons," I said. "He knows me and what's going on." I heard her relay this to her partner. When she closed the door again, I realized there were no inside door handles. The adrenalin rush of the whole thing made me panicky, but I was certain that Don didn't have a case against me. At least, Sarah's lawyer cousin had said he didn't think I'd be doing anything illegal. *And now I can have him arrested for assault!* I smiled again. "Ouch!"

It took over two hours at the emergency room. I was X-rayed for fractures, examined, given an icepack for my jaw, and given ibuprofen for pain. The doctor said the wobbly tooth would probably heal itself, but to see a dentist anyway. I was discharged with instructions to rest, take the pain relievers, and call if any new symptoms emerged.

Detective Simmons was waiting for me outside the emergency room. He lumbered past me to a bench in the lobby. I followed and sat down next to him.

"We need to talk," Simmons said. He studied my face. "Looks like you're going to have a nice bruise on that jaw. The deputies who brought you in told me the story. They've picked up your husband. He's claiming self-defense, that you're on a vendetta against him and he was just trying to protect himself." He reached into his inside jacket pocket. "What's this all about?"

Simmons unfolded a flyer and laid it on the bench between us.

"You said you needed evidence that Don was a predator," I said. "I'm trying to get that evidence. If we know about two cases, there probably are more girls that Don harmed." I picked up the flyer. "And I did talk to a lawyer before posting these. He said that the way it was phrased was okay."

Simmons coughed and cleared his throat. "Yeah, I figured that. I saw these around town for a couple days and then they disappeared, so I figured you pulled back from what you're trying to do." He coughed again, almost choking, then continued. "Apparently, I was wrong."

"I was replacing the flyers. Don went around town and pulled them down."

"And he figured you'd do it again and was watching for you." Simmons grimaced. "Do you have any idea how dangerous this game is you're playing? If my people hadn't responded to a call about a disturbance at the middle school, you might have been seriously injured, maybe killed. Your husband—"

I interrupted. "My ex-husband!"

"Your ex-husband." Simmons nodded. "He's furious with you. I talked to him at the station before heading over here. He's threatening to sue you for defamation, and he's already talked to a lawyer. He's been fired from his job and told me his lady friend has broken it off with him."

"Good," I said, satisfaction dripping from the word. "He destroyed my daughter and my son. He's evil, and he should suffer."

Simmons studied me, his eyes tired and sad. "Mrs. Spencer, what you just said would lose you a civil suit for defamation. You blame him for what happened to your children and for leaving you for a younger woman. You want revenge. His lawyer would say that was your motivation."

I stared right back at him. "No. I want to get evidence that you can use to put him in prison. I'd tell the court about LaRissa's journal and what happened with Sarah's daughter."

"A judge wouldn't let you testify about those things. You don't have independent evidence, so it's just hearsay or your opinion." He stood up. "Are you going to press charges against him for assault?"

"Yes. What do I need to do?"

"Come down to the station tomorrow morning. I'll take your statement. We'll go from there. But you need to be careful. He'll likely bond out within twenty-four hours, and he might come after you again." Simmons sat down again. "Look, I agree that it certainly looks like your husband abused your daughter. Not a hundred percent, but what you've told me raises strong suspicions."

"I did get a phone call from one young girl—she sounded young, anyway—who saw the flyer. But she's scared and hung up on me twice. I think she'll call back. If I can convince her to talk to you, will you listen?"

He rubbed his forehead before responding. "Yes, I'll listen. Now go home. Don't put up any more flyers in the middle of the night. And watch out for your ex." He stood up again. "Do you need a ride to your car?"

Simmons dropped me off at the middle school and waited until I was in the car and pulling out before flashing his lights at me. I watched his taillights in the rearview mirror. Despite my sore jaw and ribs, I felt like I'd made progress. At least Simmons believed me.

Chapter 45

Wednesday, September 12

The week passed quickly, what with police reports, another midnight foray into Fairview to post new flyers, and a visit to Hinton College to talk with the head of the psychology department. The interview had gone very well—we'd talked for two hours. Professor Kim was young and had a Ph.D. from Yale. Her Ph.D. dissertation was on characteristics of pedophiles and their association with potential for rehabilitation. I learned a lot, but I didn't reveal the reasons for my interest in her research. She assured me that I would be accepted into the master's program in psychology. Her positive response and offer of a research assistantship were, I knew, because of my grant writing experience at the clinic. I wasn't too enthusiastic about writing grants again, but she assured me that part of the research assistantship would include literature reviews and actual data collection on several projects. The job paid only $500 a month, but that would cover the costs of books and fees, with some left over. By the time I left the college, I was enrolled in three classes for the January semester.

Detective Simmons had also called me twice. The first call was to let me know that Don had made bail and to warn me again to avoid him. He'd threatened me in front of Simmons, and the detective had told him threats were prosecutable offenses, especially in combination with his arrest for my assault.

The second phone call, a few days later, was to tell me that Don had pleaded guilty in return for a light sentence. "The judge gave him a six-month jail sentence but then offered him probation with the condition of staying away from you. He'll go to jail to serve out the six months if he violates probation. So, you won't need to testify." I hadn't been looking forward to being face-to-face with Don, so this news was a relief despite the light sentence and the fact that Don was free again. Before we ended the call, Simmons asked, "Have you gotten any more calls from your flyer?"

I had to admit I hadn't. I kept the burner phone in my pocket or by my side day and night, but it hadn't rung. "I did put up more flyers this week. Some at the college here in Hinton and, I know you won't approve, but I put some up again in Fairview."

"Well, let me know if you get anything," Simmons said.

Today I had nothing to do. Calendar was empty, apartment was clean, laundry was done, pantry was full enough. I'd even baked homemade chocolate chip cookies already. Wine was off my list—I'd decided to cut back after the last hangover.

It was raining, so sitting out by the pool wasn't an option. I'd unpacked my boxes of books and arranged them by category on an IKEA bookcase I'd assembled after I'd moved in. At Professor Kim's suggestion, I'd bought two abnormal psychology tomes at the college bookstore. I decided to get an early start on reading for that class.

Abnormal Psychology by William Ray was a used copy— only $48 at the bookstore. I pulled it off the bookshelf and curled up on the sofa. The prior owner had kept it in pristine shape: no one's name on the inside cover and no underlining or highlighting in the text. I skimmed the table of contents and decided to start at the beginning.

The ringtone of the burner phone startled me from a light sleep. By the third ring I was racing to the kitchen where I'd inadvertently left it. I snatched it up and hurriedly swiped Accept.

"Hello!"

"This is the girl who called you before." The voice was soft and tentative, like she wasn't sure she'd meant to call.

"I'm happy you called back," I said. "How can I help you?"

"I don't know. All I know is I have nightmares, and I'm scared all the time."

"What are you scared of?" I asked gently. I didn't want to provoke her into hanging up again.

"Him. Men. Being touched." She was breathing rapidly. "I don't know what's wrong with me."

"Do you know the man on the flyer?" I held my breath.

There was silence on the other end of the line. I was afraid she'd hang up, but I could hear her breathing. After what seemed a long time but was really only a minute, she answered. "Yes. He's the one who hurt me. And made me scared. And I don't know what to do."

"I can help. I'll try to help." I listened to her breathe. "He hurt my daughter, too, sweetie. And together we can work to make sure he doesn't hurt anyone else."

Her tone was stronger when she replied. "That's what I want too! But I don't know what to do."

"You can talk to me for now. Then we can figure out what to do. Does that sound all right?"

She murmured, "Yes."

"Do you want to tell me your name? I'm Jana Spencer. You can call me Jana."

"I'm Harriet. My friends just call me Harry." Her voice was so young.

"I'm happy to meet you, Harry." I thought for a moment, wishing I knew what a trained counselor would say next. "Are you willing to tell me when you met this man?"

"It was about two years ago, I think. I was in eighth grade then."

Eighth grade. I pushed back the rage building in me. "How did you meet him?"

"I was riding my bicycle home from tennis practice, and I got a flat tire. I live out in the country, and it's about three miles home on gravel roads," she said. "He saw me pushing my bike and stopped and asked me if I needed help. I said no, but he got out of his car and came and looked at the tire. He said it couldn't be fixed and that he'd drive me home. I knew I shouldn't get in a car with a strange man, but he seemed so nice. And it was about a hundred degrees out, and I didn't have any water." Her words ended in a wail. "It's my fault, isn't it? I knew I shouldn't get in the car, but I did."

The phone went dead as Harry ended the call. I was distraught. *That poor child, what had Don done to her? Had I made things worse by wanting her to talk about it? And what if she doesn't call back?* I sat for minutes staring at the phone. I couldn't call her back on the restricted number. I put the burner phone in my pocket and got my cell phone from the living room. I had to talk to someone, and Sarah was the only person other than Detective Simmons who knew what I was trying to do. She didn't answer, of course. It was a school day and classes were still in session. I left an urgent voicemail.

The rain had stopped. I went for a walk around the block, trying to relieve the pent-up tension in my body. Back in my apartment, I sat on the sofa and tried to return to reading about abnormal psychology.

Sarah called me back two hours later. "Are you okay? What happened? Did Don find you?" The questions came rapid-fire. My message had been for her to call me right away and that it was urgent.

"No, I'm okay. I'm sorry for scaring you. The girl who called before about the flyer called me again." I related the gist of my conversation with Harry to her. "Did I scare her off somehow, Sarah? I don't know what I'm doing or how someone trained would talk to a victim. Especially a young victim. I'm afraid she won't call back, and I'm afraid that even if she does, I'll screw it up somehow."

Sarah had listened without interrupting. "Jana," she said, when I stopped, "it doesn't sound like you did anything wrong. That child has trauma that she's never told anyone about. My limited experience says that talking about it is the first step to recovery, but you can't expect her to not be frightened and overwhelmed. I think she'll call back, but it may take her several times to open up entirely. Just be there when she calls and listen. Don't judge or react to what she tells you. Just be supportive and kind. She needs to trust you."

Sarah's advice rang true. "I hope you're right."

We talked for a while about what she and her family were doing and the trip they were planning for Disneyland at Christmas. I admitted that I was getting bored without a job or school to distract me, and she shared some ideas about volunteer work. Sarah finally said her girls were home and she had to get dinner on, and we hung up.

I flipped on the television to watch the evening news, but my thoughts were with Harry. I hoped she was okay and that I could, somehow, help her. If she called back.

Chapter 46

Friday, September 14

Harry called back two days later, and this time she was ready to tell her story.

I was crying by the time she stopped. Don had not taken her home. He'd driven down a dead-end side road. Then he'd tried to charm her. And when that didn't work, he'd pinned her down, ripped off her pants and panties, and raped her. She'd screamed and struggled, but there was no one to hear. Harry said, after it was over, he'd put his arm around her, told her how pretty she was, and asked if she'd enjoyed it. "He said we could do it again sometime, if I wanted to." I could hear her crying and wished, desperately, that I could comfort her.

"I didn't know what to say that would convince him to let me go," Harry said. "I finally said maybe. But then he grabbed my arm hard—I had bruises for a long time—and said if I told anyone, they wouldn't believe me. And if he found out I'd told anyone, he'd find me and kill me. Then he laughed and pushed me out of the car. He threw my clothes on the ground. While I was getting dressed, he hauled my bike out of the trunk and drove away. I tried to see his license plate, but it was covered with mud." She sobbed and added, "When I got home, my dad asked why I looked like something the cat dragged in, and I said I'd had a flat tire and fallen off the bike."

Harry was silent for several minutes. I let her have the time she needed. What she finally said next surprised me. "I want to stop him from doing this to anyone else."

"We'll do that, Harry. But you'll have to be very brave. Can I ask you a few questions?"

"Uh-huh." She wasn't crying, and her response was emphatic.

"Are you absolutely certain the man is the one in the picture on the flyer?"

"Yes."

"Did you notice anything else about his appearance that would help identify him?"

"He had a tattoo on the inside of his thigh," Harry said. "He made me look at his 'thing' before he raped me, and I saw it. It was a shark with big teeth."

I gritted my teeth in rage. Don did have that tattoo—the result of a drunken binge with his college buddies. Her seeing it was convincing evidence, but it also dashed any hope I'd had left that I was wrong.

"Harry, that's good. That's evidence. One more question. Did you tell anyone else about what happened to you? At the time? Maybe a friend?"

"No. I wanted to forget it. And I didn't want anyone to know I was so stupid. They'd blame me for getting in a car with a strange man." Her voice caught. In my mind I could see her tears falling again. "Ever since kindergarten, teachers and my dad have warned me about stranger danger. It's my own fault, I know."

"No! It wasn't your fault!" I nearly yelled. "He's an evil man, and you are a trusting young woman. He took advantage of that. He did something no man should ever do to you! He's the one at fault, Harry. Not you," I said more quietly. "Don't ever blame yourself."

There was silence on the other end of the line. When Harry spoke again, she sounded resolved. "What do we do next?"

"Are you willing to tell your story to the police?" This was the vital question. If she was afraid to do that, her sad story was just another in the accumulating evidence that wasn't sufficient for Detective Simmons to act.

"Would my dad have to know?"

"He would need to know, Harry. You're a minor, and the police would have to investigate. You also might have to testify in court about what happened and identify the man who hurt you." I held my breath waiting for her response.

"I don't know. My mom died three years ago, so it's just my dad and me. It would hurt him a lot knowing that something like this happened to me," Harry said. "I don't know what he'd do." After a pause, she said, "Let me think about it." And the line went dead.

She still hadn't told me her last name or phone number, so I had no way to reach her, to try to persuade her. I put the phone down and wept.

Chapter 47

Tuesday, September 18

The rundown house with flaking pink paint and a boarded-up window on the second floor didn't have a sign out front. The lawn was choked with weeds, but two flowerpots on the porch had flourishing red geraniums. I'd taken Sarah's advice and volunteered to help at the shelter for battered women in Hinton. It was my first day, and I wasn't certain this was the right activity to occupy my time and distract me. But here I was.

I rang the doorbell and heard footsteps. The door opened, and a young woman holding a can of pepper spray stood there. "Who are you?" The suspicious tone, and the pepper spray, took me aback.

I'm Jana—Jana Lane," I said. "I'm a new volunteer." It felt odd to say "Lane" again. My maiden name hadn't rolled off my lips for over twenty years. But I could no longer bear to carry the last name of the man who had abused my daughter.

The guardian at the door lowered the pepper spray and smiled. "Oh, welcome. I'm Mandy. Sorry for the reception, but we sometimes have problems with angry husbands or angry wives. Come in. I'll take you to Louise, our director." She closed the door and pointed toward the long narrow hallway that led to the back of the house. "We don't have many volunteers who are willing to come here and help our women. Mostly volunteers fundraise and donate clothes and food. Do you know what you'll be doing?"

"Not yet. I talked to Louise last Saturday. She asked me a lot of questions about my background and said she'd make good use of me." I smiled. "But she didn't say how."

The kitchen was filled with boxes. Most of them held food, and two large ones were overflowing with clothing—pants, shirts, nightgowns, sweaters, and other items. A large, heavyset woman with gray hair piled high on her head was standing at the stove, stirring a large pot of something that smelled tasty.

"Louise, your volunteer's here," Mandy said in a singsong voice.

"Come stir for me, Mandy," Louise said, waving a wooden spoon in the air. "This stew is almost done, and I don't want it to scorch the bottom of the pan." Mandy took over stirring duty, and Louise turned to me. "Welcome. It's Jana, right? We'll sit in the conference room, also known as the dining room, the study, and the kids' playroom."

I followed her back down the hall and into a large room dominated by a long table and bookcases. The bookcases held books, games, toys, and stuffed animals. "I see what you mean. Definitely a multipurpose room," I said. "Are there children living here too?"

"Mothers usually bring their kids. Abuse doesn't focus on only one person," Louise responded. "Sit down. I'll give you the synopsis of what we do here."

I sat and listened. The Hope Center had been founded ten years ago as a refuge for battered women. Its location wasn't advertised other than through word-of-mouth. Most of its clients came through referrals from the hospital and police. There were five women and four children there at the moment. "We're full up, unfortunately. The average stay here is three months, and during that time we work with our clients to help them find jobs, get permanent housing, and obtain public services like food stamps, Medicaid, and TANF. We also work with two lawyers who help our folks navigate the legal system. Restraining orders against the abuser, divorce, and other legal help is provided *pro bono*. Mandy and I are the only full-time paid staff. We provide counseling, transportation, and other assistance. Our clients help with cooking and cleaning. A state grant covers our salaries, the rent and utilities for this house, and a vehicle. We rely on our board and volunteers to raise funds and donations for food, clothing, and other needs."

I frowned. "I'm not sure what role you have in mind for me. I'm willing to help out two or three days a week until January when I start working on my master's degree."

"Oh, I have an important job for you—if you're willing," Louise said with a wide grin. "We need someone to tutor our clients to help the moms get their GED before they leave here. Three of our current residents never finished high school, and they're ashamed of that. Getting a GED will increase their self-confidence and better equip them to find a job. Also, two of the children here are behind in school. You could help them catch up."

I was intrigued. This sounded like a job I'd enjoy and feel good about. "I'd love to do that," I told Louise. "When do you want me here?"

"Can you do one morning, maybe Wednesdays, and Tuesday and Friday afternoons?"

We settled on a schedule, and Louise went to the bookshelves and pulled out a large yellow paperback. "Here's the GED prep book. Study it and work out a plan. I think you should meet with the three students individually first. Then, if you think it will work, you can hold classes with all three." She shrugged. "They may be at different levels and need individual sessions. Up to you. Now let me take you on a tour of the house and introduce you to our clients."

After the tour and introductions, I headed back to my apartment. It felt good—I felt good—for the first time in months. This was something useful that I could do. If it worked out well, I might even be able to continue after I started school.

After a Lean Cuisine dinner, I opened the GED prep book and began making notes about where to start with the students I was to meet with the next day. My focus was so intense that when the burner phone rang, I was startled. *Harry!* I grabbed it off the table and swiped Accept.

"Harry, I'm so glad you called back," I exclaimed.

"This isn't Harry," a deep gravelly voice responded. "This is her father, Amos. Is this Jana?"

"Yes, sir. How can I help you?" My excitement faded. *She must have told him. Is he going to tell me to never contact her again? Threaten me?*

"My daughter told me what happened to her and that she's been talking to you," Amos said. "I want to know who that man is. You know, and you need to tell me." His voice was threatening, abrupt, and angry.

I stared at the phone, knowing exactly how he felt. Instead, I said: "It's better to turn this over to the police."

"Fuck the police. I'm going to kill the son of a bitch. He doesn't deserve to be on the same planet as my daughter!" His fury was palpable. "I'm thinking a baseball bat will take care of him in about two minutes. Instant justice."

"Mister, uh, Amos, we can best punish him by going to the police. They'll arrest him, and he'll be in prison where he can't hurt your daughter or anyone else." I tried to sound reassuring and logical. "If you go after him, you'll end up in prison, and Harry wouldn't have you to care for her."

"He'd probably be out in a couple years and back to it, don't you think? Is it worth my daughter's revealing what happened to her to the world, if he only serves a few years in prison? And what if he isn't convicted? Then what?"

"If he's not convicted, I wouldn't say a word if you took him out," I told him. "That's what I'd like to do, myself. He hurt my daughter too." *And my son's in prison for twenty years, possibly for longer than Don would be.*

He responded to the bitterness and anger in my tone. "I'm sorry, ma'am. About your daughter," he said more gently. "But that man has to be destroyed."

"He will be if Harry puts him in prison. Men who hurt children are not treated well by other prisoners." *Visions from TV shows about prisons passed through my mind. I had some thoughts about what consequences would be fitting.*

"I'm going to think about this and talk to Harry. It's a big thing for her to get up on the stand and tell the world what he did to her. She and I need to talk about it and make sure that she wants to expose herself like that," Amos said. "We'll call you back when we decide." He hung up.

I was hopeful, almost excited. Maybe, finally, Don would pay. I dialed Sarah to tell her. She, as usual, cautioned me not

212

to get my expectations up. "Honestly, I don't know whether I'd want one of my daughters to be in that position. All their friends knowing, judging her. It could be as traumatic as the original rape, Jana."

After we hung up, I looked down at the huge GED prep book and sighed. For the first time in a couple weeks, I regretted not having wine in the apartment. I put on a pot of coffee, opened the book again, and resumed making notes.

Chapter 48

Thursday, September 20

Amos called while I was in a tutoring session and said he and Harry wanted to meet me on Saturday. But Saturday was visiting day at the prison, and I couldn't miss seeing Kyle. He suggested Friday, instead, at a small Mexican restaurant in Hinton. We agreed, and I hung up.

"Is everything okay, Ms. Lane?" Jewel, the eighth grader I was helping with her geography lesson, looked at me anxiously. She was small and very thin, her light brown hair pulled back into a tight ponytail. She would have been pretty, except for the constant worry evident on her face. Her stepfather had beaten her mother unconscious in front of her, and when she'd tried to stop him, he'd backhanded her. She bore a scar on her forehead from hitting a table when she'd flown across the room. It wasn't surprising that she was struggling in school.

"It's all fine, Jewel," I said with a smile. "Just making plans to meet some friends tomorrow for dinner." We went back to memorizing the capitals of South America.

Working at the shelter was good for me. It got me out of my apartment for part of three days a week and prevented me from obsessing about LaRissa, Kyle, and the Don situation. But the experiences of these women and their children broke my heart. If I worked here long enough, I wondered if I'd ever be able to trust any man again. Not that it was likely that I would anyway.

I 'd admitted to Louise that I had experience writing grants and groaned silently when her eyes lit up. "There's a major grant that would give us funds to remodel this place and add two more bedrooms. Would you help us with it?" Given that I wasn't working and had nothing on my schedule other than volunteering at the shelter and visiting Kyle every other Saturday, I'd reluctantly agreed. Though I did remind her that when school started in January, I wouldn't have time for more than tutoring a few times a week. Grant writing is an intensive process, with obscure and unique requirements for every application and tight deadlines.

After Jewel, I had one more tutoring session on today's schedule. Angela had dropped out of high school after getting pregnant at sixteen. Her mother had kicked her out of the house after the baby was born, and Angela had bounced around Hinton, sleeping on friends' couches for months before finally getting a job cleaning motel rooms. The motel manager had wooed her and convinced her that moving in with him would be a nice, stable arrangement. She'd been happy there until she discovered he was selling opioids on the side. She threatened to turn him in, and the beating he'd given her put her in the hospital. He'd fled the city, DCS had placed her baby with its grandmother, and Angela was here, trying to put her life back together. She was working hard to prepare for the GED, but it was evident that studying, focusing, didn't come naturally to her. But at least she showed up regularly, unlike the two other women Louise had told me needed GED tutoring.

I was exhausted when I got home. A peanut butter and jelly sandwich and store-bought coleslaw were all I could eat for dinner, and then the grant loomed large. I couldn't face it right away, so I took a brisk walk through the October sunset. It helped a little, but not much. I sank into a chair at the kitchen table, powered up the computer, and spent the next three hours banging the narrative out. After spellchecking and reviewing what I'd written against the requirements, I went to bed. My last thought before falling asleep was *Tomorrow we can finally put Don in handcuffs.*

Chapter 49

Friday evening, September 21

Harry's father was a big man—well over six feet tall, with a long red beard streaked with gray. He wore overalls and a flannel shirt, and his hand, when he shook mine, was rough and callused. Harry was seated, looking like she was trying to disappear into the corner of the booth at the Mexican restaurant. From her voice, I had envisioned her as slight, light-haired, and very young-looking. Instead, she appeared older than her age and robust. She had short curly red hair and deep green eyes. Her face showed worry and fear. That was the only aspect of her I had gotten right.

"Hello, Harry," I said, extending my hand. She reached out and put her hand in mine briefly, then leaned against her father. "I'm glad you decided to meet me." I glanced at Amos. "And I'm happy you told your father." I sat down across from them.

"We haven't decided what we're willing to do, ma'am," he said. "No last names for now. If we don't decide to press charges against this son of a bitch, I don't want you tracking us down." He spoke softly, looking around to be sure there were no other customers close enough to overhear.

"I understand," I said. "My interest is in making sure this man doesn't hurt any more girls. He molested and terrorized my daughter and tried to victimize the daughter of our next-door neighbors. I went to the police, but they said they couldn't do anything without a witness who would testify against him."

"Why not your daughter?" Amos asked, staring at me intently. I pressed my lips together, trying to think how to tell him about LaRissa.

Just then, the waitress strolled up and asked for our orders. Amos ordered the chicken enchilada plate for himself and Harry. I couldn't think of food. "Just a glass of tea, please," I told her.

After the waitress left, Amos repeated, "Why not your daughter? You want my daughter to go on the record, expose what happened to her to everyone. Shouldn't your daughter be in the same position?"

I opened my mouth to reply, but nothing came out. I realized my cheeks were wet. I swiped at them with a napkin before answering his question. "My daughter's dead, and it's his fault."

Amos and Harry listened quietly as I related what had happened to LaRissa and to Kyle, how I'd found LaRissa's composition book, and the horrors I'd learned about Don. "I know he's guilty. I know he's done this to other girls and women. He needs to be removed from society because he'll keep doing damage if he remains free. But the police say LaRissa is dead, and what she'd written can't be verified. And my friend's daughter's testimony wouldn't be sufficient to convict him. That's why I posted the flyer. I was hoping someone who'd been hurt by him would come forward." I looked at them. "And someone did."

Amos was the first to speak. "Ma'am, I'm so sorry for what you've been through. You've lost both of your children to this man." He reached out and patted my hand. "I'm going to see that he's punished for what he did to my Harry, one way or the other." The anger in his voice and face was convincing. "But whether Harry testifies or not is up to her. She's the one who would be putting herself out there. And people are hard. Some would turn their back on her, others would whisper about her. The teen years are hard enough without dealing with something like this in public." He turned to Harry, whose eyes were brimming with tears. "Harry, it's up to you. I'll support you either way you decide. You know that. And you don't have to decide right this minute."

Harry buried her face in her hands. She didn't look up as she murmured, "I just don't know."

"It's all right, Harry," I said. "I don't know what I'd tell my own daughter if she were still here. But think about it, please. Think about the next girl that he might attack. You could prevent that." I refrained from saying "Think about your father," though I suspected that if Don wasn't arrested and convicted, Amos would take matters into his own hands. There was a certain satisfaction in imagining Don getting pounded into the ground, but I also envisioned the consequences—Harry's father in prison for assault or murder.

Harry raised her eyes and met mine. "I don't know yet. I'm afraid of testifying, telling all those people what happened to me and how dumb I was. But I also want to put him in prison."

When the food came, Amos asked the waitress to box it up to take out. As she walked away, Amos slid out of the booth. "Okay, then. Harry will think about it. When she decides, I'll call you. Thank you for meeting with us. And telling us your story." He touched my shoulder as Harry slid out and stood beside him. She was taller than I'd thought. She gave me a sad smile and followed her father out of the restaurant. *She's brave,* I thought as I watched them leave. *Please, God, let her be brave enough.*

Chapter 50

Saturday, September 22

The long drive through the mountains to Greyson State Prison gave me time to think. My trips to visit Kyle so far had been devoted to talking about how things were going for him and the changes I was making in my life. He did know that his father and I had separated and divorced. I'd reassured him that it wasn't because of him. But I hadn't told him about Don's role in this whole disaster or what I was doing to seek justice for LaRissa and for him. I wasn't sure if I should. Sarah had advised against it—at least until something developed that ensured Don would be arrested and prosecuted.

"You don't know how he would react to this, Jana," Sarah had said. "It might confirm to him that he was flawed somehow, since he has the genes of a father who could do something like that. And it could make him feel even more guilty about LaRissa's death—like he should have been protecting her, not judging her and being angry at her behavior. Maybe you should talk to a professional before you decide to tell Kyle what's going on."

I'd decided not to talk to Kyle about the situation unless Harry went to the police and Don was arrested. If that happened, Kyle might read about it in the newspaper; he'd asked me to have the local paper sent to him at the prison. My decision changed fifty miles outside the prison gates when my cell phone chimed. The caller ID screen read Restricted, and I knew it was Harry or her father. I pulled over to the side of the road.

"Hello."

"This is Harry."

"Harry," I said, holding my breath.

"I'm going to go to the police, and I'll testify," she said, her voice strong and determined.

"Does your father agree with you?"

"Yes, he does," Harry said. "I made the decision, though. You're right. We shouldn't let any other girl experience what I did. And I can stop him. I *will* stop him," she asserted, her voice rising.

"Thank you, Harry. You have no idea how proud I am of you, and how grateful." I whispered. "Thank you."

"What do we do next? My dad's here. Talk to him."

"Ma'am? This is Amos—Amos Lynch. It's time for last names. But I don't want, yet, to know your ex-husband's name. Because I might be tempted to find him," he said grimly. "What are the next steps?"

"I understand," I replied. "I dropped my husband's last name when I divorced him. Jana Lane is my name. As far as next steps, Detective Alphonse Simmons is with the county sheriff's office in Fairview. I've talked to him. I also told him I'd let him know if anyone got in touch with me through the flyers. Are you willing to text me your phone number and address? He will probably want to talk to you directly to schedule."

"I'll do that right away." His voice dropped. "Harry's gone to the kitchen. I do want to thank you. I knew something was going on with Harry. She had become quiet and withdrawn, but she always said nothing was wrong. Now I can help her. Maybe find a good therapist for her. I've been reading up on this and . . . well, there can be bad things after a girl goes through something like this."

"That's a very good idea, Amos. I'm glad she has you to help her through all this," I replied. "Please tell her again for me that I appreciate her courage, and I'll be there for her every step of the way."

We hung up. A few seconds later, my cell phone chimed with the text with address and phone number. I stored them in my contacts list, then called Detective Simmons. His voicemail invited me to leave a message, and I did. Then I texted Sarah before I drove on. She deserved to hear the good news too.

220

Kyle was limping when the corrections officer brought him into the visiting area. But he smiled when he saw me sitting at a table in the far corner of the room.

"What happened—" I started.

"What's wrong—" Kyle said.

"You first," I said. "What happened? Why are you limping?"

Kyle laughed. "Just a basketball injury. There's a bunch of guys who play during outside time. I joined in and proved that I haven't gotten any better since eighth grade. Twisted my ankle." He pulled his pants leg up a few inches to show me the elastic bandage around his ankle. "Now you tell me what's up. You looked worried when I came in."

I wasn't sure how to begin. Kyle had to know about his father. It might be in the newspaper next week, and it wasn't right for him to learn about it that way. I wanted to soften it, make it more palatable, for his sake. But there wasn't any way to do that. I reached out for his hand. He pulled it back.

"No touching, remember. What's going on?"

"Kyle, it's about your father," I said.

"Is he sick?"

"No. Well, maybe. Kyle, your dad is probably going to be arrested for raping a young girl," I blurted out.

Kyle's mouth dropped open. "What? That's crazy. He wouldn't. I mean, I know he's always been a ..." He shook his head. "I never told you this, but I caught him one time with some woman. In your bedroom. But a young girl? How young?"

"She was thirteen at the time. I've talked to her. Her story is credible, Kyle," I said. "She's going to talk to the police, and they'll probably arrest him. I wanted you to know in case it made it to the newspaper." *In my bed? He fucked someone in my bed? And Kyle caught him?* I clasped my hands tight enough that my fingers turned white. I fought down my rage, though, because today was about Kyle and helping him through this. "I'm sorry you saw something like that," I said. "It must have upset you."

"It did. He knew I saw him, but he never mentioned it. I slammed the door and left the house. Mostly, I didn't want you to know." He was shaking his head. "I can't believe this."

He grimaced. "I know he was hard on me, but he's my father. Thirteen? How could he do that?"

"I don't know. I really don't. He must be mentally ill," I responded.

Kyle stared at the wall behind me. I didn't know what he was thinking and waited.

"Oh, my God!" The words burst from his mouth. "They'll send him to prison, won't they?"

I nodded. "If he's convicted, most likely."

His eyes darted frantically around the room. "What if they send him here? I know what these people think about pedophiles. What if they kill him for what he did? What if they think I'm one too?"

My heart was breaking. It wasn't enough that he was going to spend years in prison for a situation Don had caused. Now, even there, Kyle could face blowback because of Don. I'd been relieved that the violent depictions of prison life I'd seen on TV didn't seem to have been Kyle's reality, at least so far. But now?

"I'll talk to the prosecutor, the judge, everyone," I said quickly. "I'll do everything to make sure your father is sent somewhere else." I didn't know whether I could influence that decision, but I would try.

Kyle slumped in his chair, defeated. "I know you will, Mom. I know you'll try. But that's not how things work around here." He stared bleakly at me for a minute. "I can't talk more right now." He stood up and motioned to the corrections officer near the door. "I love you, Mom, and I'm sorry our family is so screwed up. You don't deserve this." He walked toward the exit without looking back.

It took several minutes for me to compose myself and get up to leave. Kyle's reaction had been worse than I'd hoped. But how could it not be? I'd been worried that Kyle might internalize his father's sins and begin to believe that he was genetically condemned to commit similar evil. But I hadn't considered practicality. What if Don did end up at Greyson? What would it mean for Kyle's welfare if it was known that his father had raped a young girl? A dark thought passed through my mind: Should I . . . would I . . . try to convince Harry and Amos to not talk to Simmons? Would I be willing to leave Don free to prey on others, if it meant protecting my son?

Chapter 51

After a sleepless night, tormented by thoughts of Kyle being attacked by large men in orange jumpsuits, I got up Sunday morning and made a list of pros and cons of my alternatives. It was a short list.

Alternative one was to proceed with pursuing justice for LaRissa, Harry, Bridget, and the unknown number of other girls Don had hurt. The pros were obvious: Don wouldn't be able to harm anyone else, at least for the time he was in prison, and he'd be on the sex offender registry, which might reduce his ability to find future victims. The con? Kyle would be at risk.

Alternative two was to convince Harry and her father that pressing charges would have detrimental effects on Harry's life and they should reconsider. The cons to this one were clear: Don would be free to continue harming girls, Harry would live her life in fear and possibly guilt for not coming forward, and Harry's father might go after Don. The latter would be okay with me, except for the fact that Harry would lose her father. The only pro was that Kyle would be protected from potential harm from other inmates. Of course, that wasn't guaranteed, both because Don might eventually be found out and prosecuted and because there's always the possibility for violence in prison.

The answer to my indecision was obvious. I needed to pursue justice for LaRissa, even if there were repercussions for Kyle. I put down the pen and picked up my phone. Sarah answered on the first ring.

"Hey, I expected to hear from you yesterday," Sarah said. "How's Kyle doing? Did you tell him?"

"I sort of told him," I said. "Just that his dad was probably going to be arrested for rape of a thirteen-year-old. And that I wanted him to know before he read it in the newspaper. But I didn't say anything about LaRissa or Bridget."

"Yeah, I understand. He doesn't need to feel even worse than he does about LaRissa."

"That's what I thought. What happened with LaRissa and Bridget won't need to come out in a trial. His attack on Harry should be enough to put him in prison. At least, I hope. But I need to get your advice about something. Kyle's reaction to the news wasn't what I was expecting. He was upset, of course. But he was mainly worried that if his father went to prison, he'd be at Greyson. And there could be implications for how other prisoners viewed Kyle. Son of a pedophile?"

Sarah sucked in a breath. "Whew. Yes, I can see that. Kyle may be right to worry about guilt by association."

"He seems to be adjusting to prison all right. He talks about things he enjoys doing and is looking forward to taking college classes. Right now, things are better than I expected," I said. "But what if Don ends up there? The pedophile label is bad enough, but what if Don . . . I don't know . . . bullies Kyle? Tells other inmates that Kyle was always a loser? Kyle doesn't need that." I stopped to organize my thoughts. "Sarah, on the way back, I was almost thinking of trying to dissuade Harry from coming forward, to protect Kyle," I blurted the words out.

Sarah was silent.

"I know that's wrong. I can't do it. But how can I protect Kyle?" I was begging her for a solution, an idea, something, anything I could do to help my son.

"Jana, I don't know the answer," Sarah finally said. "Can you talk to the prosecutor? The judge? Whoever makes the decision about where a convict goes for prison? You need to find out and then do what you can to convince them that Don shouldn't be placed with Kyle."

"Maybe that will work," I said, doubtfully. "I'll talk to Detective Simmons and get his advice."

"Remember, Don first has to be arrested, then tried, and then sentenced. That all takes time. You're persistent, you can go up whatever chains there are to persuade someone to send Don elsewhere," Sarah reassured me. "I have faith in you. And if there's anything I can do, I'll do it. Changing topics, have you heard back from your detective?"

"Not yet, but it's Sunday. I'll hear from him tomorrow. I hope."

"Well, let me know. If he needs anything from me or Bridget, we'll be there. How're things going at the shelter? I'm thinking of volunteering there during the summer when school's out. Could you ask the director if she needs any help from a home ec teacher?"

We talked a bit longer about the shelter work and hung up so Sarah could get ready for church. The day stretched in front of me, rainy and gray—which eliminated going for a walk or a swim. I had no other friends to call. It's amazing how so many so-called friends disappear when tragedy strikes, especially double or triple tragedy. Talking to my mother wouldn't help either. She would criticize me or do her impression of a solicitous mother, neither of which would make anything better. There wasn't anything on TV that looked good, and I'd already read the two books I'd checked out of the Hinton Public Library— which was closed on Sunday.

There was nothing left but to lug out the abnormal psychology text and start reading again. *At least I'm getting a head start on all the twenty-two-year-olds who'll be in class with me.* It was interesting but not very informative on issues I was particularly focused on. It did make me think, though. What did I really want to do with a psychology degree? I put the book down. Where did I imagine I would be in five years?

I closed my eyes and visualized myself sitting with a young girl who looked like LaRissa—listening to her pain and confusion, leading her to understanding. It wasn't her fault, terrible things happen, and they're not due to anything a person did to deserve them, she was a random victim, the evil that was done to her was solely the fault of a mentally sick person and she'd been an opportune victim. I'd tell her to think of what happened to her as an automobile accident caused by someone who was driving while drunk. Her being hit by the car was a random occurrence; she wasn't at fault for being in the crosswalk. But she could legitimately blame the driver for his decision to get behind the wheel—and maybe blame society for not sufficiently cracking down on drunken driving.

Would this be the right approach? I wasn't sure. That's why I had enrolled in the master's degree program—to learn the best therapeutic avenues to improve the outcomes for children and young women who had been harmed by sexual assault. Like LaRissa.

I had a mission, I realized—one that would take time and hard work, but I would do it. I sat up and opened my eyes, resolving to talk to Louise about it at the Hope Center next week.

Chapter 52

Monday, September 24

Harry's father called a little after noon. I'd slept well and was on my way to the Greek hole-in-the-wall restaurant to buy a gyro.

"Jana, your detective called me just now. I told him what this was about, and he asked us to come to see him this evening. Can you meet us at the sheriff's office in Fairview at five-thirty?"

"Absolutely," I said. "Did you tell him I'd be there?"

"Yup. He didn't sound thrilled about it but said it was up to me."

"Good, I'll see you there." I hung up and practically skipped the half-block to the restaurant. Back at the apartment complex, I decided to sit out by the pool, enjoy the seventy-degree day, eat my gyro, and read more psychology.

I was immersed in the chapter on personality disorders when Eddie loomed over me. He was carrying a bottle of water and two bags of corn chips.

"Hi, Mrs. S. I'm on lunch break. Can I join you?" He plunked down in a chair next to me without waiting for a response.

"Hi, Eddie. It's Ms. Lane now, but you can call me Jana. How're you doing?" He'd slimmed down over the past couple months and was wearing black jeans and a loose red T-shirt with an incomprehensible slogan on it. His blond hair was cut short—better than the straggly man-bun he'd had when I moved in.

"Pretty good," he said, smiling. "I got into Hinton College for the January semester. I'll be taking a full course load and working as a computer programmer part time."

"Wonderful! Maybe I'll see you there. I'm starting a master's program in psychology and counseling in January. What are you going to be studying?"

"Computer science." He took a sip of the water bottle and pulled open the bag of chips.

"Good for you. Kyle's hoping to take a course in coding."

Eddie nodded. "Dope! I got a letter from him last week, but he didn't mention that." He gazed off in space for a moment. "I'm glad he's going to be able to do that. It must be boring there. He said in the letter that he was on kitchen clean-up duty for about four hours a day. Besides that, there wasn't much to do but read." His eyes lit up. "But he is reading. Just finished the Lord of the Rings trilogy and asked me for suggestions on what to read next."

"Do you write to him often?" I asked. I was curious. Kyle hadn't mentioned keeping in touch with friends outside.

"Yeah, about once a week after you gave me his address. Bob over at Final Quest asked some of the other regulars to write to Kyle every week too. He said it's important for Kyle to know he still has friends."

I love Bob, I thought. *I'll have to write him a note, thanking him.* "And Kyle writes back?"

"He does. He's a pretty good writer too. Did you know he's writing stories? Fantasy in the two he sent me. I told him he should send them to *Fantasy Magazine* to see if they'll publish them."

I was startled by Eddie's revelation. Kyle had hated writing papers for school and hadn't ever expressed an interest in writing fiction. "No, he hasn't mentioned it. What's *Fantasy Magazine*?"

"It's a digital magazine. They have a podcast too. You should check it out!" He fished around in the bottom of his second bag of chips, licked his fingers, and stood up. "Well, lunch break's over. I better get back. Nice to see you and say hi to Kyle for me when you see him. We do miss him at the Quest." He gave me the Vulcan salute and hurried off.

I was bemused by what I'd learned from our brief conversation, but grateful that Kyle had friends and to know he was reading and writing. Maybe I could donate books to the prison library. Abnormal psychology beckoned me back. I picked up the book and began reading about personality disorders.

Amos and Harry were sitting on a bench outside the sheriff's office when I arrived at five twenty. I waved and walked over to them. Harry was jiggling a foot and wide-eyed. Amos was somber. I sat down beside Harry and took her hand.

"Are you nervous? Of course, you are," I said to Harry. "It'll be fine. Detective Simmons is a kind man. He'll ask you questions and listen to you. Just answer the best you can."

Harry looked at me. "I know I need to do this, but I really am scared. What if he doesn't believe me? Or, like he told you, there has to be more evidence before he can do anything." Her hand convulsively squeezed mine. "Can my dad and you be with me when I talk to him?"

Amos stood up. "I damn well will be with you, Harry. Don't you worry about that. This prick has to be stopped, and this is the legal way to do it. If people like you don't come forward, he'll just go on doing what he did to you. It's time. Let's go in." The large, red-bearded man in overalls looked more like a biker than the gentle father I knew him to be.

Inside the sheriff's office, we waited while the front desk person rang Detective Simmons. He came shuffling out of the hall to the left and motioned for us to follow him. The room he led us to was small, with a square table and four chairs. There was a camera above the door and a sign announcing that video and audio recording might take place. The small sign on the door said it was a conference room. I thought as we entered that it didn't seem any different from an interrogation room.

"Thanks for coming in," Simmons said after introductions were made. "Ma'am, it would probably be best if you waited in the lobby. I know your concerns, but Ms. Lynch needs to tell me what happened in her own words."

"We'd like her to sit in," Amos said. "How about if I pull a chair back to the wall and she can listen?" Amos glanced at me and added, "Just listen, okay? Not talk."

"I'm sorry, but no," the detective said. "Please wait in the lobby. I promise we can all talk after Ms. Lynch and I are done, to the extent that she is agreeable."

"Whatever you think best," I said. "I don't want to risk compromising your investigation." I left the room and closed the door. In the lobby, I waited on the hard wooden bench. People came and went, some in handcuffs, others in uniforms, and some just looked like they were having a normal day in a normal office. It wasn't as interesting as I might have envisioned a sheriff's office.

It was over an hour before Simmons appeared at the end of the hallway and invited me back to the conference room. Harry's face was streaked with tears, and her father had an arm around her.

"Harry's experience was horrific," Simmons said abruptly. "It also is credible, especially since she identified a tattoo on the leg of the perpetrator. I assume you can confirm that the tattoo exists?" I nodded. "I'll take this to the district attorney's office and lay out what the evidence is. I want to caution you all that there are some complications." He looked at me. "One is that you posted your husband's picture all over Fairview and Hinton. A defense attorney might argue that Harry saw the picture and the words on it and mistakenly identified it as of the man who raped her. Which means when ... if ... Harry identifies him in a lineup, she might be identifying the man she saw in the picture rather than her actual assailant. In addition, her contact with you might let a defense lawyer argue that you described the tattoo to her." He frowned. "It would have been better if Harry had come to the police when it happened and described the man who attacked her, including the tattoo. Then the defense would have less of an argument—even with the posters."

We were all silent for a few moments. Amos's face was getting red, and his fists were clenched. "Are you saying the district attorney might not take the case?" The words burst out of him, loud and angry.

"I'm saying that's a possibility. If there was DNA evidence or if you'd told anyone else about the attack when it happened, the case would be stronger," Simmons said.

Harry held up a hand. She was shaking. "There might be DNA evidence," she whispered.

Simmons swung around and looked at her. "What do you mean?"

"I tore off my clothes after I finally got home and took a shower," Harry said, her eyes downcast. "I threw the clothes in a corner of my closet, behind some boxes, and I haven't touched them since then. I couldn't. They would remind me . . . bring the whole thing back." She slumped back in her chair and started crying again.

Detective Simmons turned to Amos. "Do you give permission for us to go to your house and retrieve those items?"

"Yes," Amos said. "Of course." He pulled Harry close to him and hugged her. He murmured something and she nodded. "Harry gives permission too."

"All right. I'll need your keys and a description of which room is Harry's. It'll take a couple hours to do this. If you want, you can go get some dinner . . . there's a McDonald's and a couple restaurants just down the road . . . then come back. We'll need you to confirm that the clothes we find are the ones you were wearing when you were assaulted, Harry. Once you do that, I can send the clothes to the state lab for DNA testing." Harry nodded again, not looking up from where she'd buried her face in her father's shoulder.

Detective Simmons hurried out, and I sat quietly. Harry finally sat up straight. "I'm not hungry, but you and my dad can go if you want."

"How about if I go to McDonald's and bring something back?" I asked. "Maybe just burgers and fries?"

"That sounds good," Amos said. "I'll stay here with Harry. But I think we could use some food since it sounds like we'll be here awhile. There's a soda machine in the lobby. I'll get the drinks."

I nodded and left the conference room. By the time I returned, Harry had washed her face and appeared more relaxed. She ate every bite of her order, and half of my french fries.

Over the next hour and a half, I learned a lot about Harry and her father. Harry was a sophomore in high school, played the tuba in the marching band, and was an outstanding soccer player. She wanted to go to college and study to become a phys ed teacher. Amos was a forklift diesel mechanic. He'd gone to college for two years but then married Harry's mother and dropped out to support his family. He, Harry's mother, and Harry had been close and enjoyed going to movies, watching the Miss America pageant to make fun of the contestants, and every year lavishly decorating the inside and outside of their house for Halloween, Thanksgiving, and Christmas. Harry laughed as she described the last time they'd decorated for Halloween as a family of three—with Peanuts characters on the lawn and the Great Pumpkin, held up with wires, rising from their garden patch. Harry and her father had recreated that scene each year since, because it had been her mother's favorite.

I couldn't help but think about my family, which I'd always thought of as happy but wasn't. *This is what a happy family looks like. No underlying darkness. Tragedy, yes, but then resilience and love.*

Detective Simmons came back, escorted by a deputy carrying an evidence bag. He put on gloves, then sat down at the table and slowly took out jeans, a sweater, shoes and socks, a bra, and a pair of white cotton panties. He turned on the video recorder, then held up each item. "Ms. Lynch . . . Harry . . . do you recognize these clothing items?"

"I do," Harry replied.

"When did you last wear them?"

"The day I was raped," she said, her voice steady, then added the date and time of the rape had occurred.

"Thank you." Simmons turned off the recorder. "I'll send these off to the state lab. That may take several weeks, but I'll ask for expedited analysis." He shrugged. "Sometimes that works, sometimes it doesn't. But as soon as I get the answer, I'll call you."

"Will it be enough if there's DNA?" Amos' worry was evident.

"If the DNA matches the suspect's, yes. We have his DNA already from when LaRissa died, Jana. But all of this will take time."

"So, he'll be free to attack other girls for months?" Amos growled.

"We'll identify him as a person of interest, Mr. Lynch. We'll bring him in and interrogate him about his whereabouts on the day Harry was attacked. He'll know he's in trouble and, I hope, that'll keep him from doing anything criminal for the time being."

"Can't you have him watched?"

"I wish we could. Not enough resources, but I'll have our deputies cruise by his residence a couple times a day." Simmons held up his hands. "Best I can do, but I understand your concerns. I have them too."

We didn't leave the sheriff's office until half past ten. I hugged Harry and told her I was proud of her. "We'll get him, Harry. And it'll be because you're brave enough to come forward."

She hugged me back and got in the car with her father. I watched them drive off and walked to my vehicle. As I turned the ignition key, Detective Simmons knocked on the window.

I lowered the window. "Detective, thank you for your help," I said. "Harry said you were kind with her."

"She broke my heart, ma'am. And I'm determined to get justice for her," Simmons said. "And for your daughter." He cleared his throat. "Ah, I wanted you to know that I haven't been ignoring your story, even though there was nothing legal I could do for you or for your neighbor's daughter. I've been keeping an eye on your ex-husband. He's living in an apartment on Pine Street, just outside the city limits, since he separated from the girl he was with," he smiled. "Your flyers put the kibosh on that relationship. Anyway, we'll be bringing him in in the next couple days to answer some questions. I know he attacked you and got off with probation, but you be careful. He may come after you after we talk to him. I'd recommend you stay away from Fairview for the time being."

I promised him I would do that and drove off. It had been a long day, and I was exhausted. My dreams that night were of LaRissa, happy and smiling at me.

Chapter 53

Thursday, September 27

L ouise was busy doing entry paperwork for two new residents of the Hope Center on Wednesday. I'd left a note on her desk asking to meet with her, and we finally had time to talk Thursday afternoon. Over the past few days, I'd given thought to the project that I wanted to present to her. I'd made a power point, but I'd also printed it out to present to her in a three-ring binder.

Louise settled into her desk chair and leaned back. She ran her fingers through her hair, further disarranging it, and sighed. "What a week. I'm going to need you to work with Suzy, our newest resident. She dropped out of high school senior year and has been working as a motel maid, and she can't support her two kids on what she makes. Her husband beat her up when she complained that he'd run up several thousand dollars on credit cards he took out in her name. She has bruises and a fractured wrist, but she'll heal. I don't know about the kids. They seem frightened and withdrawn. She seems bright, so you may be able to get her ready for the GED in just a few sessions." She sighed again. "I hope. I don't suppose you have any experience teaching keyboarding?"

I smiled. "I keyboard, but no. No experience teaching it. I could give her some tips but, if she has a fractured wrist, typing may be difficult until it's healed."

Louise sat up and leaned forward. "Okay, do what you can. What did you need to talk to me about?" She stared me, looking apprehensive. "You're not going to tell me you need to quit, are you? Please tell me that's not what you want to talk about."

"No, no," I said, laughing. "I really like volunteering here, and it looks like I'll be able to continue after school starts in January if I can move some sessions to work around my classes."

"Good," Louise said. "You're doing good work, and the ladies like you. So, what's the topic?"

"You know I'm going back to school to get a degree in psychology and counseling, but you don't know the reason." I went on to tell her my sad story—daughter dead, son in prison, husband discovered to have been sexually abusing my daughter, and how the sexual abuse had led to her death. I spoke in a quiet voice, not making eye contact.

When I finished, I looked up. Louise was watching me with the saddest, most compassionate expression I'd ever seen. In that moment, I wished she was my mother so I could collapse against her bosom and cry.

"I'm so sorry, Jana. I can't even imagine how that must have affected you. Some women would become bitter and hardened by what's happened, but you chose to help these unfortunate women. I'm so grateful." Louise rose from her desk chair and came around to sit next to me. "But I still don't know what you want to do that involves me and the Hope Center."

I bent down and retrieved the binder from beside my chair. "I'm hoping that you'll want to expand your mission." I handed the binder to her. "There's a lot known about the effects of sexual abuse on the lives of child and teen victims." I began turning pages. "Nearly one in four girls experience sexual abuse in this country, and it affects all aspects of their lives from then on. They're more likely to attempt suicide, experience mental and physical health problems, abuse alcohol and drugs, run away from home, become delinquent, and become sexually active at an earlier age. And they are less likely to finish high school or go to college." I ran my fingers down the page listing the negative outcomes. "This is partly because there's not a lot known about the most effective ways to help child survivors of sexual abuse. I'm early in my research, but so far I'm not finding evidence on what works best to promote positive outcomes for these children."

Louise nodded. "I'm aware of the negative outcomes. Many of the women who show up at our door were sexually abused when they were young. It seems related to the choices they make in male partners—who are prone to physically abusing them."

"Right! If we could help them earlier, soon after the initial sexual abuse, we might be able to shift those outcomes!"

"But, Jana, we don't have sufficient resources to help all the women who come to us right now. You're suggesting we expand our mission to include young victims of sexual abuse, if I'm following you. That would require possibly another building, money for food, clothing, transportation, and more. And counselors—experienced ones. Then, too, would the victims live here? That would involve guardianship or parental approval." Louise was shaking her head. "I hear you about the need. But this would be a major expansion, and I don't see how it would be possible."

I turned two more pages in the binder. "It could be possible, Louise. Especially if you're willing to view it as a long-term project. There are mental health grant opportunities—some for brick and mortar, some for staff and services." I read off a list of government agencies and foundations that provide funding for programs that address mental health needs of children and adolescents. "We could start small—maybe get a grant initially to fund one or two counselors who are trained to work with victims of child sexual abuse. You probably have young mothers and children here already who need those services."

"I'm sure we do. I know we do. But grant funding? They fund a couple years and then the money goes away."

"In the meantime, we market the program—to child welfare agencies, churches, schools, hospitals, other institutions that may support the program. We partner with those agencies and get referrals and financial assistance!"

Louise frowned. "And how do we do that? I have enough trouble keeping this shelter going from year to year. We have two employees—me and my assistant—and a half-dozen volunteers. We're stretched to the limit meeting the needs of the women and children we help."

"I'll look for and write the grant applications, Louise. That's something I'm good at. I brought in over $5 million in three years at the clinic. And we can recruit volunteers to help us develop and implement a marketing plan to bring in community partners."

I could see Louise was beginning to buy in. We talked for another hour, and I left the binder with her. It contained a dozen pages describing the incremental approach to the development of a resource center for child victims of sexual abuse, a step-by-step plan—one that I, when my master's degree and counseling internship were completed, could play a significant role in.

Louise had promised to read it and think about it. That was all I had hoped to accomplish. I was elated as I drove home. LaRissa wouldn't have died in vain if her death could result in providing help, support, and services to other girls who were struggling with the aftermath of abuse.

Chapter 54

My life settled into a routine. Three half-days a week at the Hope Center, visiting Kyle every other Saturday, studying, and—a recent activity—daily exercise. The apartment complex fitness center had a personal trainer who planned a tailored exercise program and a weekly support session for only $100 a month. Over the past eight months, with all that had happened, I'd gained fifteen pounds. That was on top of the twenty extra pounds I'd been carrying since LaRissa was born. So now, every morning, I spent a half hour or more at the fitness center. It had only been two weeks, but I'd lost three pounds and was already feeling more fit.

I was in the middle of a cardio session with the personal trainer when my cell phone rang. I let it go to voicemail and waited till I'd finished, showered, and dressed to check it. Detective Simmons had left a voicemail that the DNA lab had completed the analysis of the sample from Harry's clothing against Don's DNA and it was a match. "I wanted you to know because your ex-husband may begin to feel we're closing in and might blame you. Be careful. Don't come to Fairview. It'll still be a couple weeks before we can present the findings to the grand jury and get an indictment. Once that happens, we can arrest him. Call me if you have any questions or if you hear from or encounter him."

Progress was being made, but I was frustrated with the snail's pace. It had been months since I'd first suspected Don and met with Simmons. And six weeks since Harry had first called in response to the flyer. And now it might be at least another two weeks before he was arrested. *How many more girls has he already attacked over the past eight months? How many may he assault somehow in the next month?* Detective Simmons had said his deputies were keeping an eye on Don and that he would be brought in for questioning. I hoped that would be enough to deter him from new offenses. But I worried.

It was one of my Hope Center afternoons, and I headed there after a light lunch of avocado toast and V8. Louise had been right when she'd told me that the new client, Suzy, was bright. She was my last tutee of the day. I liked her. She was only nineteen years old but had two children, ages one and two-and-a-half. Suzy wore black-framed glasses that highlighted her pale complexion and short blonde hair. She was plain, with a thin mouth and a nose that looked as though it had been broken and not set properly. Her skin was pocked with acne scars. Despite her timid behavior, she was determined to get her GED.

"I need to do this to make a better life for my kids," she told me, her voice soft. "And I need to do it for me. I don't ever want to be a punching bag for some man again."

Louise hadn't told me much about her background or the circumstances that had brought her to the Hope Center. Client confidentiality was a strong principle at the center. But the fading bruises around her neck and the cast on her wrist were obvious.

And Louise had been correct in assessing her as intelligent. She had zoomed through the sessions we'd already had and was ready to start taking practice GED exams. I was amazed when she finished the first practice test in twenty minutes and scored 100 percent.

"Wow! A perfect score, Suzy. Do you want to try another?"

"Sure, Jana. That one was easy," Suzy said, flushing. "Maybe the next one will be harder."

It wasn't. She finished in even less time and, again, had a perfect score. I shook my head, smiling. "I think you're ready to take the GED social sciences and language arts tests. But let's do the other two practice tests. Math and science might be harder for you."

"Maybe," Suzy said. "But I always did well in math and science. I thought I might want to be an engineer when I was a little girl." She laughed. "Strange choice for a girl, but I used to help my dad build and fix things. He was good at working with his hands on engines and anything with electrical systems. Before he died." A sad expression passed over her face, but she recovered quickly. "Okay, let's do the other two tests and see if I remember what I learned in high school."

I wanted to ask about her father. When he'd died, how he died, and what happened to her after that. I suspected his death had been a factor in how she had ended up with two tiny children, battered, and hiding out in a shelter at age nineteen. But I didn't. Louise had firm rules about volunteers prying into clients' lives. "Okay, math first."

An hour later, Suzy had finished the last two tests with perfect scores. I congratulated her and told her I'd arrange a time for her to take the online version of the GED tests that the state offered. "Hope Center can cover the costs, so you don't have to worry about that," I told her.

"Thank you, Jana. I'm excited to get my GED," Suzy said, a wide grin on her face. "Just tell me when, and I'll be there."

I grinned back. "You're a superstar! You should think about college. I'll be happy to help you with preparing for the ACT test and with applications."

Her face fell. "I wish. But with two kids to feed, I won't be able to. I'm just happy that maybe I can get a better job that pays more once I have my GED." She thanked me again and went upstairs to relieve the volunteer who was babysitting.

Louise saw I was free and stuck her head in the conference room. "I know you have another tutoring session now but come see me before you go home."

I nodded and waved my next student into the room. Two hours later, after a less successful session of tutoring, I grabbed my coat and purse and went to Louise's office.

She was on the phone arguing with a food supplier about the quality of the last shipment. When she finally hung up, she looked at me. "Why do people think we should be grateful for rotten fruit and flour with weevils?" She rubbed her temples with both hands, then smiled. "But that's not what I called you in for. I discussed your proposal with our board. Your step-by-step, incremental approach impressed them. They're willing to have us go forward with the first step you laid out."

"Woo-hoo!" I shouted, leaping out of my chair. "That's finding funding for at least one social worker who's worked with children who've been sexually abused?"

"That's the step," she agreed. "They said if we can get that funding, they're willing to decide on further steps after they've had a year to assess the need and effectiveness of a youth sexual abuse treatment program. It will have to be an outpatient arrangement, though. The board feels that we shouldn't divert resources from our primary mission."

I sat down. "You may have clients already here that may need this type of service. And I can reach out to child welfare and the sheriff's office and ask for referrals. I'm sure we can find enough clients to keep one social worker busy full time."

"One of our board members also volunteered to help with the outreach and recruitment. Maisie Diller has lots of contacts everywhere in the county," Louise said. "I'll put you together with her when the time comes. But it's up to you to get the funding first. Nothing happens until we have an award."

"I know," I said. "There are two grant announcements coming out soon that I think we have a shot at. I can do most of the writing, but you'll need to give me background information on the center, some statistics on who we serve and our outcomes, and you'll need to do the budget." I was talking rapidly, excited and ready to go.

"Will do. Just let me know when." Louise's phone rang. She glared at it, smiled at me, waved goodbye, and answered.

I threw my coat on and left the Hope Center, smiling. It was only the beginning of the first step, but someday, I was determined, there would be a LaRissa's Hope Center.

Chapter 55

Thursday, November 22

Thanksgiving was a pleasant day with Sarah and her family. It was the first time I'd been in Fairview since Detective Simmons had warned me to stay away. Sarah had insisted, though, and even driven to Hinton to pick me up so my car wouldn't be in her driveway in case Don drove by. It was strange—almost hallucinatory—to be back on the street where I'd lived for twenty years. My house had been painted off-white, and the flower beds lining the walkway had been replaced with bushes. A wave of sadness washed through me as I stared at the house, wondering what happy or unhappy family was now occupying it.

My mood didn't improve as I followed Sarah through her front door. We'd always entered each other's homes through the back doors—kitchen to kitchen. I couldn't remember the last time I'd used the foyer.

Thanksgiving dinner was, of course, a feast. Sarah was a home economics teacher and a creative cook. How could it be otherwise? But I ate little, not tasting the food, as memories of happy times around Sarah's table intruded: LaRissa laughing, excited to be with Sarah's girls. Kyle, the only boy, being teased and enjoying the attention. The warmth and scents of turkey and sage and pumpkin spice brought it all back. I'd been content at those Thanksgivings, I'd loved how fortunate we were to be a close family with dear friends to share the holiday—not knowing, never envisioning, the current world I lived in. Being in the present was hard. I ate politely, complimented Sarah on the meal, thanked her and Bill for inviting me, hugged Bridget, Siobhan, and Mary, and asked Sarah to drive me back to Hinton early.

It was dusk when I hugged Sarah and she drove off. I entered the apartment complex, stopped at the convenience store to buy milk, then headed to my second-floor apartment, keys in hand. There was no one in the courtyard as I started up the stairs, but I heard the scuffling of footsteps behind me as I reached the second-floor landing. Keys in hand, I walked rapidly toward my door. The footsteps behind me accelerated and, as I inserted the key, a heavy hand landed on my shoulder.

"You bitch!"

I could smell alcohol fumes in Don's words. I whirled around and shoved him. "Get out of here!" I screamed, "Help!" and kicked at Don. He grabbed me again and slammed me against the wall. I slung the carton of milk at his head and it clipped his ear—which only infuriated him more.

"You're ruining my life!" he shouted. His hands encircled my throat. Don was tall and at least fifty pounds heavier than I. I tried to pry his fingers loose, but it was futile.

"There's a restraining order," I gasped. His hands tightened, and I could hardly breathe. I smashed my knee into his groin, and he let me go and stared at me, his eyes red and angry. I heard a door open and saw one of my neighbors stick his head out, then duck back in and close the door. I hoped he was calling 9-1-1.

My keys were still in my hand. I pushed one between two fingers and lashed out at Don's face. He ducked, but the point of the key caught his nostril, ripping it and causing a gush of blood. Don backhanded me and took off running as a siren wailed in the distance.

He turned and snarled, "You'll never be safe from me," before he pounded down the stairs.

I sank to my knees, sobbing. My neighbor opened his door again and stood watching me.

"The police are on the way," he said. I nodded. "Do you need anything?" He seemed reluctant to approach me. I shook my head, and he remained stationary, ten feet away, until two

243

police officers ran up the stairs. Then he stepped back into his apartment and quietly closed the door.

The officers ran to me. One bent and helped me up. The other took out a notebook and pen. "Ma'am, are you hurt? Is the person who hurt you still here?" When I shook my head and stood up, he added, "Tell us what happened."

"It was my ex-husband. He attacked me. I have a restraining order, and he's on probation for attacking me before," I said. I leaned against the wall, my legs trembling. "Can we go in my apartment? I need to sit down."

Inside, I collapsed into a chair. One of the officers went to the kitchen and came back with a glass of water. He handed it to me, then stood, waiting. I told them Don's name and asked them to call Detective Simmons at the sheriff's office in Fairview. "He's aware of this situation. He also has my ex's address and said his deputies were keeping an eye on him." I laughed, a bit hysterically. "At least they're supposed to be watching. It's Thanksgiving, though. I suppose even the police want to be home on Thanksgiving."

"I'll see if I can reach him," the first officer—Cummings, according to his nametag—said. He stepped away from us and made a phone call. The other officer asked me to relate what had happened. I did, in detail and with occasional non sequiturs. My mind was roiling, both with fear and anger. When I finished, the officer continued writing for a couple minutes then put his notebook and pen in his jacket pocket.

"Detective Simmons is on his way, ma'am," Officer Cummings said. "He asked us to stay with you in case your ex comes back." He peered at me closely. "We could take you to the ER if you feel you need medical help. Did he hit you anywhere else other than your neck and face?" He nodded at the other officer. "Tom, get the camera from the cruiser. We need to take pictures of those marks."

I rubbed my throat with one hand. It was sore to the touch, but I wasn't having any trouble breathing. "I think I'm okay. We'll just wait here for Detective Simmons."

It was more than a half hour before Simmons arrived. While we waited, the officers took a half dozen pictures of my bruises and a scrape on my hand. Officer Cummings left to talk to my neighbor who'd called 9-1-1.

244

I made a half pot of coffee and offered a cup to the police officers. They declined, and I sat clutching my cup for a few minutes before going into the bathroom to wash my face and brush my hair. The image in the mirror shocked me. The marks on my throat were evolving from red to purplish-blue. *Don really might have killed me if my neighbor hadn't intervened. I should thank him later.*

A light knock on the apartment door announced the arrival of Detective Simmons. He thanked the two officers, and they left. "How are you doing?" He sat on the sofa next to me, looking tired and concerned.

"I'm okay, really. He tried to strangle me. I fought back, but it was my neighbor coming out to see what was going on that scared him off." I pointed to my throat, pulling my sweater down a bit to show him the bruises.

"Well, you won't have to worry about him. He got pulled over for erratic driving just inside the Fairview City limits. The deputy smelled alcohol and arrested him for DWI. He's in the Fairview jail, and he'll stay there awhile. Since he was on probation for his previous assault on you, this will send him to jail for at least six months. If you press charges for this tonight, his sentence might be longer."

"Let me think about it," I said. "Right now, I'm tired and can't figure out what I want to do."

Simmons stood up. "Well, call me if anything else comes up. The grand jury is meeting next week. I've had Don in twice for questioning, so he knows he's under suspicion. I should mention that he's hired a lawyer, James Barrow?" I grimaced. Kyle's lawyer. Simmons went on: "Nothing can move forward till the grand jury meets, but I'm hoping we can charge him next week with the rape. I'll contact you right away if he's released from jail, but I doubt it'll happen for a while."

I thanked him and walked him to the apartment door. After he left, I went around the apartment and checked to be sure all the windows were locked. Then I propped a kitchen chair under the doorknob. I still didn't sleep that night.

Chapter 56

Thursday, November 29

"He's being charged, Jana," Amos said.

My cell phone awakened me at eight fifteen a.m. I'd been studying till the wee hours and slept in. Amos' words sent a wave of adrenalin through my body, and I leaped out of bed.

"The grand jury indicted?"

"Five minutes ago," Amos said. "He asked if Harry could come and identify her rapist in a lineup this afternoon. She wants to do it and get it over with, so we'll be there at four thirty."

"Can I come too? I'd love to be there when she identifies him, and when he's arrested for what he did to her." My heart was beating rapidly. The DNA match and Harry's lineup identification would mean it was over. Don would be charged, arrested, convicted, sent to prison—hopefully for a long time, given Harry's age when he'd raped her—and prevented from harming anyone else.

"Detective Simmons said I could tell you the news, but he asked that you stay away from the process—particularly when Harry's involved. He's worried that the defense lawyer may claim you influenced Harry or gave her cues that would help her identify your ex."

I frowned. "Even with the DNA match? I'd think the match would prove conclusively that Don was her assailant. The lineup identification shouldn't even be necessary."

246

"Same here. But Simmons said we have to think about the trial and how the defense might spin this. You're the ex-wife. They might argue that you're intent on getting revenge because your husband left you for another woman. That you somehow managed to set all this up to frame him." Amos paused for a moment, then went on. "I'm sorry for saying that . . . just repeating what Simmons said. I know you're seeking justice for Harry and your daughter and anyone else your ex hurt." His sympathetic voice quashed the angry words that had formed in my mind.

"Thanks, Amos. Simmons is right. I need to let the system work," I said. "But I hope you'll keep me informed."

"I'll call you tonight and tell you how the lineup went, okay?"

"Thank you. Talk to you then." I ended the call and sank down on my bed. I was happy that it looked like Don would be brought to justice. At the same time, somehow, I was sad. Don being punished didn't change what had happened to Harry and to LaRissa and to Kyle. And to my life. Nothing would change the past—for them or for me.

For a few minutes, I drifted into despair. The creation of a treatment program for sexually abused young people would be a drop in the bucket. Thousands of children and teens were abused—sexually, physically, emotionally—each year. The treatment program I had envisioned might help a few dozen of them. Even if I were able to help hundreds, there would still be so many predators harming new victims—most of them undetected and unstopped. It all felt futile, like something I was trying to do just to make myself feel like I was doing something, anything. Tears leaked from my eyes, and I fell back on the bed and buried my face in the pillow.

An hour later, I got up, took a shower, and got dressed. I made coffee and took it out on my small balcony to sit in the sun. It was one of those beautiful fall days that only occur in the Southwest: a balmy sixty-eight degrees with a light breeze, sunny and restorative. By the time I finished my second cup of coffee, my mood had lifted. My plan for a treatment center might only help a few people, but for those few it could be life-changing. That would be enough to honor LaRissa's memory, knowing that something positive resulted from her tragedy.

A sudden thought caused me to stand up abruptly. *Kyle!* If Don were imprisoned at Greyson, it would affect Kyle. I grabbed my phone and speed-dialed the sheriff's office. Detective Simmons was out of the office, the receptionist said. I left a message, and it was after lunch before he returned my call.

"You can't be here when we have the lineup," Simmons said in response to my "Hello."

"I'm not calling about that. I know I need to stay out of this," I replied. "I'm calling about something else."

"I'm glad you understand," Simmons said. He sounded relieved, like he'd been expecting me to argue with him. "So, what can I help you with today?"

"If Don is convicted, who decides which prison he goes to? Kyle is at Greyson, and he said it would be bad for him if his father was sent there."

"I can see that," Simmons said. "But the decision is made by the Department of Corrections. Greyson is a low-security prison. Your son was probably assigned there due to his age and his lack of prior violent offenses."

"No prior offenses at all," I corrected.

"Yes. Your ex-husband has prior offenses—specifically, his attacks on you. And the crime he'll be tried for is rape of a child. My guess is he'll be assigned to a medium- or high-security prison. I don't think you have anything to worry about, but once he's convicted you might want to talk to the prosecutor about his sentencing recommendation."

A wave of relief swept over me. "You're saying it's unlikely Don would be sent to Greyson? That's good. And will it really be possible for me to talk to the prosecutor?"

"Check with me after the jury comes back. I can explain the situation and ask him to give you a hearing."

"That would be wonderful! Thank you so much," I said. "And not just for this. You've been a support to Harry and her father, throughout everything that's happened. I hope the people you work with know how helpful you are to victims."

Simmons harrumphed and didn't respond immediately. When he did, it was only to say, "Thank you."

After we hung up, I made notes to myself about the conversation. I would be visiting Kyle in a couple days and could finally give him some good news. He was doing well in prison:

reading, exercising, and looking forward to starting college classes in January. But our last two visits had been awkward, as his concerns about his father being assigned to Greyson clouded his positive attitude. Now I could reassure him.

Chapter 57

Tuesday, December 25

Christmas Day and I was still in bed at ten. I'd awakened at six and lay there thinking of past Christmases when Don and I had worked till late at night assembling bicycles and other toys for Kyle and LaRissa to discover when they woke. The wonder on their young faces as children, the smiles and delight at the largesse in their teens were good memories. Don would make pancakes, sausage, and bacon while I cleaned up. Traditions were important to all of us.

This year there was no reason to get up. No tree with sparkling lights, icicles, and hand-made ornaments. Those were all in a box in the storage unit I'd rented. No presents, wrapped or unwrapped, no Christmas carols, nothing to make the day special. Sarah and Bill had invited me to go with them to Disneyland. I'd thanked them but declined the invitation. They and their girls didn't need a melancholy hanger-on to bring down their joy in the day. My mother had also invited me to come to Florida for Christmas week.

"You shouldn't be alone for the holidays," Mom had said. "The condo association has activities planned. We could go caroling and to midnight services, and there's a Christmas Eve party." I turned down her offer, too, despite the plaintive tone to her invitation.

"I need to be here for Kyle, Mom," I explained. "I told him I'd visit him at the prison on the Saturday before Christmas."

"Well, that sounds dreary," she responded. "Can you at least take him some presents?"

"They don't let anyone bring gifts," I said. "But I've put money in his commissary account so he can buy snacks and things. And I ordered several books for him on Amazon. We can send him books by mail, in case you want to give him a gift."

"I'll keep that in mind. Send me the address." We'd hung up after a few more minutes with promises to talk again soon. Conversations with my mother often left me feeling like I'd somehow disappointed her. But over the past year I had become somewhat immune to her criticisms, and she'd become gentler with me. It was a small positive in a bad year.

I finally got out of bed, showered, got dressed, and made coffee. I sat out on the balcony for a half hour and tried to read, but my nerves were on edge. I needed a change of scenery. I picked up my keys and my purse. I wasn't sure where I was going, but I needed to go somewhere, to be moving.

I had a full tank of gas, so I headed east and drove for an hour and a half before stopping at a diner along the highway — it was the first sign of civilization I'd seen for twenty minutes. Inside, Christmas carols were playing and garlands of fake evergreens with red berries hung on the walls. I settled into a booth and looked at the menu. A cheeseburger with bacon and onions and a chocolate malted looked good, though they were a departure from my usual semi-vegetarian and low-calorie fare. The waitress bustled over to take my order. She was thin to the point of emaciation, looked about eighty years old, and had short hair obviously dyed coal black. Her nametag said Maggie.

"Merry Christmas, sweetie," she said in a hoarse voice. "You're only our third customer today. Not much call for us to even be open, but we advertise twenty-four/seven so here I am."

"Not a great way to spend Christmas for you," I said. "I hope you have something planned for later."

She grinned, revealing a gold tooth. "Nah, I volunteered for the shift today. No family left to visit — I've outlived them all. I might as well let the other waitresses enjoy the day. How about you?"

"No family I can visit either. I'm just out for a drive, enjoying the scenery." We looked out the window at the dry, flat, landscape dotted with sagebrush and rocks. In the distance, I could see a major highway overpass.

"Sure thing. Nothin' like a pleasant drive in the country," Maggie said. She raised her pad, pen poised. "What can I get you today?"

I ordered the burger and malt, and they were as good as I expected. I devoured them and was thinking about ordering a piece of peach pie with ice cream when Maggie cruised by and asked if I wanted anything else. The uncomfortable fullness in my midsection overwhelmed my desire for dessert.

"No, thanks. Just the check," I said. I pointed out the window. "What highway is that?"

She laid the check on the table. "That's I-15. Takes you to Vegas, but there's not much else between here and there."

"Thanks," I said. I fumbled in my purse and extracted a twenty and a ten. "Keep the change."

"Well, bless you, honey," Maggie said, pocketing the ten and heading to the cash register with the twenty. "Have a good trip wherever you land. And merry Christmas."

Back in the car, I rolled down the windows and used my cell phone to verify that Interstate 15 went all the way to Las Vegas. It did, and it looked like I could be there by six o'clock. I started the car and pulled out.

I'd been to Vegas twice—once for a wedding and once in college with friends. It was a town of bright lights and twenty-four-hour activity, as I recalled, and it seemed like a fittingly ridiculous place to spend my first Christmas alone.

Traffic was light, so I made it in less than three hours. From twenty miles out, the city glowed on the horizon. Unlike my two previous trips, there were few cars and buses on the road as I entered the city limits. When I'd stopped for gas, I checked my cell phone again for hotels and picked out The Flamingo on South Las Vegas Boulevard. I made the exit from I-15 and followed the cell phone navigation through the surface streets to a parking lot within walking distance of the hotel. Twenty-four dollars and five minutes later I was in the hotel lobby.

The casino was to the right, and the slot machines were ringing and playing music to entice me. Two receptionists were at the front desk. Within five more minutes, I was a registered guest with a "High Roller" rate on a room with a king-size bed and a view of the Ferris wheel. The bellhop offered to take my luggage up to the room, but I didn't have any. I asked him if there was a gift shop and tipped him five dollars for pointing it out to me. If necessary, I could pick up toothpaste and a toothbrush there. I couldn't think of anything else I might need for an overnight stay.

That night I wandered the casino for hours, not playing any of the games or slots. I felt like a space alien studying earthlings. There were old ladies—some with canes, one with a walker—sitting at slot machines, sometimes playing two or three at a time and guarding their spaces. A man in a full *thobe* robe and a *ghutra* head covering was accompanied by two bodyguards. He walked by a roulette table and threw a hundred-dollar bill on the table. One of the bodyguards stopped to observe the play and picked up the winnings. The blackjack and craps tables were the most active. I watched a young couple dressed in matching blue flannel shirts, dirty jeans, and worn Western boots play blackjack for nearly an hour, winning repeatedly— and accepting every free drink brought around by the scantily clad server. His girlfriend kissed him before every play and hugged him after. They should have stopped after ten wins but didn't. When they finally quit, they had lost all they'd won. The woman was crying, and the man looked grim.

By midnight, I was hungry. The food court was closing, but the coffee shop was open. A cappuccino and a bag of mini doughnuts that melted in my mouth restored me. I went back to the casino and watched the blackjack players for another hour. Two large men dressed as Santa Clauses held my attention that long. They weren't very merry, and not a ho-ho-ho left their lips as they lost game after game. One stumbled and fell as he staggered away from the table, and security guards descended on him and escorted him away. By that time, my body was screaming with exhaustion. The elevator discharged me on the eighth floor. I unlocked my room, turned on the lights, and sank fully clothed onto the softest bed I'd ever felt.

When I woke the next morning, I felt relaxed and happy. I stood at the window and observed the coming and going of people and cars for a while, then took a quick shower, brushed my teeth with the washcloth, and got dressed. Twenty minutes later I had liberated my car and was back on the road. Christmas was over, and I'd made it through. *I'm going to be okay,* I remember thinking as I pulled onto Interstate 15 and headed west.

Chapter 58

The jonquils were in bloom along the cemetery path as I walked to LaRissa's grave. Today was the first anniversary of her death. I carried a yellow rose, her favorite, and laid it in front of the marker that had been erected. "LaRissa Yvonne Spencer, May 2, 2002 – April 5, 2018."

I lowered myself to the grass beside her grave and tucked my legs up under me. The sunny day and smell of new-cut grass enfolded me, and I could hear the Fairview Middle School marching band, a block away, practicing Sousa's "Washington Post March." It was a perfect spring day. A day that LaRissa, if she were still with us, would have reveled in, digging out summer shorts and sandals, getting ready for the end of the school year, and making plans for a busy summer of fun.

I'd taken the day off from the shelter. The events that had cascaded into the tragedies of LaRissa's death and Kyle's incarceration haunted me, even though I knew that there would be justice for Don's evil. Another young girl had come forward after the newspaper had identified Don as the suspect in Harry's rape. Her story had been eerily similar to Harry's—broken bike, man stops to render help, offers to take her home, and then attacks her. Detective Simmons told me Don was certain to be found guilty and that Barrow was trying to negotiate a plea bargain for a twenty-five-year sentence.

"Oh, LaRissa, I miss you," I whispered. "I hoped for so much for you." My eyes were dry and sad. I'd cried a lot the past year; there weren't any tears left for today.

I kept talking, telling LaRissa that Kyle was doing well: "He's taking college courses now. He's still devastated by what happened. He didn't mean for you to die. But he takes responsibility now, and that's good. Taking responsibility is the right thing, isn't it?" I wondered, briefly, whether LaRissa would care what Kyle was doing. They'd never been close, but still he was her brother. She'd died before she was old enough to even begin to understand how their mutual history would be important someday. There wasn't a someday for her. She'd never graduate from high school or college, experience the joys and frustrations of the working world, meet someone to love and cherish, have children to delight in and despair of, or grow old with grace. And I would never have the joy of watching her gain the world that should have been hers.

I sat beside her grave for hours. I told her about going back to school and my hopes for LaRissa's Hope Center—a safe place where children who'd experienced the horror of sexual abuse could be helped to understand and overcome their traumas. Just two days before, the Hope Center had been awarded its first grant to hire a sex-abuse counselor for children—the first step on what I hoped would be that long-term path. "Your memory, your legacy, LaRissa, will be the better lives of other children," I told her. "I wish you'd been able to come to me—or someone—about what was happening to you. I understand why you didn't, but I wish you'd been able to, so we could've made it stop."

I stayed until the sun was low in the sky and the wind became cool. Then I stood, reluctant to leave . . . to have this day over. To know that years stretched ahead where I would think of her and miss her and never understand how she could be gone. Where I'd miss her laugh and teasing wit, the quick hugs when she left the house, the glimmers of insight she was beginning to demonstrate, and the bright future I'd envisioned for her. It was all gone.

When it was nearly dark, I brushed the grass off my pants and stood to go. I looked back when I reached the path. The headstone with the yellow rose was all that remained of her, except my memories. *I miss you, my sweet girl. Every day. Every year. Forever.*

Other Books by K.L. Kovar

The Angie and Bernie Mystery Series

A Dangerous Winter
The Spring Militia
The Dog Days of Summer
A Fall of Bones

Darya of Algaron
A teen/young adult science fiction story

Available on Amazon in Kindle and paperback.

Other Books by K.L. Kovar

The Angie and Bernie Mystery Series

A Dangerous Winter
The Spring Militia
The Dog Days of Summer
A Fall of Bones

Darya of Algaron
A teen/young adult science fiction story

Available on Amazon in Kindle and paperback.

Acknowledgements

There are many people I need to thank and appreciate for their support and encouragement. As always, the Bearlodge Writers group continues to provide amazing support and encouragement to me and many other writers out here in the remote areas of northeast Wyoming. K.D. Gearhart, fellow writer, BLW member, and friend, always offers a sharp eye for finding the gaps in consistency, logic, and completeness of my first (and second, etc.) drafts. Thank you to all of you.

Jennifer Goode Stevens is an exemplary editor, who points out my lack of knowledge in areas where I do lack knowledge. An excellent editor to work with and whose advice I (almost) always take. Any remaining errors are clearly on me.

Dione Moon designed the wonderful cover art for this book. A great talent and a good friend.

Cheryl Taylor provided amazing and efficient technical support to make this book happen. Especially appreciated for reducing my stress and ensuring I have more time for writing.

And, as always, my patient husband helped enormously, by not complaining about my hiding out in my office to write, bringing me tea and snacks, and keeping our two unruly dogs at bay. Couldn't have done this without you, Stu-Bob!

About The Author

K.L. Kovar lives in very rural Wyoming, with two dogs and a patient husband. She enjoys reading mysteries, political thrillers, science fiction, and astronomy and geology textbooks.

Prior to turning to writing, she was an economist who specialized in health economics and financing and worked for private research agencies and the Federal government in Washington, DC. After fifteen years of statistics and writing up results of studies, she abandoned the East Coast in favor of moving out West and working with American Indian Tribes to obtain funding and implement programs to address the very significant health disparities in Indian Country.

This is her sixth book and first stand-alone novel. She is currently writing the first of the Charlie Johns, P.I. mysteries, featuring a hard-bitten former cop, set in late 1970s Chicago.

Made in United States
Orlando, FL
24 September 2023

37241122R00148